He lounged or ___ ___ *indolent and f*___

With his chiseled goo___ ___ ___ scruffy attire and his devil-may-care attitude, Travis McCall looked like a cross between a movie star, a pirate and a biker.

He glanced her way, and Rebecca saw the subtle stiffening of his body, the frown that replaced his lazy grin. She bit her lip.

After a moment, he hitched himself off the stool and headed for her. He walked with a loose-limbed, hip-rolling saunter, his thumbs hooked in his low-riding jeans, his gray eyes boring into her from beneath half-closed lids.

Rebecca felt her stomach clench. He looked annoyed . . . and dangerous. . . .

Dear Reader,

Happy February! Happy St. Valentine's Day! May this year bring you love and joy. And to put you in the mood for hearts and roses, Silhouette **Special Edition** is proud to bring you six wonderful, warm novels—stories written with you in mind—tales of love and life that you can identify with—romance with that little "something special" added in.

This month, don't miss stories from Patricia Coughlin, Tracy Sinclair, Barbara Catlin and Elizabeth Krueger. February marks the publication of *Ride the Tiger,* by Lindsay McKenna—the exciting first book in the wonderful series MOMENTS OF GLORY. Next month brings you *One Man's War,* and *Off Limits* follows in April. February is also the month for *A Good Man Walks In* by Ginna Gray—a tender tale featuring characters you've met before in earlier books by Ginna.

In each Silhouette **Special Edition** novel, we're dedicated to bringing you the romances that you dream about—stories that delight as well as bring a tear to the eye. And that's what Silhouette **Special Edition** is all about—special books by special authors for special readers!

I hope you enjoy this book and all of the stories to come.

Sincerely,

Tara Gavin
Senior Editor

GINNA GRAY
A Good Man Walks In

Silhouette Special Edition

Published by Silhouette Books New York

America's Publisher of Contemporary Romance

SILHOUETTE BOOKS
300 East 42nd St., New York, N.Y. 10017

A GOOD MAN WALKS IN

ISBN: 0-373-09722-0

First Silhouette Books printing February 1992

Printed in the U.S.A.

Books by Ginna Gray

Silhouette Special Edition

Golden Illusion #171
The Heart's Yearning #265
Sweet Promise #320
Cristen's Choice #373
*Fools Rush In #416
*Where Angels Fear #468
If There Be Love #528
*Once in a Lifetime #661
*A Good Man Walks In #722

Silhouette Romance

The Gentling #285
The Perfect Match #311
Heart of the Hurricane #338
Images #352
First Love, Last Love #374
The Courtship of Dani #417
Sting of the Scorpion #826

*The Blaines and the McCalls of Crockett, Texas

Silhouette Books

Silhouette Christmas Stories 1987
''Season of Miracles''

GINNA GRAY

A native Houstonian, Ginna Gray admits that since childhood, she has been a compulsive reader as well as a head-in-the-clouds dreamer. Long accustomed to expressing her creativity in tangible ways—Ginna also enjoys painting and needlework—she finally decided to try putting her fantasies and wild imaginings down on paper. The result? The mother of two now spends eight hours a day as a full-time writer.

A Good Man Walks In continues the story of the Blaine twins' extended family from *Fools Rush In* and *Where Angels Fear*. Expect to see more of the Blaines and McCalls of Crockett, Texas, in future Special Edition novels by Ginna Gray.

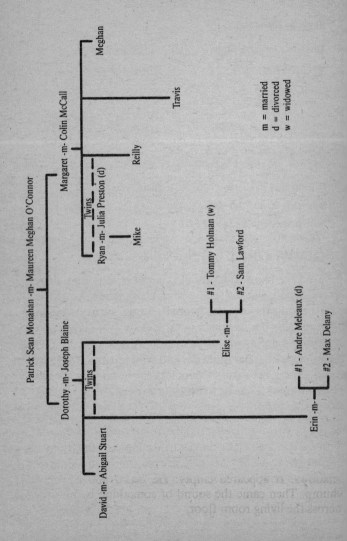

Patrick Sean Monahan -m- Maureen Meghan O'Connor

Margaret -m- Colin McCall

Dorothy -m- Joseph Blaine

David -m- Abigail Stuart

Twins

Meghan

Travis

Reilly

Ryan -m- Julia Preston (d)

Mike

Elise -m-

#1 - Tommy Holman (w)

#2 - Sam Lawford

Erin -m-

#1 - Andre Meleaux (d)

#2 - Max Delany

m = married
d = divorced
w = widowed

Chapter One

Travis awoke instantly. He lay still—listening.

It came again, the soft sound that had jerked him from sleep. A thump followed, then another. The hair on Travis's nape prickled.

He slipped his hand beneath his pillow and pulled out his 10 mm automatic. Silent as a cat, he rolled from the bed. He stepped into the denim cutoffs he'd tossed onto the bedside chair hours before and moved toward the open bedroom door.

Arm bent, Travis held the weapon at ready beside his right shoulder, the barrel pointed at the ceiling, and flattened himself against the wall beside the doorway. Cautiously, he peered out.

Except for the faint glow of moonlight seeping in from the other bedrooms, the hallway was shrouded in black shadows. It appeared empty. He heard another muffled thump. Then came the sound of something being dragged across the living room floor.

Travis slipped out of the room. He moved swiftly down the hallway toward the sounds. Hugging the wall, he darted past each doorway, a lethal, silent shadow flitting through the darkness, his bare feet soundless on the wood floors of the beach house.

At the point where the hallway opened into the living room he halted and flattened himself against the wall again. Hesitant footsteps tapped against the floor, moving away from him. Travis edged forward and peered around the corner.

Long rectangles of moonlight spilled into the room through the two sets of French doors. The pair nearest to him stood open. In the center of the room, a shadowy figure groped through the darkness.

The guy was small, but Travis knew that didn't mean a whole helluva lot, since he was probably armed. He debated on barking out an order for the man to halt but decided against it. If he was nervous, he just might turn and fire. Travis crouched and moved into the room.

When he'd crept to within a few feet of the man, he stuck his automatic into the back pocket of his snug cutoffs. He launched himself at the intruder and caught him in a flying tackle that sent them both sprawling.

The man let out an *"Oof,"* and Travis cursed when his elbow whacked the hardwood floor. He cursed again when the guy almost wriggled out of his grasp.

Though small, his opponent was agile and desperate. Making frantic, gasping sounds, he kicked and bucked and twisted, at one point nearly unmanning Travis with a sharp thrust of his knee. Amid grunts and thumps and scuffling noises, they grappled together in the darkness, but the intruder was no match for Travis. The fierce struggle lasted only seconds, and when it was over Travis sat astraddle the man's back, holding him face down on the hard floor with his arm twisted behind his back.

"All right, knock it off," he snarled when his captive continued to buck and pitch. "You give me any more trouble and so help me, I'll break your arm."

The intruder sucked in a sharp breath and froze.

"Tra-Travis? Travis McCall? Is that you?" a feminine voice asked.

"What the hell!"

Travis raised up on his knees just long enough to flip his captive over, then sat back, straddling slender hips, and swiftly skimmed his hand over the body penned beneath him. He cursed long and fluently when his palm cupped a full breast.

The woman jerked at the contact and make a shocked sound, but when she squirmed and tried to bat his hand away, he grabbed her wrist.

"Be still." Holding both her wrists in one hand, he stretched out his other arm and switched on the lamp on a nearby end table.

The woman was still gasping, her chest heaving with each agitated breath, and he could feel the tremors that shook her whole body. At the base of her throat her pulse hammered wildly. During their tussle, her rich mahogany brown hair had come loose from the chignon coiled at the back of her head, and several curling tendrils lay across her face. Frightened blue eyes stared back at him from between the wild strands.

Frowning, Travis roughly brushed the tangled locks aside. At first he didn't recognize her. Then her gaze skittered away from his and settled somewhere in the region of his chest. The reaction struck a familiar chord, and Travis's eyes narrowed. He examined the classically beautiful features, carefully set now in a cool mask, and his jaws clenched.

It had been years since he'd seen her. Nine or ten at least. She'd grown up, gotten older and, if possible, even more lovely than the nineteen-year-old he remembered, but he'd never forget that face.

"Rebecca Quinn." He muttered her name in a flat, hard voice that held not the slightest trace of gladness or welcome. "What the hell are you doing here? And why were you sneaking around in the middle of the night?"

Her gaze jerked back to his. "I—I wasn't sneaking around. I co-couldn't find the light switch, and I was feeling around for a lamp." She paused and licked her lips, watching him warily. "And I'm, uh...I'm here at Erin and Elise's invitation. They said I could stay here for the next few months."

"What!"

Rebecca felt Travis's body jerk. His head snapped back as though he'd received a punch to the jaw.

"The hell you say! You must have misunderstood. They told *me* I could use the beach house for the rest of the summer."

She stared at him, appalled, and drew in several more deep breaths, trying to bring her galloping heart under control. The terror she had experienced when he attacked her was fading, but a new uneasiness was rapidly taking its place. "Bu-But...there must be some mistake."

"That's right. And you made it, lady." Releasing her hands, Travis sat back, crossed his arms over his bare chest and pinned her with a blistering stare.

To Rebecca's surprise and dismay, she experienced a long forgotten but familiar stab of hurt. Without a doubt, Travis McCall had the sexiest, most come-hither eyes of any man walking the earth. Silvery gray and surrounded by long dark eyelashes that any female would kill for, they surveyed the world with lazy amusement, and surveyed women with a sensual gleam that was both flattering and wicked...except when they focused on her. On those occasions they invariably turned hard and cold. How many times, growing up, had Travis looked at her in just that way? she wondered sadly.

Shaking off the depressing thought, Rebecca strove, as she always had, to hide her feelings behind a facade of cool dignity. "I had breakfast with Erin and Elise not more than sixteen hours ago. When I flew into Albuquerque, they drove over from Santa Fe and met me at the airport to give me the keys to this house. They assured me I would be safe h—" She stopped and bit her lip, appalled at what she'd nearly blurted out. "Uh... that I'd have plenty of privacy here. They didn't mention you at all."

She should have known that Travis would catch the slip. For all his lazy, laid-back air, he was quick and intelligent and his training as an FBI agent had honed his powers of observation to the point where almost nothing got past him.

He frowned. "Are you in some kind of danger?" His scowl deepened and so did his voice. "You're not in trouble with the law, are you?"

"No! Of course not. That was just a poor choice of words. That's all."

He studied her through narrowed eyes, clearly doubting.

Apprehension fluttered through Rebecca. Unable to meet that penetrating stare, she lowered her eyes, but her uneasiness worsened when her gaze skimmed over wide, bare shoulders and down his muscular chest and the thatch of golden hair covering it.

She became suddenly aware of the intimacy of their position, and the shocking alignment of their bodies. His bottom was pressing against her upper thighs, his sex nestled warmly at their juncture. Through her silk slacks, she could feel his heat, the hard strength of his legs clamped against her sides.

Rebecca's gaze trailed down over his flat belly, then lower still, and she nearly gasped when she encountered the widespread V of his unbuttoned cutoffs. She stared at the spot where the thin line of silky blond hair that arrowed downward over his belly began to spread and merge with the thatch of tighter, darker blond curls, barely visible at the base of the open placket.

Her heart picked up speed and her eyes widened. Shocked, she realized that, except for those threadbare cutoffs, Travis didn't have a stitch on. It dawned on her then that he must have been sleeping when she arrived. Completely nude.

The thought so rattled Rebecca that she experienced a rush of panic. Every nerve in her body twanged with awareness. The incredible intimacy of their position had an alarming effect on her sensory perception as well, making it suddenly acute.

She felt his strength, his hardness, his heat. She became aware of the muscular breadth of his chest and shoulders, the sleekness of his bronzed skin, his male scent—tantalizing and musky, and tinged with soap. She could even smell the minty aroma of toothpaste on his breath, see each individual eyelash and the tiny flecks of charcoal floating in his silvery irises.

A trembling began deep inside Rebecca, and she instinctively sought to hide it. Tipping up her chin, she met Travis's skeptical gaze with cool politeness. "Since you surely know by now that I am not a burglar, would you mind letting me up? This floor is not exactly comfortable." Nor are you, she thought, but she was doing her best not to draw his attention to their position.

The attempt was wasted; she could tell the instant Travis became conscious of their erotic closeness. His mouth hardened even more, and he jerked off of her as though she had suddenly become hot to the touch.

"Sorry," he said curtly.

He sprang to his feet, hesitated, then extended his hand to help her up. The instant she was standing, he released her and stepped away, putting several feet between them.

Rebecca's heart leaped. "Oh, my word! You've got a gun!" she exclaimed, staring at the weapon sticking out of his back pocket.

Travis turned back and looked at her. "That's right. You're lucky I didn't blow your head off."

He was trying to scare her, Rebecca knew. And he was succeeding brilliantly. Her nerves were already frayed. It didn't help matters any that he still had not bothered to button his pants.

She watched him pace the spacious room, and gradually she became aware of things about him that she had been too shaken to notice before.

Travis had always been a laid-back, daring devil who sauntered through life with a cocky grin and a twinkle in his eyes, laughingly defying convention. But even in his wildest high school days, she had never seen him look quite the way he did now. His thick, blond hair, though cut short on the top and sides, hung below his shoulders in the back. His face sported reddish brown stubble that was at least three days old and he had a tattoo of a snarling leopard on his upper right arm. A round, puckered scar, which Rebecca had the sickening suspicion was the result of a gunshot wound, decorated his right thigh. But the crowning touch was the two-inch long earring in the shape of a dagger that dangled from his left ear. He looked rakish and tough and sexy... and dangerous.

"Look," he said suddenly, startling her. "There's obviously been some sort of foul-up. We both can't stay here all summer."

"No, of course not," Rebecca agreed nervously. Watching him, she plucked the remaining pins from her hair and tried to finger-comb the heavy mass into some order. "I, uh... I suppose we should call Erin or Elise and straighten things out."

"Yeah. But it's too late to call tonight. Elise would probably have heart palpitations if I called her at two in the morning, and if Sam didn't have my head for scaring her, Erin would." His mouth twisted. "Somehow, I doubt that either one of my cousins would consider this situation an emergency."

"True," Rebecca agreed with a wan smile. Elise and Erin, though identical twins whom most people could not tell apart, were as different as night and day. Bold, outspoken Erin wouldn't hesitate to tear a strip off of Travis for waking her over anything less than a catastrophe, and she was as protective of her more gentle sister as a mother grizzly was of her cub.

"By the way, how did you get here at this hour? There are only two ferries a day between the main island and this one, and the last run was hours ago."

"I know. The only plane I could get to Alhaja Verde was the red-eye, so when we landed, I hired a fisherman to bring me over."

"I don't suppose you asked him to wait, did you?"

Rebecca shook her head.

Travis's mouth twisted. "Well, I guess we'll just have to make the best of it. It'll be hours before we can call Santa Fe and straighten this mess out, so we might as well get some sleep."

"Fine. If you'll just point me toward the bedrooms, I'll say good night."

"Take your pick. Erin and Elise and their husbands own the place jointly, so it was built to accommodate two families at once. It has two separate bedroom wings," he said, pointing out the hallways that opened off either side of the living room. "Each with a master suite and two guest rooms. Although... since I'm staying in Erin and Max's wing, you might want to choose a room in Elise and Sam's."

In other words, stay as far away from you as I possibly can, Rebecca interpreted silently. She felt again that old stab of hurt, but her face remained impassive. "Fine," she repeated, and headed for the pile of luggage she had managed to drag inside from the deck, where the fisherman had deposited it for her.

"Good grief! Is all that yours?"

Rebecca looped the strap of a shoulder bag over her arm and reached for two more cases. "As I explained, I came to spend the summer. That requires more than just a few changes of clothes."

"Huh. Looks to me like that's everything you own."

It was, but Rebecca wasn't about to tell him that. "Which wing is Elise and Sam's?" she asked, hefting the cases.

"C'mon, I'll show you," Travis grumbled, and snatched up the other four.

He led her to an airy bedroom in the right wing, and dumped the cases at the foot of the queen-size bed. "The bathroom is through there. It's stocked with anything you could possibly need, so make yourself at home. For tonight, anyway," he added pointedly, giving her a hard look. Before Rebecca could reply, he headed for the door. "I'll see you at breakfast."

Rebecca stared after him for a moment, then walked over to the bed and sat down on the edge. Sighing, she shook her head. It seemed that some things never changed. Travis McCall was still handsome as sin, even with his current, scruffy rebel look. He was still lean and fit, and he still moved with that easy, hip-rolling saunter that drew a woman's eye to his body and her thoughts to the bedroom. No doubt, he still had that heart-stopping smile as well, though it certainly hadn't been in evidence tonight.

And, of course, he still didn't care much for her.

With a rueful grimace, Rebecca picked up her overnight bag and headed for the bathroom, dismissing the man from her mind. She had more serious things to worry about than her hometown's local hunk and his opinion of her.

Like how she was going to elude Evan.

By now he would be looking for her. Rebecca set her cosmetic case down beside the sink and stared at her reflection in the mirror. God help her if he managed to track her down.

The thought sent stark fear slicing through Rebecca. She closed her eyes and gripped the edge of the counter hard with both hands. For a moment she gave in to the terror and trembled violently, as though in the grip of a hard chill.

She gulped in several deep breaths and struggled for control. When she had regained a modicum of calm, she opened her eyes and stared into the mirror at the pale woman with the wildly disarrayed hair and haunted eyes. What would she do if Erin and Elise said she couldn't stay? She had no place else to go.

Don't be silly, she told her reflection, tamping down a fresh rush of panic. Erin and Elise were her oldest and dearest friends. They knew how desperately she needed to stay and why. They wouldn't ask her to leave. They wouldn't.

Rebecca's lower lip trembled, and she caught it between her teeth. No... but Travis would.

"Rebecca Quinn." Travis muttered the name with utter disgust. Of all the women in the world, why the hell did he have to get stuck on a remote island with Rebecca Quinn?

He lay sprawled on his back, legs spread, his hands stacked beneath his head, scowling through the darkness at the ceiling above the bed. Every muscle in his body was drawn taut as a fiddle string.

Dammit! What had Erin and Elise been thinking of? They knew why he had asked for the use of their beach house. He had some heavy thinking to do, decisions to make—decisions that would affect his whole life. He sure as hell hadn't taken a leave of absence from the Bureau just to lie on the beach in the sun all day. Or to entertain their friends.

Unable to lie still another moment, Travis made an aggravated sound and bounded from the bed. Naked, he stomped to the window.

The guest bedrooms ran along the back of each wing of the house. From them the view consisted of sand dunes and salt grass, tinted a pale blue by the moon. Beyond the sand, the forest took over and began its climb toward the mountains. Travis stared out, his feet braced wide, fists propped on his bare hips, blind to the eerie beauty.

He flexed his shoulders, but the tightness did not ease. The taut restlessness was foreign to his nature, but it was not new. It had been plaguing him off and on for the past year or so—in the past few months with more and more frequency. He felt...antsy...and vaguely dissatisfied, and he didn't know why or what to do about it.

When his cousin David had gotten him the job with the FBI, it had seemed like a dream come true. Going away to college had whetted Travis's appetite and made him anxious to experience more of the world outside the sleepy little east Texas town of Crockett where he'd grown up. He'd craved excitement and adventure, longed to see new places, experience new things, flirt with danger.

Unconsciously, Travis's fingers massaged the puckered scar on his thigh, and his mouth twisted. He'd found excitement, all right. Maybe more than he'd bargained for.

He was good at his job, though. Damned good. Especially undercover work. But lately... lately, he just hadn't enjoyed it like he used to. As time went on, the thought of spending the rest of his life going from one dicey situation to another held less and less appeal.

Sighing, Travis slipped his hand under the thick fall of hair at the back of his neck and kneaded the tight muscles there. Hell, maybe he was just getting old. He'd be thirty-one in a few weeks—not a great age under normal conditions, but a man burned out fast when he lived on the edge.

Travis sighed again. When David had left the Bureau a few years ago, he had thought his cousin was nuts, but now... now he wasn't so sure.

About the only thing he was sure of at that point was he needed a change.

Maybe the job David had offered him with Telecom International was the answer. The pay was more than double what he was pulling down with the Bureau and, God knew, that wouldn't be hard to take. Plus, he'd get to travel all over the world, which meant he'd have plenty of excitement without the risk of getting his throat cut in a dark alley some night, or of blowing his cover and having some drug kingpin waste him in one of any number of unpleasant ways. Yeah, anyway he looked at it, the Telecom job was a cushy one. He just wasn't sure it was right for him.

Which was precisely why he was on Rincon Island. He'd hoped that in the quiet and solitude he would be able to think clearly and come to a decision about his future.

Now, here was Rebecca Quinn.

Only it wasn't Rebecca Quinn anymore, he reminded himself. It was Rebecca...? Rebecca...? What the devil was the name of that rich Dallas big shot she'd married? Edgar

Howe? Hull? No...no, Hall. That was it. Edgar...no, Evan. Evan Hall.

The guy was always getting his picture in the papers, hobnobbing with the movers and shakers in Texas politics, attending society events, closing one big deal after another.

Travis's mouth twisted. He remembered Erin showing him a clipping of Evan Hall and Rebecca coming out of the church on their wedding day five or six years ago. They had looked the picture of fairy-tale bliss. Rebecca, as usual, had been drop-dead gorgeous, in that elegant, quiet way of hers, and her groom had radiated confidence and masculinity.

Erin and Elise had been Rebecca's maids of honor, and they had oohed and ahhed over what a great catch Evan was—so charming, so bright, so good-looking. Remembering that arrogant face with the cold eyes and practiced smile, Travis snorted. He'd thought the guy looked like a calculating bastard.

Which, come to think of it, probably made him the perfect husband for Rebecca.

He'd never liked her. Erin and Elise had always argued that he wasn't being fair, that if he'd just get to know her he would change his mind. Shoot, he knew her. They'd grown up in the same town, for Pete's sake. He'd known her all his life, and she'd always irritated the living hell out of him.

Even as a small child Rebecca had been standoffish and quiet, always looking so perfect, with her long dark curls tied up in a pink ribbon, and dressed in fancy clothes with never so much as a scuff on her Mary Janes.

As a teenager she'd been downright stuck-up. False modesty aside, Travis knew that in high school he'd been the big man on campus. He'd been captain of the football team and class president, and he'd been voted most handsome *and* most popular. Every other girl in school had flirted with him and vied for his attention, but not Rebecca. Oh, no. Not Miss Nose-in-the-air Rebecca Quinn. Most of the time she had looked right through him as though he didn't exist.

Her father, Richard Quinn, was the wealthiest man in Crockett. Hell, he was the wealthiest man in Houston

County, and Travis always figured Rebecca's aloofness was her way of reminding everyone of that.

As far as he was concerned, she was just a spoiled little rich girl with the personality and charm of a block of ice. He'd never been able to figure out what Elise and Erin saw in her, but the three had been friends since their preschool days.

Which had made it damned difficult for him to avoid her. Back in Crockett, the McCalls and the Blaines lived only a stone's throw apart, and the kids of both households had worn a path through the woods between the two places. All of his life Travis had been as at home in his cousins' house as he had been in his own. He'd practically spent half his childhood running in and out of the Blaines' old Victorian barn of a home.

Unfortunately, Rebecca had also, or at least, it had seemed so to him. Every time he'd turned around she'd been underfoot, always quiet, her expression solemn and unreadable.

For as far back as he could remember, she'd always been there on the fringes of his life, right up to the time he'd left Crockett to join the FBI upon graduation from college. Since then he hadn't seen much of her, and that had suited him just fine.

Now, here she was again.

"Not for long though," he swore. Travis stomped back to the bed and flung himself down on his back. He flounced over on his side and punched his pillow. Come morning, she was outta there.

After a few hours of restless sleep, Travis arose at dawn. He made coffee and paced the kitchen while he sipped the hot brew, checking the clock every few minutes. By six, he had convinced himself that most normal people were awake and ready to start the day, and he reached for the telephone.

Travis placed the call to the cousin he figured was most likely responsible for the awkward situation in which he found himself. On the sixth ring Max answered, and at his slurred, "Yeah. Who is it?" Travis remembered the time zone difference and winced.

"It's Travis. Look, I'm sorry to wake you, Max, but I've got to speak to Erin. It's important."

"For your sake, buddy, it better be," Max said over a yawn. "You know how she is when someone wakes her up."

"Yeah, I know," Travis muttered. About as cheerful as a grizzly getting a root canal.

He turned and leaned back against the long curving counter that separated the kitchen and living room. On the other end of the line he heard a rustling noise and soft murmurs as Max tried to coax Erin awake. The man obviously knew his wife well.

"Travis McCall, you wretch," Erin's sleep-raspy voice snarled into his ear a moment later. "This had better be important or I'm gonna skin you alive."

Ignoring the threat, he snapped, "What the devil do you mean, sending Rebecca Quinn down here and telling her she can stay for the summer? *I'm* here for the summer. Remember?"

"That's it? *That's* what you woke me up for? Travis, it's the middle of the night! It's still dark outside!"

"Not here, it isn't. And don't change the subject. I want to know what you're going to do about Rebecca."

"Nothing."

"*Nothing!* What the devil do you mean, nothing?"

"Look, Travis, I'm not going to turn Rebecca out, so you're just wasting your breath. She's recovering from a very bad...experience. She desperately needs solitude and peace for a while."

"Dammit! So do I! But I sure won't get any with Rebecca here! How could you do this to me, Erin? You and Elise know that I can't stand the woman. One of us will have to go."

"There is absolutely no reason for either of you to change your plans. After all, it is a big house. Surely the two of you can manage to stay out of one another's way for a couple of months."

"You can't be serious!" Travis snorted. "Share a house with Rebecca Quinn?"

"Rebecca Hall," Erin corrected.

"Whatever. Look, cousin. It'll never work. I promise you. Rebecca doesn't like me any more than I like her. Which is zip. Zero. Zilch. Not at all."

"Tough. You're just going to have to make the best of it and work out some arrangement between the two of you, because I am not going to tell Rebecca to leave. Not after what she's been through."

"Erin! You can't do this to me!"

"Sure I can. Now you be nice to Rebecca, you hear. Bye, Cuz."

"Erin! Erin, don't you dare hang up on—"

The phone clicked in his ear. Travis jerked the receiver out at arm's length and glared at it, then turned and slammed it back into its cradle and cursed.

It was then he looked up and saw Rebecca standing in the middle of the living room.

Chapter Two

Travis winced. She had obviously heard the whole thing.

For the space of maybe two heartbeats, Rebecca gazed at him, her expression stricken. Then she blinked and raised her chin a notch, and her features assumed that composed, slightly aloof perfection that Travis had always despised. She hadn't, however, been quite quick enough.

For that brief moment he had glimpsed her vulnerability and her pain, and he knew an instant of sheer amazement. He hadn't thought Rebecca capable of feeling any emotion that deeply.

Guilt and embarrassment flooded Travis. He didn't like her, it was true, but he hadn't meant to hurt her. He was fond of women, and he'd been taught to honor and cherish them. It went against everything he believed in to hurt any woman. "Look, Rebecca, I..." He grimaced and made a feeble gesture toward the telephone. "I, uh...that is..."

"I'll leave on the next ferry," she said with immense dignity, cutting him off.

Her cool acceptance made Travis feel worse. For a second he was tempted to accept the offer, but his conscience simply wouldn't let him. As a result, he reacted with anger when she turned and headed back to her room.

"Dammit! Will you wait!" He darted around the end of the counter and sprinted after her, overtaking her before she reached the hallway. Stepping into her path, he forced her to a halt and glared. "Look, there's no need for you to go. Okay?"

"But you just said—"

"I know what I said." He raked his hand through his hair and heaved a sigh. "Look. So I don't like you? So what? You've always known that. And I'm sure the feeling is mutual. The point is, you're a friend of my cousins and you're here at their invitation. They'd both have my hide if I ran you off."

"But you're family. And you were here first. I can't expect you to leave."

"Damned straight. I don't intend to budge, either. But that doesn't mean you have to go."

Rebecca tipped her head to one side and looked at him warily. "Then what are you suggesting?"

"That...well..." He cleared his throat. "That, uh...that we both stay." It pained him to voice the words, and he grimaced. Lord help him, he couldn't believe he was doing this. "As Erin pointed out, this is a big house. We're both adults. Surely we can come to an arrangement."

"What kind of arrangement?"

"We could work out a schedule for using the kitchen and laundry facilities, and...I don't know...just generally stay out of each other's way, I guess. It shouldn't be too difficult."

Rebecca chewed at her lower lip. The small sign of nerves intrigued Travis. He'd never known her to be agitated or indecisive about anything before. He half expected her to turn him down flat with a polite, "No, thank you" but to his surprise, after a moment she nodded.

"All right. I suppose we could try it for a few days. If it doesn't work out, I'll leave."

"Fine," he said through clenched teeth. "Then let's sit down and make a timetable."

They spent the next fifteen minutes ironing out a schedule that would accommodate them both. Since Rebecca was habitually an early riser, they agreed that she would take the first shift in the kitchen, and that she would have use of the laundry facilities on Mondays, Wednesdays and Fridays. They would stick strictly to their separate wings, and on alternate nights, each would have sole use of the living room.

The last was Travis's suggestion. "That way, if either of us is, uh...entertaining, we'll be assured of privacy," he drawled suggestively.

With his bare heels hooked on the bottom rung of the bar stool, his knees spread wide, he swiveled around, propped his elbows on the counter behind him and fixed her with a heavy-lidded look.

He was once again dressed in a pair of skimpy cutoffs and nothing else, and everything about him—his lazy sprawl, his half smile, the heated, insolent gleam in his eyes, his near-indecent attire—taunted.

His attitude was blatantly provocative, a deliberate attempt to make her squirm. Travis knew it was not the way to promote harmony, but he couldn't seem to help himself. He'd never been able to resist needling Rebecca. Something about her got under his skin like a heat rash, making him prickly and aggressive.

The reaction was alien to his basic nature. He was normally even-tempered, always laid-back and casual, especially in his dealings with women. He never asserted himself or went out of his way to draw their attention or provoke a reaction of any kind. He never had to. Women came to him. They always had. Somehow, though, whenever he was around Rebecca, he felt an all-consuming need to shake her up and wipe that look of serene indifference off her face any way he could.

Travis knew his reputation with women. Hell, he'd done all he could to foster it. The image of a ladies' man came in handy at times, especially when he worked undercover; no one took a womanizer seriously or viewed him with too much suspicion.

Not that it was all for show, of course. He liked women. A lot. And he'd learned early in life that women liked him. But if even half the stories about his exploits were true he'd be a physical wreck by now.

Since arriving on the island he hadn't given so much as a thought to making contact with any of the local lovelies. He'd come there to do some serious thinking, and he didn't need or want that kind of distraction, but the chance to make Rebecca uncomfortable had been too tempting.

"Is that arrangement all right with you?" he asked with a sardonic lift of one burnished gold eyebrow.

Delicate color rose in Rebecca's cheeks. She shifted on the rattan sofa, her gaze darting around in an effort to avoid his bare torso. Travis grinned.

"Certainly," she replied with a hint of frost in her voice. "I'll do my best to stay out of your way, I assure you."

When they were done, Rebecca excused herself and went to her room. A few moments later, Travis had just poured himself a cup of coffee when she returned carrying a straw tote bag.

She gave him a stiff smile. "You may go ahead and use the kitchen first this morning if you'd like. I have to go into Chapulta for supplies."

"You don't have to do that. I stocked the cupboards when I arrived a week ago. There're plenty of groceries here."

"Thank you. That's very generous of you, but I prefer to buy my own. If we're going to make this work, I think we have to remain separate in every way."

"Oh, for crying out loud. It won't hurt you to have one meal on me before you go traipsing all that way. It's two miles to Chapulta. Besides, you're not going to find much there beyond a few staples. It's just a fishing village. You need to take the ferry back to Alhaja Verde to do any serious shopping.''

''I realize that, but I'm sure I'll find enough to last me a few days.''

''Fine. Suit yourself,'' he practically snarled, but Rebecca paid him no mind. She murmured a soft ''goodbye'' and stepped out through the open French doors.

A moment after she had gone, Travis carried his coffee outside. The large, airy living room/kitchen formed the center of the beach house and the wings on either side angled off of it in a wide-spread V. A spacious deck ran all along the front, facing ocean. Sipping his coffee, Travis stood by the rail and watched Rebecca stroll away down the beach.

She walked with her back straight, her shoulders erect, her head held at a proud angle, her hips swaying gently with each stride of those long legs. Damn. Even slogging through ankle-deep sand, she still managed to look graceful and elegant . . . and as aloof as a princess.

He probably should have offered to let her take the speedboat that Max and Sam kept docked in the boathouse. Or, if she couldn't handle a boat, then the dune buggy that Erin used to zip around the island. He hadn't suggested either because merely being around Rebecca made him so agitated he couldn't think.

Hell, knowing her, she probably would have refused both offers in that ultra-polite way of hers, he told himself.

Rebecca. Jeez, he couldn't believe he'd agreed to spend the summer sharing a house with Rebecca Quinn. The maddening female had all the warmth and depth of feeling of a beautiful marble statue. How on earth was he going to tolerate the snooty woman for three months? Hell and damnation.

Rebecca walked on steadily, head high, jaw set, fighting the trembling ache deep inside her and the foolish urge to cry. It hurt. It shouldn't, but it did. Terribly.

Which was perfectly ridiculous. She had gotten over her girlish crush on Travis long ago. His opinion no longer mattered to her in the least.

Anyway, after all these years, heaven knew, she should be accustomed to his animosity. She'd been on the receiving end of it since she was five years old.

However, she was discovering that it was one thing to tell yourself that someone disliked you, and quite another to hear that sentiment put so bluntly into words.

The problem was, emotionally she was still raw and bleeding. Erin and Elise's summer house on Rincon Island was a refuge for her right now, a place of safety, but she had also come there to heal and regain her strength. She simply was not in any shape at the moment to deal with Travis's dislike.

The best thing for both of them would be for her to stay out of his way, as he'd insisted.

Swallowing her hurt, Rebecca trudged on toward the village at the south end of the island. There was some comfort, at least, in knowing that Travis had been oblivious to her adolescent crush all those years ago.

A wry smile tugged at her mouth. Actually, her feelings for Travis went back much further than her teenage years. Rebecca had adored him even as a child.

She had been five to his seven when they had met, the first day that Erin and Elise had brought her home with them from preschool to play. For the next eight or nine years, she had endured his little boy nastiness and malicious pranks and taunts. With that ancient, instinctive wisdom that all females, even those of her tender age, possessed, she had known that his boorishness wouldn't last forever.

When Travis had finally emerged from his obnoxious pubescence, however, it hadn't been Rebecca who had captured his interest. It had been Emma Lou Perkins. And after her had come Mary Beth Johnson. Then Caroline Abbot and Ida Jo Delacourt.

Almost every passably pretty girl in school had caught his eye at one time or another, Rebecca recalled, her mouth twisting wryly. They'd flocked to him, like flies to honey, drawn by his blatant masculinity, the newly emerged deep drawling voice, that hip-rolling sexy saunter, and the wicked promise in his eyes. He had responded to all of the love-struck teenage girls with an easy, off-hand charm that had set their hearts to fluttering. To all of them, that was, except her.

At the memory, Rebecca shook her head and chuckled weakly. Travis had been so popular and so good-looking she had known that she hadn't a chance with him. She had been too painfully shy to flirt with him or to reveal her attraction to him in even the most subtle way. Besides, Travis had made his feelings toward her more than clear. Her only defense had been to pretend indifference.

Rebecca was profoundly grateful that she had. How much more humiliating and painful that scene this morning would have been if he had known that she had once been head-over-heels in love with him.

She had gotten over him, of course. Travis had gone off to college, and two years later so had she. Then he'd joined the FBI and left Crockett for good...and she had met Evan.

Despite the warmth of the sun a shiver rippled through her. Rubbing her arms briskly, Rebecca forced her thoughts back to Travis and those painful teenage years when she'd suffered in silence. She would be forever grateful that she had not confided her feelings to a living soul—not even to Erin and Elise.

The very idea produced a chuckle. Elise might have been a safe confidante, but never in a million years would Erin have been able to keep her mouth shut. She would probably have lit into Travis and demanded to know if he was deaf and blind as well as stupid.

At least, she had been spared that humiliation. To this day, thank God, neither of the twins even suspected that for most of her life she'd secretly nursed an unrequited love for their cousin.

* * *

In Santa Fe, New Mexico, in the high mountain aerie that Max and Erin Delany called home, Elise Lawford perched herself on a bar stool in the kitchen and eyed her twin's smug expression with suspicion. "Don't just stand there smirking like a Cheshire cat. Out with it. Was Travis terribly angry when he called?"

"He was livid," Erin replied with a gleeful grin. She hitched herself up on the next stool and sipped her coffee, her eyes twinkling over the rim of the mug. "For such an easygoing devil, he can sure blow a gasket when he does get his temper up. For a minute I thought he was going to reach right through the phone line and strangle me."

"Oh, dear." Elise did not return her twin's contagious grin. She worried at her lower lip with her teeth, the look in her eyes apprehensive. "Maybe we've made a mistake, Erin, sending Rebecca down there. I mean...we've always known how Travis felt about her."

"Nonsense. This will be good for him. For both of them. Haven't we always said that if Travis would just take the time to really get to know Rebecca, he would like her?"

"Yes, but—"

"Well here's his chance. Anyway, what other choice was there? Between relatives and tourists, the family's cabin in Vail is booked for the summer. Besides, Evan knows about it."

"Oh, dear. Do you think he's looking for her?"

Erin sobered. Her mouth tightened, and her brown eyes snapped with anger. "After what Rebecca told us? You bet. To tell you the truth, I'm darned glad that Travis is there with her. He may grumble and grouse and he may be a bit of a devil with the ladies, but he's a white knight at heart."

Her irrepressible grin flashed again. "And who knows, something may develop between those two during the next few months. I've always thought they were perfect for one another."

Elise rolled her eyes. She looked at her sister and shook her head, her gentle smile tinged with exasperation and amusement. "You can't be serious. Rebecca and Travis? Why she pays him no more mind than if he were a pesky gnat. And as for him, he reacts like a cat whose fur has been stroked the wrong way whenever he's around her."

Erin smiled smugly, a wicked light dancing in her eyes. "I know. Interesting, isn't it?"

Travis was gone when Rebecca returned from the village.

After lunch she changed into a swimsuit and headed for the beach.

The waters of the Gulf of Mexico were warm and docile. The sun-spangled blue expanse undulated with only the gentlest swells that crested and broke in a thin line of frothy white lace. The water was so clear Rebecca could see the bottom even when she swam out many yards from shore. The salty liquid flowed against her skin, caressing her body like warm silk.

Rebecca gloried in the sensual pleasure of it and in the wonderful sense of freedom. Of peace. For hours she swam and dove and frolicked like a child. When she grew tired, she floated on her back until she caught her breath, then started in again.

Finally, exhausted, she waded ashore, spread a towel under a palm tree and flopped facedown onto it in the shade. Within seconds she was asleep.

Hours later, the faint chill of the air woke her. She raised up on her elbows and saw that the sun was rapidly slipping behind the inland mountains. Vibrant pink and mauve clouds streaked the sky, and the surf had turned a molten red.

Rebecca fumbled in her beach bag for her watch. Peering at it, she saw that it was after seven o'clock; she had slept the afternoon away.

The interior of the house was dim and shadowy when she entered, lit only by the warm glow of the sunset seeping in through the skylights that dotted the living room ceiling. The empty, slightly forlorn atmosphere told Rebecca that Travis still had not returned.

After she had showered and eaten and cleaned the kitchen, Rebecca curled up on the sofa and thumbed through a magazine, but her gaze continued to stray every few minutes to the empty pier. Finally, after reading the same article three times without absorbing a word of it, she tossed the magazine aside and stared out at the moonlit water.

Rebecca drew up her legs, looped her arms around them and propped her chin on her knees. She wondered if Travis had decided to give up his claim to the beach house and leave. If so, she ought to feel relieved. She should, in fact, be delighted. She wasn't though.

Sighing, Rebecca realized that, for all of Travis's grumpiness and animosity, she didn't want him to leave.

She was perfectly safe, she assured herself. Sleepy, remote and sparsely populated, Rincon was the smallest in a chain of small islands off Mexico's eastern shore. Few people even knew of its existence. There was only the fishing village and four other vacation homes scattered around the island, and the closest one to her was over seven miles away on the other side. She had privacy, and, outside of Erin and Elise and a few simple fishermen, no one knew she was there. Still, it was comforting to know that Travis was with her.

Around ten o'clock the drone of an inboard engine sounded across the water. Rebecca looked up to see a boat's running lights bobbing toward the pier, the beams stabbing through the darkness and reflecting on the calm surface like a silvery spill.

Her heart gave a little jerk. Common sense told her it was Travis, but all the same a frisson ran over her skin.

She went to the French doors. Standing to one side, she peeked around the edge of the jamb. The boat reduced speed as it approached the pier, the roar of the engine dropping to a throaty rumble. Suddenly the door to the boathouse began to rise, and a growing rectangle of yellow light shot out onto the shiny surface of the water. The boat entered the spill of light at a slow idle. Rebecca released the breath she'd been holding, the tautness draining out of her at the sight of Travis's blond hair blowing in the breeze.

She watched him guide the sleek craft into the boat-house. The rumble of the engine ceased, and the big overhead door rolled back down into place, leaving the dock area once more lit by only the dim light over the small side door. A few moments later it opened, and Travis stepped out onto the pier, carrying an ice chest, and headed toward the house. With a start, Rebecca jumped back from the window and scampered for her room.

She heard him come in, heard him thump and bang around in the kitchen and smiled at the image of Travis, who had been petted and pampered and catered to by women all of his life, ineptly preparing a meal for himself.

It was early yet, but Rebecca put on a nightgown and propped herself up in the bed with a lurid mystery novel someone had left on the bedside table. Feeling strangely content and secure, she settled back for a good read.

The next morning, as usual, Rebecca awoke before the sun. In the kitchen she found a note taped to the refrigerator.

Fresh fish in the freezer. Caught more than I can eat. Help yourself.

Terse and to the point, without a single pleasantry. How typical—at least, where she was concerned. With every other female between the age of nine months and ninety years, Travis was a charming flirt. Rebecca made a wry face and tossed the crumpled note into the trash.

So, Travis had spent the day fishing, had he. Funny. She would never have thought of that. Lolling on a secluded beach with a willing woman or sauntering through the posh watering holes on Alhaja Verde, yes, but never something so tame as fishing.

An hour later Rebecca was strolling along the beach a short way from the house, when Travis emerged. Barefoot, dressed in cutoffs and an unbuttoned shirt that flapped behind him like a flag in the breeze, he loped down the steps, carrying a cooler balanced on one shoulder and a boom box in his other hand.

If he saw her he gave no indication, but simply headed down the pier for the boathouse. Five minutes later, the sleek boat eased out of its berth and roared away toward the open waters of the Gulf.

As time slipped by, their days followed the same pattern. Travis disappeared in the boat every morning and returned late. Rebecca spent her time either roaming the island or swimming, or simply walking on the beach, never coming within speaking distance of Travis, but drawing comfort from his presence.

They had been sharing the house for almost a week when Travis returned about a half hour before sunset one evening. Rebecca was on the beach as usual, at some distance from the house. She sat motionless on the sand with her arms around her updrawn knees, gazing at the undulating waters. Remotely, she noted Travis's arrival but she remained as she was, content to let the peace of the island work its spell.

For so long she had lived on raw nerves, always apprehensive, tense. Now, in the calm and lulling solitude, the knot that had been in the pit of her stomach for so many years was beginning to ease.

Pensive and still, Rebecca watched the water change from blue to gold, and let the pervasive peace of the island seep into her soul.

Since arriving on Rincon Island she'd had time to do a lot of thinking and soul-searching. It was an excruciating process, something she had shied away from in the past, but the counselors and the support group at the crisis center had made her see that it was essential. She had to come to terms with all that had happened and shed the paralyzing mantle of self-blame before she could truly get on with her life.

So, in the quiet and solitude of the island, she examined it all—the early loneliness and disappointments of her childhood, the hopes and dreams and constant striving that had been doomed from the start, then later, the pain and terror. And worst of all . . . the humiliation, the feeling of utter worthlessness.

They were feelings that she still had to battle; the conditioning of a lifetime could not be undone overnight, she was discovering. But she was getting better every day, stronger. She was there, wasn't she? Somehow she had found the courage to take charge of her life.

In rehashing the past, Rebecca was consumed with sadness, but she felt anger, too—anger directed at herself, at Evan, at her father.

Her father. Picking up a handful of sand, Rebecca let it trickle through her fingers and pondered the awesome power a parent had over a child, its long-reaching effects. She had spent her childhood and most of her adult life yearning for her father's approval and love. Rebecca's mouth quirked. What a waste. She realized now that Richard Quinn would go to his grave bitterly resenting her for being female instead of the son and heir he had wanted. The only time she had truly pleased him was when she had married Evan.

Her father enjoyed having a wealthy and powerful man like Evan for a son-in-law. He was exactly the kind of son that Richard had always wanted. One thing was certain; her father would not be pleased when he returned from Europe and learned what she'd done.

The thought brought a rush of the old panicky feeling, but Rebecca managed to quell it. A reckoning would come. It was inevitable. But not now. Not yet. Not until she was stronger. Please, God.

Resting her cheek on her knees, Rebecca hugged her legs tighter and pushed the troubling thought away. She wouldn't think of that now.

With her eyes half-closed, she gazed at the brilliant display of fiery sky and sun-drenched waters. She sat so still she might have been made of stone, her only movement the steady rise and fall of her chest and shoulders. With each breath she absorbed the utter peace and tranquility, drew it deep into her as though it were a sweet scent hanging in the air, and let the whisper of waves breaking on the sand and the endless, mesmerizing movement work its healing magic on her troubled spirit.

What the devil was she doing down there?

Perched on the railing with one foot on the top plank, the other braced on the deck, Travis scowled at the huddled figure far down the beach. He took a swig of beer, then draped his arm over his updrawn knee, holding the long-necked brown bottle loosely in the circle of his thumb and forefinger, and regarded her steadily.

Every evening for the past week she'd been out there when he'd come home, either strolling along the water's edge or sitting on the sand watching the sunset. The sight of her, so remote and solitary, bothered him, and he found himself wondering about her. What did she do with herself all day while he was gone? What had her life been like these past years? What kind of marriage did she have? And what the devil was she thinking about so hard?

She hadn't moved since he arrived, and that had been twenty minutes ago. What problems could Rebecca possibly have that required that kind of deep thought?

A cynical smile tugged at Travis's mouth. Something trivial, no doubt. She'd always led a privileged life. She'd lived in the biggest house in town, worn the best clothes, had a fancy car at age sixteen, all the comforts and perks that money could buy.

Travis took another pull on the beer and scowled. He'd been so angry when she'd first arrived that he hadn't given a thought to why she had come to the island, especially alone, but now he wondered.

Erin had mentioned a bad experience. Had Rebecca had a spat with her husband? It was difficult to imagine her becoming aroused enough to quarrel with anyone, but he supposed it was possible. Maybe she'd come to Rincon without her husband's knowledge to worry him and teach him a lesson. That sounded like something Miss Butter-wouldn't-melt-in-her-mouth would do, he thought sourly.

The next instant, another, more worrisome thought struck Travis, and his eyes widened. His spine stiffened and he sat up straight, his indolent slouch abandoned. What would Evan Hall think if he knew his wife was sharing a house with another man?

If Rebecca were his woman, Travis knew he'd damned well be furious.

A sudden vision of an irate husband swooping down on him with murderous intentions brought him bounding off the rail with a burst of profanity.

In a blink he was across the deck and loping down the steps. Propelled by righteous ire, Travis stormed down the beach, his bare heels digging into the sand with each long stride. Dammit! He should have followed his instincts and sent her packing that first night.

He glared toward where Rebecca sat. In the gloaming all he could see was a shadowy form huddled on the sand, sitting utterly motionless. She seemed unaware of his approach until he drew to an abrupt halt directly in front of her.

She started and looked up, her eyes wide and blinking. "Travis," she whispered with obvious surprise.

She looked small and lonely and defenseless. Travis felt a pang of concern, but steeled himself against it.

"I want to know two things," he barked. "First, does your husband know that you're here? And if so, how is he going to react when he finds out you're staying in the same house with me?"

He stood over her like an avenging angel with his feet braced wide and his balled fists planted on his hips, but Rebecca met his glower with a steady look.

"Is that why you're so agitated? There's really no need for you to worry," she replied calmly.

She rose gracefully to her feet and brushed the sand off her seat then shook out the skirt of her lavender sundress.

She looked at him and smiled—that polite, distant smile he remembered so well—and he gritted his teeth.

"Evan poses no threat to you, Travis. I divorced him two months ago."

Chapter Three

Travis stared at her, speechless.

If Rebecca noticed his stunned reaction, she chose to ignore it. She gave him another ultrapolite smile and eased away a step. "Now, if you'll excuse me, I think I'll call it a day. Good night, Travis."

Without waiting for a reply, she walked away. He watched her retreating form fade until she was just a slender, slightly darker shadow moving through the dusky twilight.

So that was it. She had come to the island to lick her wounds. Funny. The idea that Rebecca might be divorced had not occurred to him. Probably because she and that cold-eyed bastard seemed ideally suited. Plus, Rebecca was so detached he couldn't imagine anything getting under her skin to the point that she'd put herself through that kind of gut-wrenching upheaval.

Sticking his fingertips into the back pockets of his jeans, Travis strolled back toward the house. Then again, theirs had probably been one of those "civilized" divorces, all very polite and unemotional.

He wondered who had initiated the split. Odds were, it was Evan. Rebecca wouldn't risk alienating her old man by making a move like that.

Ambling along at the edge of the surf in ankle-deep water, Travis eyed the lighted house thoughtfully. Man, oh man. He bet it had really hit the fan when Rebecca told her father. Old Richard Quinn had probably thrown a vein-popping, fire-breathing, wall-eyed fit. The whole town knew how proud he was of his big shot son-in-law.

Come to think of it, that was probably why Rebecca had taken refuge on the island—not because she was upset, but to escape her father's wrath and give him time to cool down.

When he reached the pier, Travis left the surf and climbed the beach to the house. On the deck he paused to hose the sand off his feet and legs and brace himself to face Rebecca again.

It was her night to use the living room, but when he stepped inside she was nowhere in sight.

He looked toward the right wing. The faint strains of a piano concerto were coming from her room. The music was the kind you played when you were melancholy or upset, and for the first time Travis wondered if beneath that calm exterior Rebecca wasn't more affected than she appeared.

Frowning, he went into the kitchen and rummaged in the refrigerator for the makings of a sandwich. A small ham, a bowl of potato salad and a lemon pie sat on the shelf that Rebecca used. He eyed the items sourly and pulled out a package of bologna and a jar of mustard.

When his makeshift meal was assembled, he carried it and a tumbler of milk into the living room. Dropping onto one of the rattan sofas, he slouched on his spine with his bare feet propped on the coffee table, the plate balanced on his flat belly. He bit off a fourth of the sandwich and chewed slowly, his unseeing gaze fixed on a wall hanging of seashells and driftwood.

So, Rebecca was divorced. Travis's mouth twitched. If she were anyone else, their situation might prove interesting. In his time he'd consoled many a despondent newly single

woman and helped just as many other gay divorcées cele-
brate their freedom.

He sobered at once. Of course, there was no chance at all
of anything like that happening in this case.

He took a swallow of milk and wiped his mouth with the
back of his hand. He should be relieved that Rebecca was
divorced. At least he wouldn't have to contend with a jeal-
ous husband.

Travis frowned. Somehow, though, he felt even more
uneasy than when he'd thought she was married.

The next morning Rebecca left the house early and walked
to the village. There she caught the ferry to the town of San
Cristobal, on the main island of Alhaja Verde.

Rebecca had made the trip once, and she had planned to
make it again in a day or so for more supplies, but after the
encounter on the beach and an almost sleepless night, she
was more anxious than usual to avoid Travis. Removing
herself from the island before he woke seemed the most
certain way of accomplishing that.

The problem was, she felt guilty. She hadn't been completely honest with Travis. She may have obtained a divorce, but she knew perfectly well that would not mean
anything to Evan.

If he ever found out that she was sharing a house with
Travis he would be livid. It wasn't a matter of jealousy. For
that Evan would have to love her, and Rebecca doubted that
he ever had. She didn't think he was capable of loving anyone. But he was a possessive man; what was his, remained
his... until he was ready to let it go.

How much of a threat he was to Travis remained to be
seen. Brawling with another man, especially one as fit and
potentially dangerous as Travis, wasn't Evan's style. He
never entered a battle he wasn't certain he could win.

It was unfair of her not to explain the situation to Travis,
but she was afraid if she did he might leave, and she didn't
want that. Anyway, the very thought of admitting to him
that she had been a battered wife made her cringe. God

knew, he had a low enough opinion of her as it was. She had no difficulty at all imagining his disgust if he were to learn the truth about her marriage to Evan.

The ferry reached San Cristobal around noon. Hungry, Rebecca headed straight for Pepe's Cantina, which was located on the beach road, a block from the harbor. As usual, during the short walk, small children crowded around, hawking their wares—everything from chewing gum to straw hats and pottery. Before she reached the cantina Rebecca had succumbed to the blandishment of several pairs of pleading brown eyes.

"Ay yi yi! Señora Hall, you have done it again," Constanza Moralles cried, throwing up her hands when Rebecca entered the cantina loaded down with a serape, two straw hats and a crudely carved wooden statue of a burro. "I told you, you must tell those *niños* to go away. You cannot buy something every time you get off the ferry. They take advantage of you, *señora.*"

"I know, Constanza," Rebecca replied sheepishly. "You're right, of course. I promise I won't do it again."

The motherly Mexican woman rolled her eyes and muttered a string of rapid-fire Spanish. "That is what you say the last time." Still shaking her head, she took the purchases from Rebecca and waved her toward the back of the room. "Come. Sit down. I will put these away and bring you something to eat."

"Pepe!" she yelled at her husband. "Wine for the Señora! *Pronto! Pronto!*"

Constanza bustled away toward the family living quarters at the rear of the cantina, and her scrawny little husband hopped to do her bidding. Stifling a grin, Rebecca settled into a booth.

For a large woman, Constanza moved with amazing speed. Only seconds after Pepe arrived at the table with a bottle of wine and three glasses, she returned carrying a tray loaded down with platters of spicy enchiladas, tacos, rice and beans.

"Ah, Señora Hall," Pepe greeted, smiling broadly. "We are so happy to see you again. Only this morning Señora Delany, she called, asking about you."

"Erin? Called here? About me? But why?"

"Your friend, she was worried." Pepe slid onto the seat across from her and filled the three glasses with red wine. His wife unloaded the tray and sat down on the bench seat next to Rebecca. "The *señora,* she tried several times to reach you at the beach house but you did not answer, so she called here to see if Pepe and Constanza had seen you."

"Oh. I see. I'm sorry she bothered you. You see, I'm usually out on the beach. I—"

"Ai yi yi! Do not worry about it, *señora.* It was no bother. Pepe and I, we talk to the *señoras,* and to their *hermano,* their brother, Señor David and his wife, *frecuentemente.* How you say...very off-teen. *No es nada.*"

"Si, *señora.* I myself told Señora Delany not to worry. Pepe will look after you," the little man said, thumping a fist against his chest dramatically.

Rebecca lifted the glass to her lips to hide another grin. Erin and Elise had told her all about their friends, the Moralleses. Despite his scrawny build, Pepe considered himself to be a *muy macho hombre.* Apparently so did his wife, though she stood three inches taller than her excitable husband and outweighed him by at least seventy-five pounds.

Until he had gotten embroiled with David Blaine and Abigail Stuart in an international intelligence operation the previous month, Pepe had also fancied himself a potential James Bond. According to the twins, however, the hair-raising episode had dulled his enthusiasm for espionage work. Pepe was still fascinated by David's and Travis's tales about their past assignments with the FBI, but he no longer hankered quite so much for a life of living dangerously.

"The *señora,* she wanted to know if you were getting along with Señor Travis," Constanza added, spooning another helping of rice onto Rebecca's plate.

Rebecca's fork halted halfway to her mouth. So... Erin and Elise *hadn't* forgotten that Travis was staying at the beach house after all.

"I told her that there was no need to worry. Señor Travis, he is a gentleman." Darting a look around, Pepe leaned closer and in a conspiratorial whisper, added, "Besides, what better protection could you have than one of your own government's agents? Eh?"

"He is also *muy atractio,* this *hombre,*" Constanza added with a sly look that made Rebecca uneasy. "Who knows? Perhaps soon you and Senor Travis will be more than just old friends."

Rebecca almost choked on a bit of enchilada. More than friends? Good, Lord. She and Travis had never been even that. She did not tell Constanza and Pepe that, of course, but she did make it clear that there was no possibility of anything developing between herself and Travis, much to the disappointment of the romantic-minded pair.

Still, they continued to extol Travis's virtues and his sexy good looks and hint at what an excellent match the two of them made. Uncomfortable, Rebecca quickly finished her meal and excused herself to finish shopping, leaving her earlier purchases with them to be picked up on her way back to the evening ferry.

Rebecca spent the afternoon wandering through the marketplace, where her senses were swamped by the mélange of sights and sounds and smells—the array of colorful wares, the babble of voices speaking in Mexican and English, the bleat of goats and bray of burros, the rattle of vendors' carts, the scents of spices and tortilla and frying meat that hung in the air along with the pungent smells of animals, straw, dust, leather and humans. Blending with it all was the occasional whiff of the island's profusion of wild flowers. Rebecca was enchanted.

By late afternoon she had two carryall bags filled with groceries—vegetables and fruit she had purchased from the street vendors and staples from the town's lone supermarket. She had been so enthralled that time got away from her

and it was late when she started back to the harbor. She
covered the distance to the beach road at a pace just short
of a run.

"Whoa, *señora!* Slow down, slow down," Pepe urged
when she rushed into the cantina. "Here, sit and rest yourself. I will get you something cool to drink."

"I can't, Pepe," she gasped. "No time. I've got to hurry
or I'll miss the ferry."

"Ah, but there is no need for you take the ferry, *señora.*
Señor Travis, he is here. See. There, at the other end of the
bar. He will take you back to Rincon. I will go tell him that
you have arrived."

"No! Wait! Pepe, don't—" Rebecca began, but the wiry
little man had already darted toward the opposite end of the
bar, calling Travis's name.

"Oh, no," Rebecca moaned.

Travis was talking with the couple sitting next to him.
Relaxed and laughing, he tossed a handful of peanuts into
his mouth and washed them down with a swallow of beer.

Rebecca stared, something about the tabloid catching her
unawares. This was vintage Travis, she realized with that old
familiar pang. The real Travis. The one the rest of the world
saw—relaxed, amiable, a charming devil who sauntered
through life with a wink and a grin.

He lounged on the bar stool in that loose, boneless way
he had, looking somehow indolent and formidable all at
once.

He wore faded, holey jeans, disreputable tennis shoes
with no socks, and a much-washed T-shirt with the sleeves
cut out, revealing the snarling leopard tattoo on his upper
right arm. Around his forehead was a folded bandanna tied
as a sweatband. His long blond hair hung down his back,
almost to his shoulder blades, glittering in the dim light, in
sharp contrast to that of the dark-haired patrons all around
him. The stubble he had sported the night she arrived had
grown into the beginnings of a shaggy, reddish-brown
beard.

A slow grin created fine crinkle lines around his eyes, and as he shook his head in response to a comment from one of his companions, the two-inch saber dangling from his earlobe swung rakishly. With his chiseled good looks, his scruffy attire and his devil-may-care attitude, he looked like a cross between a movie star, a pirate and a biker bum.

Rebecca watched as Pepe caught his attention and chattered away to him over the bar, arms waving. She saw the subtle stiffening of Travis's body, the frown that replaced his lazy grin. He looked her way, and Rebecca bit her lower lip.

After a moment he hitched himself off the bar stool and headed for her. He walked with that loose-limbed, hip-rolling saunter, his thumbs hooked in the belt loops of his low-riding jeans, his gray eyes boring into her from beneath half-closed lids. He looked annoyed... and dangerous. Rebecca felt her stomach clench.

"Pepe says you need a lift back to the island," he said in a flat voice.

"No. Really. That won't be necessary. I'll take the ferry. I just stopped by to pick up some packages I left here."

"Nonsense, *señora*. You cannot want to ride that old rust bucket ferry when you can return in the speedboat with Señor Travis. He insists that you ride with him. Isn't that right, Señor?"

"Yeah, sure," Travis drawled, but Pepe missed the sarcasm in his voice. Rebecca started to protest again, but Travis grasped her elbow and turned her toward the door. "C'mon. Let's go."

"Wait! I have to get my things."

"Here they are, *señora*." Constanza came hurrying around the bar and handed the bundle to Travis. He slung the straw bag over his shoulder and said good-night to the Moralleses. With a steel grip on Rebecca's elbow, he steered her out the door.

"You can let go," she said the moment they were out of sight of the beaming couple. "You're off the hook now."

He snorted. "Oh, yeah, sure. In a pig's eye."

"Travis, you don't have to do this. I can still make the ferry if I hurry."

"You don't get it, do you? Between them, Pepe and Constanza are related to over half the people on this island. Nothing goes on that they don't hear about. If I let you take the ferry now, they'd know it before that tug cleared the harbor. And they'd be giving Erin and Elise an earful five minutes after that. Not only would my cousins have my hide, my name would be mud on this island."

"Couldn't we simply explain the situation and our agreement?"

"No. Take my word for it, they'd never understand."

"But—"

"Drop it, Rebecca. I'm taking you back in the speed-boat. I like Pepe and Constanza and I like coming to San Cristobal now and then to unwind. I'm not going to be labeled a villain because of your bad timing."

"I'm terribly sorry if my presence here has made difficulties for you," she said, casting an anxious look at his profile. He hustled her along so fast every third step she had to do a little hop and skip just to keep up with his angry stride. "That certainly was never my intention."

"Yeah, well, you're sure doing a good job of it."

His boorish behavior cut Rebecca to the quick. Instead of lashing back, she did what she always did when hurt; she withdrew into herself, erecting an invisible barrier between them against further pain. Her expression remote, she allowed him to lead her down the pier to the boat, accepted his helping hand with a polite "Thank you" as she climbed aboard, then took a seat as far away from him as she could get and folded her hands in her lap. During the entire twenty-mile trip she stared out at the ocean and uttered not another word.

Once clear of the harbor, Travis sent the small craft skimming over the water at full throttle. Throughout the trip, except for her hair streaming out behind her and grabbing the seat every now and then when they bounced over a wave, Rebecca remained as composed and still as if she were in church. Her insouciance made Travis do a slow burn. Didn't the woman ever react to anything?

He knew she wasn't to blame for the awkward situation. She hadn't known he was in San Cristobal any more than he'd known that she was, but his ire needed a target.

The irony of that was not lost on Travis. Anger and frustration were foreign to his nature. At the Bureau he had a reputation for being unshakable, nerveless. If a case called for an unflappable attitude and a cool head, he was the one they assigned. His personal philosophy was that life was too short and too ridiculous to sweat the small stuff. Anyway, there was very little worth getting bent out of shape over. Generally, he dealt with what he could and the rest he ignored.

The exception was, and always had been, Rebecca. Just being around her set his teeth on edge.

He watched her, his jaw set. Gradually he became aware of the way the wind molded the cotton sundress to her breasts, the long curves of her legs, the creaminess of her skin, the delicate perfection of her features. She was, he admitted grudgingly, one of the most beautiful women he'd ever seen, and without even knowing it, she exuded a quiet sexuality. All of which made him furious. God! What a waste.

They made the return trip in less than half the time it took the ferry. When the boat was secured and they were standing on the pier, Rebecca turned to him with a stiff smile. "Thank you for bringing me back. In the future, however, if you will let me know when you're planning to visit San Cristobal I will remain here. That way we can avoid any more awkward encounters." With a nod, she hefted her purchases, turned and walked sedately up the pier to the house.

Travis watched her go, gritting his teeth. It was a sensible suggestion. Eminently sensible. But, dammit! He was spoiling for a fight! He didn't want to hear sensible suggestions!

At the end of the pier a lifebuoy lay atop a coil of rope, which tethered it to a piling. Making a frustrated sound, Travis hauled off and kicked the floatation ring as hard as he could, sending it sailing out over the water, the rope unfurling behind like a long snake.

For the next six days their routine remained unchanged; Rebecca arose early, ate breakfast and left the house before Travis emerged and disappeared in the boat. On the seventh day, however, exactly one week after the encounter on Alhaja Verde, he decided he could use a change, and spent the morning in the boathouse, giving the inboard engine on Max Delany's speedboat a tune-up.

High-speed engines, whether in cars, planes, motorcycles or boats, were one of Travis's passions, tinkering with one his favorite way to relax. After five hours and three skinned knuckles, the boat was running like a top, and he emerged from the boathouse tired, hungry, covered with grease and feeling pleasantly mellow.

The last lingered only as long as it took him to reach the house. The moment he stepped through the door and his senses were assaulted by the delicious smell of something cooking, his mood took a nosedive.

The source of the heavenly aroma, he discovered, was a simmering Crockpot of stew on the kitchen counter. As usual, Rebecca was nowhere in sight.

His mouth watered and his stomach growled. Almost snarling, Travis snatched a can of chili from the pantry, dumped the contents into a bowl and zapped the spicy glob in the microwave. Sitting at the counter, he shoveled the unappetizing concoction into his mouth and glowered at the simmering stew.

The woman was driving him crazy, just as he'd known she would. Oh, sure, she'd lived up to her end of their bargain. With a vengeance. He rarely caught so much as a glimpse of her. Hell, even when it was her night to use the living room, when he returned in the evenings she always scurried off to her room before he reached the house—as if he were some kind of ogre, or something. It irritated the hell out of him.

Out of sight or not, he was always aware that she was there. How could he not be? There were constant signs of her presence everywhere—one of her books left on the sofa, a glass in the sink with lipstick on it, a faint drift of perfume in the air, the sound of music coming from her room. The other day he found a pair of scanty lace panties she'd left in the dryer. He sent another black look at the Crockpot. Worst of all, the smell of her cooking was driving him nuts.

That had come as a shock. He hadn't expected Rebecca to be able to cook at all. Nor to know how to keep house. The Quinns had always had domestic help. Since her mother's death, when she was five or so, there had been a string of housekeepers to run the Quinn home and see to Rebecca's needs. Yet, if smell were anything to go by, she was an excellent cook. She also kept the living room and kitchen, and what he could see of her side of the house, neat and clean as a pin. By comparison, his bedroom was beginning to look like a disaster area.

Giving a disgruntled snort, Travis slid off the bar stool and sauntered around the counter. No sooner had he put his bowl and glass in the sink then he stepped on something sharp.

"Hell and damnation!" He hopped around on one foot, cursing vividly and holding the injured foot in his hand. Finally he leaned against the counter to examine the injury, and uttered a choice expletive at the sight of the small gold earring embedded, post first, in the sole of his foot.

His inhaled breath whistled between his gritted teeth when he plucked the ornament out of his flesh. He slammed the earring down on the counter and limped through the living room and down the hall to his bathroom in search of alcohol and a Band-Aid.

Hellfire! Living with Rebecca was like living with a damned ghost!

By the time Travis had showered and doctored his foot the rare burst of temper had subsided and his usual indolent, sunny outlook had returned.

It was too late to go fishing, but he wasn't in the mood to just lie around the empty house. Besides, he was tired of his own company. What he needed was a night in Alhaja Verde. He'd go to Pepe's Cantina, have a few beers, enjoy some of Constanza's great cooking, shoot the breeze with her gregarious little husband. Maybe he'd even dance with a pretty *señorita* or two.

Cheered by the prospect, Travis shoved his bare feet into a pair of deck shoes and headed for the boathouse, whistling a snappy tune as he sauntered down the pier with his hands in his pockets, his long blond hair lifting in the Gulf breeze.

"I just love a man with a tattoo," the redhead purred. Giving him a sultry look, she traced the snarling leopard with one long scarlet nail. "It's so manly."

"Oh yeah?" Travis shot her an amused glance and took a sip of beer.

"No really. I mean it." She leaned closer and rubbed her breast against his arm. Her eyelids grew heavier and her fingers crept up over his shoulder and threaded through the hair at his nape, the long nails lightly scoring his scalp. "There's something so sexy about it. So...deliciously primitive. And this earring..." She flipped the dangling saber. "Oh, baby." The last came out on a breathy whisper that feathered about his ear.

Travis grunted and resisted the urge to scratch the annoying tickle. Her perfume, undoubtedly expensive, was suffocating him, and her breath smelled of gin and cigarettes.

He wondered why what had seemed like such a good idea a few hours earlier had lost all appeal.

For the past hour, Bootsie Whatever-her-name-was had been coming on to him with all the finesse and subtlety of a sailor on a three-hour pass, but for some reason he wasn't even tempted.

She simply didn't appeal to him, he told himself, nor did her life-style.

Bootsie—Travis shuddered just thinking the ridiculous name—was with a party traveling on one of the luxurious private yachts in the harbor—one of the idle rich, seeking a diversion from boredom. From the moment she and her friends had wandered into Pepe's, loudly demanding service, she'd latched onto him.

She probably thought, from his appearance, that he was a shady character. Not that he blamed her. So had the slimeballs he'd busted on his last undercover assignment on the Miami docks.

He liked women. Hell, he adored women. All kinds. Short, tall, thin, chubby, brunette, blonde, young, old—he thought they were all terrific. He enjoyed their company. He liked the way they looked, the way they smelled, the way they talked, the way they walked. Hell, he even found their thought processes fascinating. But when it came to intimacy, he did have certain standards. And they didn't include letting himself be seduced by a spoiled socialite looking for a cheap thrill.

The trouble was, in the beginning, when the idea of a little feminine company had still held appeal, he'd made the mistake of flirting right back. The longer he'd talked to her, however, the more he'd been put off. Now he had to find a graceful way of extricating himself.

He'd cooled his response, but the subtle approach was wasted on Bootsie. Travis glanced at Pepe, then at Constanza, and sighed. He'd get no help from that quarter. For some reason, the Moralleses had been glaring disapproval ever since the redhead had perched herself on the bar stool next to him.

Bootsie pressed closer, and Travis felt a sharp nip on his lobe. "Travis, honey," she murmured in his ear. "Why don't you and I go back to my stateroom on the *Ilona*. We'll have privacy there so we can..." She traced the swirls in his ear with the tip of her tongue and made a purring sound. "...really get to know one another. What do you say?"

Her hand settled on his thigh and began a slow foray upward but Travis caught it and leaned away, breaking contact with the woman's voracious tongue and hot breath. "Sorry," he said with what he hoped with a regretful smile. "But I can't."

"Why not?"

"Because . . . I'm, uh . . . I'm involved with someone. Seriously involved."

Bootsie narrowed her eyes. "I don't believe you. If you're involved with someone, what are you doing on Alhaja Verde alone?"

"I'm not. I'm vacationing here with my fiancée."

"Vacationing? You?" She gave him a slow once-over, from his sockless feet to his long mane of hair, and a cynical smile curled her lips. "Frankly, honey, you're a good-looking devil, but you hardly look like a tourist. Or the type to have a fiancée."

Travis shrugged. "Sorry, but I am. And I do."

"Oh, yeah. Then where is she?"

"Shopping. You know how it is with us guys and shopping," he said with a sheepish half smile. "She's meeting me here when she finishes."

Bootsie took a deep drag on her cigarette and blew a stream of smoke toward the ceiling. She watched Travis, her gaze frankly disbelieving. "It's getting dark out. The market closed a half hour ago. You wouldn't by chance be trying to give me the brush-off, now would you, Travis? If you are, I warn you, I don't give up that easily."

"No, really. She should have been here by now." Feigning worry, Travis looked toward the entrance, just in time to see Rebecca push through the door with a shopping bag on each arm. On impulse, he slid off the stool. "Ah, there she is now," he said, and headed for her.

He strode purposely through the crowded room. Rebecca, her gaze sweeping the dim cantina for an empty table, didn't see him until he was only a few feet away. The shock of recognition flashed in her eyes when she spotted him bearing down on her, and she instinctively took a step back. Her eyes grew even wider when he came to a halt in front of her and grasped her shoulders.

"Darling," Travis exclaimed. "Where have you been? I was beginning to worry."

Before she could stammer out a reply, he hauled her up against his chest and caught her mouth with his.

Chapter Four

Rebecca stood ramrod stiff within Travis's grasp, her eyes wide and startled.

His lips rocked over her unresponsive ones for a moment before he pulled back a fraction and muttered, ''For God's sake, loosen up and kiss me back, will ya? I'll explain latter.''

She barely had time to draw a breath before he wrapped his arms around her and recaptured her gaping mouth in a kiss that she felt right down to her toes.

She had no choice but to do as he asked; every muscle in her body went weak and trembly, melting like wax as a searing heat poured through her veins. Slowly, the handles of the shopping bags slid from her arms, and the straw carryalls thumped to the floor. Her eyelids drifted shut and she went limp against Travis's chest. Of their own accord, her arms slid around him, her hands clutching the worn T-shirt stretched taut across his broad back.

Her heart banged against her ribs. Dazed and disoriented, Rebecca clung to Travis, the only solid thing in a suddenly topsy-turvy world.

A moment ago, she had simply been standing there minding her own business, tired and thirsty, her feet aching from hours of wandering through the market. The only thought on her mind had been finding a table and getting a cool drink before she had to leave to catch the ferry. The last thing she had expected was to be snatched into a passionate embrace.

From shoulder to knee, she was locked against Travis's body, and her head swam with the smell and feel and taste of him. Her sensory perception was suddenly so acute it was as though her entire body had turned into a bundle of quivering nerve endings. She was aware of his warmth searing her, his hardness and solid strength pressing against her breasts, her abdomen, her thighs, the steely arms wrapped around her, the soft prickle of his beard against her face as his mobile lips devoured hers. Slowly, rhythmically, his tongue stroked into her mouth in an incredibly erotic caress. Rebecca moaned and clutched him harder, kissing him back with mindless fervor as her knees began to give way.

The kiss may have lasted an instant or an hour; Rebecca had no idea. It was several seconds after Travis raised his head before she realized that it was over. Slowly, as though they were weighted with lead, she opened her eyes to find him studying her with a puzzled expression.

Before she could form a coherent thought, he hugged her close once more. "I know you're confused but I'll explain all this later. I swear it," he whispered in her ear. "For now, just follow my lead. Okay?"

At that moment Rebecca remembered where they were and became aware of the amused grins on the faces of the people around them. When Travis felt her stiffen, he tightened his embrace. "Please, Rebecca," he pleaded. "Just play along."

Without waiting for her agreement, he turned and announced loudly, "C'mon, honey. There's someone over here

I want you to meet.'' He headed back to the bar with Rebecca tucked snugly against his side. Too benumbed to resist, she stumbled along beside him in a daze.

A slender, expensively dressed redhead watched their approach with bored cynicism. When they stopped in front of the woman, Travis gave Rebecca's waist a warning squeeze. ''Sweetheart, I'd like you to meet Bootsie...uh...''

''Wellingford-Tremaine,'' the redhead supplied. ''Bootsie Wellingford-Tremaine.''

''Uh, yeah. Bootsie, this is Rebecca Quinn, the one I've been telling you about.''

Rebecca managed a strained smile and mumbled a few words of greeting, but she was so busy trying to gather her scattered wits she had no idea what they were. She was uncomfortably aware of Travis's arm around her, and his lean body pressing against her side.

The redhead puffed on her cigarette and looked Rebecca over, from her windblown hair to her simple skirt and blouse, all the way down to her bare legs and sandaled feet. ''So...you're Travis's fiancée?''

Rebecca jolted and at the same time Travis gave her waist another squeeze. ''Fi-fian—?''

''Now, sweetheart, don't be angry. I know we agreed to keep our engagement secret for a while. But hey, you know how it is when people get to talking over drinks. Besides, I'm so crazy about you, I had to tell somebody.''

Rebecca looked up at Travis and experienced another shock when she found him gazing down at her like an adoring lover. A tender smile curved his mouth, and his eyes held a warmth she had never seen before. At least, not when he was looking at her.

She felt another nudge at her waist and closed her mouth. ''I, uh...I see. Well...'' She looked back at Bootsie and tried to smile but the result was merely an awkward wavering of her lips.

''Funny. I'm having a hard time picturing the two of you together,'' Bootsie drawled.

"Oh, we're together, all right. In fact, we're spending the summer together at my cousins' beach house. Isn't that right, honey?"

"Yes. Yes, that's right," Rebecca agreed quickly, grateful for a question she could answer truthfully.

"Yeah, before we announce our engagement, we thought we'd give it a trial run. You know—see how well we rub along together on a daily basis. Test how sexually attuned we are. That sort of thing," Travis added, nearly causing Rebecca to choke.

"And how's it working out?"

The challenge in the woman's voice didn't faze Travis. A grin spread over his face, his teeth a slash of white in the reddish-brown beard. His hot gaze swept over Rebecca in a look so explicitly sexual she blushed. "Terrific," he murmured in a deep, lascivious rumble, and placed a lingering kiss against her temple. "Absolutely terrific."

"Ay yi yi! I knew you it! I knew it! Didn't I tell you, *mi esposa!*"

To Rebecca's horror, Constanza, her round face beaming, bustled around the bar, plucked her from Travis's embrace, and swooped her up in a suffocating hug.

"Ah, *sí, sí! Mi* Constanza, she tell me only the other day that you and the *señorita* were..." Pepe paused to close his eyes and kiss his fingertips dramatically. "...*enamorado.* How you say—in love! Ah, *señor! Señorita!* Pepe and Constanza, we are *muy* happy for you!"

Rebecca sent a frantic look Travis's way, but he ignored it. Other than a brief frown, he seemed unconcerned. He even accepted Pepe's hearty handshake and thumps on the back with an infuriatingly self-satisfied masculine grin.

"Thanks, *mi amigo.* But hey, listen. Do me a favor and keep this quiet, will you. If Erin and Elise get wind of it the whole family will know within an hour, and Rebecca and I aren't ready to make an announcement yet."

"Ah, *sí.* Pepe understands the affairs of the heart. Do not worry, Señor Travis. Your secret is safe."

"*Traa-vis!*" Rebecca hissed. "You've got to expla—"

Snagging her waist again, Travis jerked her close, and she slammed against his side with an *oof* that cut off her protest in mid-spate. Before she could recover, he bent and planted another hard kiss on her mouth. When he raised his head, he smiled indulgently, but his eyes held a warning she could not miss.

"Don't worry, sweetheart. You heard Pepe. He'll keep our secret." He flashed his roguish grin at the others and began to maneuver Rebecca toward the door. "You'll have to excuse us, but we're going to head for home. It's a long way back to the island, and Rebecca's tired after all that shopping." He picked up the straw carryalls Rebecca had dropped.

"But Señor Travis, you must stay for dinner so that we may toast your engagement. Constanza, she will cook something *muy especial*."

"*Muchos gracias, mi amigo,* but we can't. Rebecca left dinner cooking, so we have to get back. Some other time, maybe. So long, Bootsie. *Buenas noches.*"

"Would you mind telling me what that was all about?" Rebecca demanded the instant they were outside.

Travis gripped her elbow and, with a nonchalance that Rebecca found stunning, led her down the beach road toward the marina where he docked the speedboat.

"It's simple. Bootsie was becoming a bit of a problem. To discourage her, I had to make her think I was seriously involved with someone else."

"That's it? You were just trying to give some rich jet-setter the brush off?" Rebecca exhaled a long-suffering sigh and pressed the fingertips of her free hand to her forehead. "I realize that it would probably have been the first time in living memory, but couldn't you have told her that you weren't interested?"

He slanted her a disgruntled look. "Cute, Rebecca. Real cute. In case you didn't notice, that is one tenacious female. Short of being brutal, I doubt she would have accepted that, and I don't like hurting women."

Rebecca looked at him sharply, and had to battle down a bubble of hysterical laughter. She wanted to point out that he had hurt her plenty of times. Even now, he was more concerned about a stranger's feelings than hers.

But she didn't. Mainly because she knew it was true. With the exception of herself, Travis was a cream puff where women were concerned. A modern-day Sir Galahad in sneakers and holey jeans.

"Okay, I accept that, but why me?"

Travis shrugged. "You just happened to come in at the right time. It's no big deal." They reached the marina, and he guided her down the correct pier.

"No big deal? But don't you see what a mess you've gotten us into? Now Pepe and Constanza think that we're in love and that we're...well...living together."

"We are living together."

"You know perfectly well what I mean. They think we're going to be married. And regardless of what Pepe said, sooner or later they're sure to slip and say something to Erin and Elise. Knowing Pepe, probably sooner."

"Don't worry. I'll handle it." They reached the boat and Travis jumped aboard, then extended a hand to assist Rebecca. "First thing tomorrow morning I'll come back and explain that I made the whole thing up to get Bootsie off my back."

"Fine. You do that."

"Will you quit worrying about it? It was just a harmless deception. You're acting like it's the end of the world."

"I am not. I just wish you hadn't involved me, is all." Rebecca settled herself on the padded seat and gave an annoyed sniff. "It does seem to me that a man with your experience with women could have handled the situation in a more straightforward manner."

"I handled the situation just fine. So just shut up about it," he snapped, and switched on the engine.

Rebecca pressed her lips together and fell into an offended silence. Not that it mattered. Ignoring her, Travis opened the throttle all the way the instant they cleared the harbor, sending the boat pounding over the choppy waves and making conversation impossible.

She was still smarting when they reached Rincon, and when they stepped out of the boathouse onto the pier, she turned to Travis, her expression stiff. "You will straighten this mess out with the Moralleses first thing tomorrow, won't you?"

"Dammit! I said I would, didn't I?"

"You don't have to shout. I just wanted to be sure."

"Don't worry. I'll explain. It shouldn't be too difficult to convince them that there's nothing between us. What man in his right mind would want to cozy up to an icicle like you?"

Rebecca sucked in her breath and stepped back, her face stricken.

"That's a rotten thing to say." Her voice, barely above a whisper, quavered emotion.

"What's the matter? Can't take the truth?"

"It's not true. It's not!"

"No? Well if that kiss back at Pepe's is anything to go by, it's no wonder you're divorced," Travis taunted. "Hell, even a cold customer like Evan Hall needs a responsive woman in his bed, not a marble statue."

Rebecca struggled to swallow the hurt and the anger, but for once she could not. "You know nothing!" she said in a furious voice that rose steadily in volume and intensity. "Not about my marriage and not about me. Do you hear me, Travis McCall? You know nothing! So just shut up!"

"I know—"

"I said *shut up!*" she shrieked, and lunged forward.

She caught him off-guard, ramming him stiff-armed, her flat palms striking him square in the chest, and shoved with all her might. He went staggering backward. For a moment he teetered on the edge of the pier, arms flailing, his expression comically shocked. Rebecca burst into tears, grabbed her bags and took off up the pier at a dead run an instant before he lost the battle with momentum and gravity and toppled over.

By the time Travis hauled himself back up onto the pier, she had disappeared inside the house. He stood there, wiping his face and dripping sea water. It collected in a puddle around his feet, only one of which was still in a shoe.

"Dammit. These were my favorite deck shoes," he muttered, wringing out the tail of his T-shirt.

He looked toward the house and shook his head. Rebecca had actually pushed him into the water. And shrieked at him like a fishwife. Amazing. Never, not in his wildest dreams, would he have guessed that she had that kind of fire in her.

No, that wasn't quite true. Not after that kiss. He had tasted the passion in her then, and it had thrown him for a loop. Travis pulled both hands down over his face. Ah, hell, he might as well admit it—so had his own response. He hadn't expected to feel anything, and he hadn't liked it when he had. Which was why he'd said all those nasty things to her.

He grimaced, remembering. Immediately, remorse and shame flooded him. Never in his whole life had he treated a woman so poorly, not even Rebecca. "Dammit, McCall. What the devil is the matter with you lately?" he muttered.

But he knew. He'd lashed out instinctively in self-defense. He sighed and wrung out his hair. "Stupid, masculine self-defense. And ego." He'd been so sure all these years that he had her pegged. It wasn't an easy thing, finding out that he might have been wrong, even if it was only about her ability to respond sexually.

Travis sighed. Bad as he hated to admit it, he owed her an apology. He glanced at the house again. After that little fracas, the chances of her still being in the living room were poor to nil. She was probably holed up in her room with the door barricaded, bawling her eyes out.

He found the thought strangely disturbing, and his guilty conscience pricked him even more. Who could blame her? Rebecca Quinn may be a stiff-necked, cold, pain-in-the-butt, but she didn't deserve the things he'd said to her.

Glumly, Travis started up the pier, his one shoe squishing. It was probably for the best though that he put his apology on hold, as upset as she was. He'd give her tonight to calm down and talk to her tomorrow morning.

First thing, he told himself, and ignored the little voice in his head that whispered, *Coward.*

Travis arose early the next morning. Like a child bracing for a dose of bad medicine, throughout his shower, and while he was getting dressed, he rehearsed his apology. Determined to get the whole thing over with as quickly as possible, he marched down the hall with his jaw set, muttering the stilted little speech over and over.

He expected to find Rebecca in the kitchen preparing her breakfast, but she wasn't there. He came to a halt in the center of the living room and planted his fists on his hips, thoroughly aggravated. The kitchen was neat as a pin, but the half-full pot of coffee told him that she had already eaten and gone.

Cursing under his breath, Travis stomped out on the deck and scanned the beach in both directions. It took a while, but he finally spotted her, sitting huddled on the sand with her arms wrapped around her updrawn legs. Travis scowled. What the devil was she doing down there? Hell, it was barely dawn. The sun hadn't even cleared the horizon yet.

He hated the idea of chasing after her and was considering putting off his apology until that evening, when the telephone rang.

Travis groaned and stomped back inside. At that hour of the morning there were only two possibilities: an emergency, either at the Bureau or with his family. Or it was one of the twins.

"Yeah, who is it?" he growled into the receiver.

"My, my. Aren't you just a ray of sunshine?"

Travis closed his eyes. He would have preferred an emergency. "Knock it off, Erin."

"Did you hear that, Elise? Can you believe it? That's our happy-go-lucky cousin talking."

"Goodness, Travis," Elise chimed in. "I never knew you were such a grump in the morning. I'm shocked."

"Ah, jeez. They're both on the line," he groaned at the ceiling.

"No, I don't think that's it, sis. Remember all those camping trips and sleep overs. He was always the one who was disgustingly cheerful in the morning. No, I think it's something—or someone—else that's put his nose out of joint."

"Mmm. You're probably right."

"Hey! Hey! Would you two mind not talking about me as though I weren't even on the line, for Pete's sake. What are you calling me for this early anyway? And I'm warning you, it had better be good."

"Ha, smarty! It so happens, we aren't calling you. We're calling Rebecca to wish her a happy birthday. We know what a morning person she is so we got up early especially to catch her before she left the house. Put her on, would you."

"I can't. She's not here."

"Travis McCall. You haven't run her off, have you?" Elise demanded with uncharacteristic sternness.

"No, I haven't run her off," he shot back in a mocking sing-song. "She's down on the beach."

"At this hour? What's she doing down there?"

"How should I know? As far as I can tell, she's just staring out at the water."

"Uh-oh. That doesn't sound good," Erin murmured, her voice turning serious.

"No, it doesn't," Elise agreed. "But it's hardly surprising, after what she's been through."

"What do you mean, after what she's been through? Say, are you two by any chance talking about her split with her husband?"

"She told you about that?"

"Only that she divorced him two months ago." He paused for Elise to elaborate, but all he got was silence. Finally he sighed. "So? Are you going to fill me in or not?"

"We can't, Travis," Erin answered. "It's Rebecca's personal business and we can't betray her confidence. All we can tell you is she's had a really rough time of it."

"That's right. So you be nice to her now, Travis. You hear?"

Travis snorted. "Yeah. Right. I'll stay as far away from her as I can. Will that do?"

"No, it certainly will not. Look, I don't know why you're such a jerk when it comes to Rebecca, but for today at least can't you put that aside and be your normal charming self?"

"What are you saying, Erin?" he asked warily.

"I'm saying that on top of everything else, it's Rebecca birthday and she's all alone. She's bound to be feeling blue. Couldn't you spend the day with her? Take her somewhere? Do something to cheer her up? You're good at that sort of thing."

"What! Are you nuts? No. Oh, no. Absolutely not. Forget it."

"C'mon, Travis. It's her birthday."

"No."

"*Pleeeze*. You'd be doing us a tremendous favor."

"You can cut out the wheedling. It won't work this time. And that goes for you, too, Elise, so just don't start."

"Well! I like that."

"C'mon, Tra—"

"No. And that's final."

"Oh, all right," Erin snapped. "Do you think you could at least manage to leave her a note and tell her that we called and that we'll call back tonight?"

"Yeah, I can handle that."

"Gee, thanks loads."

When Travis hung up the telephone, he scribbled out a note and stuck it to the refrigerator with a magnet. Then he poured himself a mug of coffee and wandered back out onto the deck.

Rebecca hadn't moved.

He took a sip of coffee and stared at her. She looked so...forlorn. And alone.

He looked away, then looked right back. She wasn't his problem. They had agreed to stay out of each other's way. Gritting his teeth, he bowed his head and raked a hand through his hair, bringing it all the way down the back of his head to his nape to massage the tight muscles there. He looked at Rebecca again.

Ah, hell.

He slammed the coffee mug down on the railing and loped down the steps.

This time he barely got within thirty feet of Rebecca when she spotted him. She scrambled to her feet and took several steps back, and Travis winced at her wary expression. Having a woman leery of him was a new and not very pleasant experience.

"Take it easy," he soothed. "You don't have to worry about me. I'm not angry. I just want to talk to you for a minute."

"About what?"

The faint disbelief and caution in her voice annoyed him, but he told himself he deserved it. He tipped his head toward the house. "Erin and Elise called."

Instantly her wariness turned to alarm. "Oh, my word! They've talked to Pepe, haven't they?" She groaned and put one hand over her mouth and splayed the other one over her stomach. "I knew this would happen! I knew it."

"What would happen? What're you talking about?"

"About us. About Pepe or Constanza telling them that we... that you and I are... you know."

"No, I don't kn— Oh! Jeez! That business at the cantina last night!" Travis grimaced and smacked his forehead with the heel of his hand. "I forgot all about that. But don't worry," he added quickly, holding up both hands when Rebecca made a distressed sound. "They didn't mention a word about our so-called engagement, so they haven't heard anything. You can bet if they had they would have bombarded me with questions."

Rebecca sagged visibly. "Well, that's a relief."

"Yeah. And before you ask again, I'm going to explain things to Pepe this morning. Okay?"

"Thank you."

The wariness was back; Travis could see it in her eyes. Her gaze met his, then skittered away. Only a few feet separated them. Rebecca crossed her arms defensively across her middle. Travis stuck his fingertips in his back pockets. She looked down at her feet, sunk in the white sand, then at the waves gently rolling ashore. Travis's gaze swept the inland mountains, the lacy clouds, the far headland, as though he found them fascinating. The awkward silence was broken by only the swish of waves, the dry rattle of tattered palm leaves and the occasional squawk of a mannerless gull.

"Look, uh...about what I said last night. I'm sorry. I didn't mean it." Her startled gaze shot to his face, and she stared as though she couldn't believe that she'd heard him right. Travis drew a circle in the sand with his bare foot. "I was just angry and shooting off my mouth. That's all. I didn't mean to make you cry."

"That's all right. Anyway, it wasn't you who made me cry. It was..." She made a vague gesture, then let her hand fall to her side. "A lot of other things that sort of piled up. Your remarks just pushed me over the edge is all. But I do appreciate your apology."

The explanation reminded him of what his cousins had said, and for an instant he wondered about those "other things." Then he remembered the reason for their call.

"Oh, by the way, happy birthday," he said dutifully.

Rebecca's eyes widened. "How did you know?"

"Erin and Elise told me. That's why they called. They said to tell you that they'd call back tonight."

A soft look entered Rebecca's eyes. "That was sweet of them. They're really wonderful friends. In all the years we've known one another, they've never forgotten my birthday. It means a lot to me," she added quietly, then looked away again, suddenly embarrassed.

"So, how are you going to spend the day? You got anything special planned."

"No. I suppose I'll just stay here. Maybe I'll go for a swim later."

Her lips formed a polite smile, which he was sure she intended to put his mind at ease. It didn't work. As hard as he tried not to, he noticed that her eyes were still sad.

The silence stretched out again. Travis clenched his jaw and squinted his eyes at the surf, sparkling in the brilliant sunrise. He told himself to walk away, but somehow his feet remained planted in the sand. He pulled his fingers out of his hip pockets and rubbed the back of his neck.

Ah, what the hell. It was her birthday.

"Look . . . since you don't have any plans, why don't you come with me today?" he blurted out before he could change his mind.

"What?" Rebecca blinked, stunned. "Travis, why on earth would you ask that?"

"Because I don't like the idea of you staying here alone on your birthday. It's not right."

"I see." She smiled again, a bit wanly this time. "Thank you, Travis. I appreciate the offer, but—"

"Look, I'm not talking about anything fancy. I got a call from David yesterday. His power cruiser has just come out of dry dock after a complete overhaul. He can't get away right now to take it out on a shakedown cruise and he asked if I'd do it for him. We could go over to Alhaja Verde and pick it up and take it out for the day. Do a little fishing. Maybe some swimming."

"Travis, you don't have to do this."

"Hey. I wouldn't if I didn't want to. You know me well enough to know that."

She caught her lower lip between her teeth. She wanted to accept—he could see it in her eyes—but she was torn. For some strange reason, her hesitancy made him determined to convince her.

"I appreciate the offer, Travis. Really I do, but I'm just not sure this is a good idea. As you pointed out, I'm not exactly your favorite person."

"Yeah, but we're both adults. Surely for one day we can call a truce."

"I don't know..."

"C'mon, Rebecca. You'll enjoy it. Besides, no one should spend their birthday alone. So whaddaya say?"

She searched his face. After a moment, a hesitant smile curved her mouth. "Thank you, Travis. I'd like very much to go out on David's boat with you."

Chapter Five

"Have you ever fished before?"

Rebecca looked up and realized that she'd been caught eyeing the rod and reel that Travis had just handed her as though it were a foreign object. She smiled ruefully. "Actually...no. But I'm anxious to learn," she tacked on when his mouth compressed. "Really."

That he didn't believe her was obvious. Annoyance and skepticism flashed across his face, but, with a visible effort, he reined in on both. "Yeah, well, hold on. Let me bait your line, then I'll show you how to cast."

When he had attached a hunk of squid to the hook, he led her over to the side of the boat. Several times he demonstrated the proper way to cast and how to reel in the bait to lure the fish, explaining the finer points as he went along. Rebecca paid close attention, taking in every word and movement.

"Okay, now give it a try," Travis said, and handed the rod back to her.

Rebecca flexed her wrist, bobbing the end of the flexible pole, testing its weight and balance. After slanting a tentative glance at Travis, she set her feet, drew back, and let fly. Instantly a bird's nest of tangled fishing line erupted out of the reel like a malignant growth.

"Oh! Oh! What happened? What did I do?"

"Put your thumb on it!" Travis yelped.

Put her thumb on what? In a dither, Rebecca couldn't remember, and the snarl of looped fishing line just kept growing.

Cursing under his breath, Travis reached around her and clamped his palm down on the spinning spool.

Rebecca bit her lower lip and darted a timid look over her shoulder. "What happened?"

"You just had the granddaddy of all backlashes, that's what happened. You cast so hard the line came off the spool faster than the weight on the bait end could carry it out." Shaking his head over the hopelessly snarled mess, he took the rod from her. After a few minutes of trying to untangle the volleyball-size coil, he gave up and cut it off.

When he had re-strung the rod he hesitated before handing it back to her. "Look, you don't have to do this, you know."

"No, I want to learn. Honestly."

With a shrug, he handed her the rod and stood back. "This time, don't cast so hard."

Rebecca heeded his advice so well on the next swing the line reeled out with an anemic whir to a length of only about six feet.

"Now you're not casting hard enough," Travis said impatiently. "Here, let me show you."

Before Rebecca realized his intent, he stepped up close behind her and encircled her with his arms, placing his hands over hers.

"Swing in a smooth motion and just *throoow* it out there, nice and easy," he murmured in her ear, guiding her hands and suiting action to words.

Rebecca swallowed hard and nodded. Speech was beyond her. She could barely breathe. Her heart boomed in her chest like a kettledrum.

By bending his knees, Travis had fitted his body to hers, spoon fashion. His jaw rested against her temple, and from shoulder to wrist his bare arms touched hers. As usual, his attire consisted of only a pair of cutoffs. All along her back she could feel his chest pressing against her, the silky mat of hair that covered it tickling her bare skin above her camisole-style top. His unmistakable maleness pressed intimately against her bottom, the hairy roughness and strength of his thighs rubbing the backs of her legs beneath her trim shorts. His male scent surrounded her. She could even feel his heart thumping against her back.

The incredible intimacy of their position rattled Rebecca so she couldn't think, but Travis seemed oblivious to it. Over and over, he guided her arms, swinging the rod in a smooth cast, reeling in the bait, swinging again. Through it all, Rebecca remained tongue-tied.

She had no idea whether her reaction was caused by fear or excitement. All she knew was she felt suffocated.

"Okay. Think you got it now?" he asked after they had repeated the procedure at least a dozen times.

Rebecca licked her lips. "I think so."

He stepped back, and she drew a deep breath and tried to control the trembling that threatened to buckle her knees. Concentrating fiercely, she clenched her jaw and repeated the motion he'd shown her.

The cast was wobbly and not overly long, but to her relief the baited hook sailed out over the side and plopped into the water without mishap.

"A little short, but not too bad," Travis commented. He moved away and picked up his own rod, taking up a position at the rear of the boat. "Keep it up and you'll get the hang of it."

Rebecca drew several deep breaths, deliberately slowing the pounding rhythm of her heart. She had overreacted. Just because Travis had gotten too close was no reason to panic;

she had nothing to fear from him. And there was certainly no reason to get excited. This was Travis, after all.

They didn't speak. The only sounds were the intermittent plops of their lines hitting the water and the whir of the reels. She was acutely aware of him standing just a few feet away. Now and then she glanced in his direction, but she was careful to appear unaffected.

Over and over she cast out the baited hook and reeled it in. Surprisingly, after a while the repetitive motion calmed her.

Her efforts were far from the smooth casts that Travis made, nor did they have the same results. In no time he'd caught three nice-size trout but she had not gotten so much as a nibble.

For hours they fished almost side by side without speaking. Rebecca stopped only once, just long enough to fetch a floppy-brimmed straw hat from below deck to protect her face from the burning rays of the sun. Several times she noticed Travis glancing her way, his expression puzzled, but she didn't acknowledge his interest or respond. Once she relaxed, the silence, though not exactly companionable, was soothing.

The sun beat down, creating dancing spangles of light on the water and warming her skin. Wavelets slapped at the hull of the boat and every now and then something broke the shiny surface with a splash. As far as the eye could see, there was nothing but ocean, with not another vessel of any sort to mar the great expanse of undulating swells. She and Travis might have been the only two people on earth.

The rocking motion of the boat lulled. So did the rhythmic action of casting and reeling in, and beneath the wide brim of the hat, Rebecca's expression grew dreamy.

Travis was right; no one should spend their birthday all alone.

She had almost refused Travis's offer. It had seemed the height of folly to spend the day with him, given their past history.

Rebecca's mouth twitched with amusement. During the trip to Alhaja Verde and all the while they were gassing up the *Freewind* and stocking the galley with supplies, they had treated one another with excruciating politeness, both grittily determined to keep their truce. The tension had been so thick she'd begun to regret her decision before they'd gotten two miles from shore.

Now she was glad she'd come. She was actually enjoying herself, and despite the prolonged silence between them, she was glad for Travis's company. Rincon Island was lovely and infinitely peaceful, and in the beginning she had needed solitude, but lately she had begun to feel lonely.

Rebecca executed a less-than-spectacular cast, and Travis, who had been watching, said, "Anytime you get tired of this, feel free to stop."

She glanced his way and smiled. "I'm not at all tired. I'm enjoying myself, actually."

Travis gave her a long look, then grunted, and raised his rod to cast again.

His hook had barely hit the water when Rebecca's rod bent almost double and she gave an excited shout.

"Oh! Oh, Travis! I've caught something. Quick, help me!"

"Keep the end up!" he yelled, shoving the butt grip of his own rod into a holder. "Give him line! Play him out! Keep the tip up, dammit!"

"I can't," Rebecca wailed, struggling with all her might to hold on to the taut rod. "It's too heavy." With the end of the rod propped against her hipbone, she gripped with both hands and reared back, but the bent pole wobbled and jerked and, despite her best effort, edged steadily downward.

Once again, Travis pressed close against her back and encircled her with his arms, lending his own strength to the battle, his hands gripping the rod above and below hers. This time Rebecca didn't even register the intimacy. She was too excited.

"It is a big one," Travis acknowledged with barely restrained excitement of his own. "And man, can that sucker fight. Give him his head, sweetheart," he murmured in her ear. "But keep the line taut. Now reel him in a little. Just a little. That's it. That's good. Now play him out again. Let him wear himself out before you try to bring him in. That's it. That's it."

He crooned the words in a lover's voice, his breath a hot caress feathering over her ear. The muscles in his arms and chest bunched and rippled against her flesh, but neither of them noticed.

For what seemed like hours they battled the fish, but gradually the desperate struggle grew one-sided, and with Travis's help, Rebecca managed to reel her catch ever closer.

"That's it, reel him in, honey. Reel him in. Keep that line taut. You don't want to lose him now. You've almost got him. Just a few more feet." Taking one hand off the rod, Travis reached to the side for the net. "Bring it up. Bring it up," he instructed in a low singsong, and Rebecca struggled to comply. "Easy does it now. We've almost got him."

Keeping one arm around her, firmly gripping the rod, he leaned over the side and scooped the flopping fish up in the net the instant it cleared the water.

"We did it! We did it!" Rebecca squealed. "We got him!"

She dropped the rod and hopped jubilantly from one foot to the other as Travis brought the catch aboard, and when he lifted the monstrous trout from the net she grinned at him, her face beaming with pride and happiness. "I really did it! I caught a fish!"

"You sure did," he agreed, smiling at her enthusiasm. "And it's a beaut, too. This rascal weighs ten pounds if he weighs an ounce. If I were you, I'd have it mounted."

Rebecca's grin faded. "Mounted?"

"You know—stuffed. I know a terrific taxidermist on Alhaja Verde. His prices are reasonable too."

"I couldn't do that," she protested, a look of horror on her face.

"It's that or eat it."

Biting her lip, she glanced at the fish, still flopping on the end of the line, then turned a pleading look on Travis. "Couldn't we just let it go?"

"*What?* After what we went through to catch this fish? Are you nuts?"

"Please, Travis. It seems such a shame to kill it. It's not like we need it for food. And I certainly don't want a trophy."

Travis stared at her, flabbergasted.

"Pleeese," she pleaded, and finally he sighed and rolled his eyes.

"What the hell. It's your fish." He gently removed the hook from the trout's wide mouth and, after one last, regretful look, tossed the magnificent specimen over the side.

Rebecca leaned over the railing and watched the fish swim away, a streak of silver darting beneath the surface of the water. She turned back to Travis, her face alight with pleasure and gratitude. Acting purely on instinct, she laid her hand on his arm, raised up on tiptoe and kissed his cheek. "Thank you, Travis," she whispered, and smiled warmly into his startled eyes.

Travis went absolutely still, staring at her. After a moment the look in his eyes made her uncomfortable, and she turned away.

"I don't know about you, but I'm getting hungry. Why don't I fix us some lunch?" she asked brightly.

It seemed to take a moment for her words to penetrate, but finally he nodded. "Sure. There's some sandwich stuff in the refrigerator."

"Oh, I think I can do better than sandwiches." She flashed him another smile and hurried below.

Travis watched her go, a thoughtful frown creasing the skin between his blond eyebrows. Absently, he fingered the spot on his cheek where she'd kissed him.

When he became aware of what he was doing, he dropped his hand. It irked him to realize that he found Rebecca intriguing.

He spent the next hour trying to put her out of his mind, but the rattle of pots and pans coming from the galley made that difficult. The honeyed tones of her voice, softly humming a U2 tune, made it downright impossible.

Lunch turned out to be a steaming bowl of French Onion soup and a delicious chicken salad made with grape halves and walnuts, served with frosty glasses of mint tea. Travis hadn't had a meal that good since leaving D.C., over a month ago.

"You know, you surprise me," he commented casually, using the side of his spoon to cut through the layer of melted cheese on top of his soup. He looked at her across the small table, his mouth quirking up at one corner. "I would have never guessed that someone with your background would know how to cook."

"My background?" Her faint smile held a hint of sadness. "You mean because we always had domestic help, why did I bother to learn?"

"Yeah. Something like that."

"One of our housekeepers taught me." She took a sip of tea, then shrugged. "My father was gone most of the time and I was lonely, I guess. Anyway, it was something to do. Then I discovered that I like to cook. When I was marri—" She stopped and bit down on her lip. "Later on I took a cooking course," she finished in a subdued voice.

Travis caught the hesitation and wondered at it. He was sure that she'd been about to say 'when I was married.' Why had she stopped?

"You must have graduated at the top of your class, if this meal is an example. It's great."

Surprise widened her eyes, and she looked absurdly pleased. "Thank you."

Actually, quite a few things about Rebecca had surprised Travis that day. When he'd learned that she'd never fished before he would've bet money that he was in for a miserable time. He'd expected her to be squeamish about the cut bait and to complain about the smell, but after that first time, she had rebaited her hook herself without the slightest qualm.

At the very least, he'd thought she would become bored. To his astonishment, Rebecca seemed to have genuinely enjoyed fishing, even when she hadn't been having any luck.

She was patient—he'd give her that. And, thank God, she'd had the good sense to be quiet and not scare away the fish.

Of course, Rebecca always had been distant and quiet.

Travis took a bite of salad and fought back a grin, remembering her reaction when that trout had bit her line, and how hard she'd worked to bring it in. You would've thought she'd won the lottery, she was so excited.

You could have knocked him over with a feather. Rebecca Quinn? Jumping up and down squealing with excitement? It was not a sight he'd ever expected to see.

What had surprised him most, though, was when she'd begged him to throw the fish back. That kind of tender-heartedness, though he personally thought it foolish, wasn't exactly what you'd expect of a cold woman.

And then there'd been that kiss.

There had been nothing sexual about it. The peck had merely been a show of appreciation, but coming from her it had stunned him.

Like it or not, Rebecca had piqued his interest, and he found that he wanted to dig deeper.

"So tell me, what have you been doing with yourself these past years?"

It was an innocuous question, the kind meant to open the door for small talk between people who were not close friends, and he had been careful to keep his voice casual. Yet he saw a flash of something in Rebecca's eyes that looked like wariness. Interesting.

"Nothing much, really."

"Oh, c'mon. You went away to college, got married, divorced. That's something."

"You don't want to hear about that."

"Sure I do."

Rebecca poked at her salad. "Trust me, you'd be bored silly if I told you. But what about you? You're the one who leads an exciting life. You are still with the FBI, aren't you?"

"I'm on an extended leave right now, but yeah, I'm still with the Bureau."

"Is something wrong? I mean . . . were you injured in the line of duty or something? Is that why you're on leave?"

Travis recognized the evasive tactic. The best way to avoid answering a question was to ask some of your own. He decided to allow it. For now.

"Naw, I'm fine. I had some time coming, and since I had some thinking to do, and Erin and Elise offered the beach house, I thought this was as good a time as any to take it. That's all."

He had known that Rebecca would not ask what he had to think about. She was much too polite and too reserved to pry into his personal business. Neither did he rule out the possibility that she simply wasn't interested.

"Well that's good. I mean . . . I'm glad you weren't hurt."

"Are you?"

"Certainly. Your family would be very upset if something were to happen to you. I know Erin and Elise were relieved when David left the Bureau."

"Yeah, David made the right move. He'd reached burnout and he was smart enough to call it quits before he got himself killed. Anyway, he's got it made now. He's got himself a beautiful bride and a high-paying job that he enjoys, which lets him afford a few of life's luxuries. Like this boat, for instance."

Rebecca looked around the compact cabin. The *Freewind* was an older powerboat—a custom-made one, from the look of it. Built of wood, it sported brass fittings and gleaming teak decking, and the interior had been refurbished to include all the modern conveniences. There was a certain elegance about it, a feeling of quality that was missing in the modern fiberglass crafts. "It is lovely."

"It is now, but you should have seen it six weeks ago, after Abigail got through with it."

Rebecca's eyes grew round. "David's wife?"

"Yep. They met when she came to him for help. The KGB and the CIA were both after her. Before the whole mess was cleared up the *Freewind* got shot all to hell and gone and the Russians tore the interior apart searching for a microdot that contained classified information. If that wasn't enough, Abigail, who has got to be the world's worst skipper, used the *Freewind* to ram a speedboat."

"Are you serious?"

Travis grinned, remembering the Keystone Cops chase around Alhaja Verde's harbor. "Yep. Blew two KGB guys right out of the water."

"But…Erin and Elise said that David's wife was a sweet, retiring little thing."

"She is. But Abbey draws trouble like honey draws flies." His grin flashed again. "David had to marry her to keep her out of hot water."

Travis looked around at the restored interior of the boat, and his expression sobered. "This boat is David's pride and joy. He must love her *a lot*—after the collision he didn't so much as turn a hair over the damage. All he was worried about was Abbey."

"He must love her very much," Rebecca agreed with a trace of wistfulness. Then she chuckled. "I have to admit, I have a hard time imagining David as a married man. He always seemed like such a confirmed bachelor."

"Sooner or later most of us take the plunge."

"You haven't," she came back, then immediately looked chagrined. "Or have you? Oh, Lord, Travis, I'm sorry. Just because I haven't heard about it doesn't mean—"

"No, I haven't gotten married," Travis interrupted, taking pity on her. "Heck, no woman would have me."

To his surprise, that brought a derisive snort from the elegant woman sitting across from him. "Oh, come *on*," she chided. "Who are you kidding?

"You look a little different now, I'll admit." Her gaze skimmed over his long hair, the scruffy beginnings of a beard, the leopard tattoo, and finally came to rest on the long earring swinging from his left lobe. She made a wry face. "All right, all right. So you look a *lot* different. But I can't imagine that things have changed all that much. I remember our high school days back in Crockett. Every girl in school was crazy head-over-heels in love with you."

Travis fixed her with a level stare. "Not every girl," he countered softly. "You weren't."

Her reaction fascinated him. First her eyes widened, and a look of panic flashed across her face. Immediately, a fiery blush followed. Then, with an effort, she seemed to pull herself together.

She stirred her soup, lowering her gaze to contemplate the swirling motion. "Are you sure about that?"

The soft question made Travis's heart trip over itself. His fork halted halfway to his mouth, and he went utterly still. "What are you saying?" He tried to sound casual, but even he could hear the tension in his voice.

Slowly, Rebecca looked up, straight into his eyes. Her own twinkled with rueful amusement. "I was so in love with you I thought I would die of it."

Travis's jaw dropped. His fork hit the plate with a clatter, sending chicken salad bouncing onto the table and the deck. "You're kidding! C'mon, you've *got* to be kidding," he insisted when she shook her head and started chuckling. "I don't believe it."

"It's true. I swear it. In fact..." She grimaced and rolled her eyes. "I can't believe I'm telling you this, but ... since I'm being so honest I might as well confess all of it. The truth is, I'd had a crush on you from the time we first met, when I was five and you were seven."

"Good Lord." Stunned, Travis gaped at her. He frowned and shook his head. "Wait a minute. If you were so nuts about me, then why did you give me the cold shoulder all those years? I could come into a room where you and my cousins were talking and giggling and you'd clam up. Most of the time you looked right through me as though I weren't even there. Not once did you ever let on that you even liked me, much less loved me."

"Of course not. Good heavens, Travis. I was much too shy and insecure to do that. Why, I would have died of mortification."

"Shy? Insecure? You? Hell, Rebecca. You were the daughter of the richest man in town. All your life you had everything you ever wanted handed to you on a silver platter. What the devil did you have to be insecure about? Or shy either, for that matter?"

Before he finished speaking, her smile collapsed and the sparkle faded from her eyes. Travis could have kicked himself. For the first time in their lives she had relaxed enough to open up to him, and he had to go and shoot off his mouth. She looked as though he had slapped her.

"You're wrong. I didn't get everything I wanted. This may sound like a cliché, but there really are things that money can't buy. And they're a lot more important."

The icy reserve was back, in her voice and in her eyes. Briefly, she met his gaze head on, her lovely face impassive as marble.

Lowering her gaze, she reached for his plate and stacked it on top of hers. "Excuse me. I'm going to do the dishes."

Travis's hand shot across the table and closed around her wrist. "Rebecca, I'm sorry. I shouldn't have said that. Don't go."

"It doesn't matter." She kept her face averted, refusing to look at him.

"Yes, it does matter. It was a stupid, insensitive thing to say. I guess I was just falling back on habit. Please…explain to me what you meant."

She shook her head. "I don't want to talk about it anymore."

"C'mon, Rebecca. I'd really like to know."

She looked at him then, warily, her blue eyes full of suspicion.

"Please," he urged, and rubbed his thumb across the underside of her wrist in a gentle caress.

She kept her gaze fixed on the table. Several seconds ticked by, and he began to think she wasn't going to speak. He wanted to urge her again, but he was afraid she'd retreat farther. He didn't dare push his luck.

"A housekeeper is not the same as having a mother, you know," she said finally in a flat voice.

"No, I suppose it's not."

"You're just a job to them. Looking after you is just part of the duties they're paid to do. Anyway, the longest any of them ever lasted was two years."

Travis remembered, then, hearing his mother and aunt cluck and shake their heads over the string of housekeepers that had come and gone at the Quinn home. He hadn't thought much of it at the time, but now . . .

"Still . . . you had your father."

The minute Travis made the statement, he regretted it. The ironic look she flashed him spoke volumes.

"When I was in the first grade, I marked on a calendar every day that Daddy spent in Crockett. At the end of the year I added them up. You want to know what the total was? It was eighty-seven. Eighty-seven," she repeated sadly. "He spent less than one-fourth of his time at home."

With her forefinger, she drew circles in the condensation on her glass. Her gaze followed the action, but there was a faraway look in her blue eyes. "Even when he was at home he didn't have much time for me. My father is not exactly what you'd call . . . well . . . an affectionate person."

Affectionate? Hardly, Travis thought, recalling the hard, impatient man he'd known in his youth. Using the word in connection with Richard Quinn was almost funny. Except . . . there was nothing funny about Rebecca's carefully controlled expression.

"It's just his nature. I don't suppose he can help being the way he is. But I spent most of my life trying to make him love me and wondering why he didn't. I thought I was somehow to blame. That sort of thing doesn't make you feel very secure or confident.''

She said it all matter-of-factly, as though she were talking about something as mundane as the weather, but Travis still held her wrist, and he felt the fine tremor that ran through her.

''Yet you always seemed so self-assured.''

''We all have our defenses, Travis. I discovered early that if I cried or complained in any way, my father became even more aggravated, so I learned to hide my feelings and pretend to be unaffected. It also became a way to save face, at least outwardly.''

Travis stared. The Richard Quinn he'd known had used his wealth and position to run roughshod over other people, but Travis had always assumed that with his daughter he showed a softer side. Apparently that wasn't the case.

Reading the surprise on his face, Rebecca shook her head. ''Didn't you ever wonder why I spent so much time at the Blaine house when we were growing up?''

''No, not really.''

''Their family was exactly what I had always dreamed of having. There was always laughter and warmth and love in that house. Even when the twins and David were squabbling, or when Erin would pull one of her crazy stunts and their father would punish her, you could still feel the love. I tried to pretend that I was part of the family.'' Rebecca's mouth twisted in a wry grimace. ''It never really worked, of course. Most of the time I felt like a penniless child with her nose pressed against the candy-store window. But I adored being there, anyway.''

Looking suddenly embarrassed, she straightened and forced a smile. ''Even if you did glare at me all the time.''

Travis studied her intently. Her story tugged at his heart, stirring emotions he'd never expected to feel where Rebecca was concerned—compassion, pity, sadness...and yes, dammit...guilt.

Unless she was lying through her teeth, then he had been wrong about her all those years. Terribly wrong. He didn't want to believe that. He prided himself on being a good judge of character; in his line of work you had to be. Still . . . she appeared to be telling the truth. For that matter, why would she lie? She'd been giving him the silent go-to-hell treatment for most of her life.

Old attitudes die hard, however, and he could not resist probing a little deeper. "Is that why you didn't let on that you had a crush on me?"

"I didn't dare. You were always so nasty to me, I knew it was hopeless. I figured if you ever found out you'd laugh in my face."

He didn't want to think so, but remembering the strength of his animosity back then, he knew it was possible that he would have, and he experienced another twinge of guilt. "I glared because I thought you were stuck-up and snooty."

"Stuck-up? Me?" She looked incredulous. "I was just trying to protect myself. If you pretend that someone's opinion of you doesn't matter, then their rejection doesn't hurt quite so much."

"Is that what you did with your father?"

"Yes," she answered without a second's hesitation, and the last of Travis's reservations faded away.

To suddenly see someone you know—or thought you knew—in a whole new light was disquieting.

In hindsight it was all so clear, so obvious—the string of housekeepers, the way Richard Quinn spent more and more time out of town, preferring his apartments in Dallas and New York over his Crockett home. Why hadn't he seen it?

Travis thought of Rebecca as a beautiful, too quiet child, always hanging around on the fringes of his boisterous family, watching so solemn-faced and big-eyed, and his jaw clenched. Suddenly the fancy house and the expensive clothes and the cars and privileges she'd had no longer seemed so terrific.

"God, Rebecca. I'm sorry."

"Don't be. I came to terms with it all long ago." She frowned at what she saw in his face. "I didn't tell you to play on your sympathy, Travis. I don't need or want pity. I simply wanted you to understand.''

"So I'd get off your back. Right?"

"Yes."

No hesitation, no hedging, just direct, unflinching honesty. Travis experienced a flicker of disappointment, then immediately berated himself. Hell, what did you expect? That she wanted you to understand because your opinion of her mattered? Yeah, dream on, McCall. After the way you've treated her for the past twenty years or so, you're lucky she'll even speak to you.

Pulling her hand free of his, she started stacking the dishes again. Travis could tell by her nervous movements and the way she would not meet his eyes that she was having second thoughts about letting her guard down in front of him. He understood, but he couldn't let it go just yet. There were too many things he wanted to know.

"Since you wanted a family so much, I'm surprised that you and Evan didn't have children," he probed gently.

Her withdrawal was instantaneous. He could almost see the invisible wall slam down between them. With a subtle altering, her lovely features took on that aloof, ultrapolite look that had enraged him so in the past.

This time it filled him with an aching tenderness.

"Things don't always work out the way we want them to," she replied stiffly. She reached for his glass and hers and carried both to the counter, turning her back on him in a clear dismissal. She squirted dish detergent into the sink and turned the water on full blast.

Travis watched her. He'd struck a nerve that time. *All right, sweetheart. I understand that you're feeling vulnerable right now, so I'll drop it. But sooner or later I'm going to find out what's behind that haunted look.*

Chapter Six

Fool. Fool. Fool. What on earth possessed you to say those things? To Travis, of all people. You spent a lifetime hiding your feelings—about your father, about Travis—and what do you do? You let yourself be lulled by a little friendly conversation. The first time he's halfway decent to you, you spill your guts. Idiot!

Rebecca kept her back to Travis and scrubbed a plate with unnecessary force. She could feel his gaze boring into her, and her nerves twanged like plucked guitar strings. The counselor and the others in the support group had urged her to open up and share her feelings, it was true. And it *had* helped. Their encouragement had given her the courage to tell Elise and Erin everything.

She'd stopped short of that with Travis, thank God, but still, it had been foolish to furnish him with more ammunition to use against her. As it was, he'd no doubt found her pathetic revelations hilarious.

"Say, I have an idea," the object of her thoughts announced out of the blue.

Rebecca jumped and braced herself for a hateful remark.

"I know this great little island that has a secluded cove with glass-smooth water. It's perfect for scuba diving. So how about it? You game?"

The suggestion, the tone of his voice, were so far removed from what they had been discussing, from what she expected, for several seconds she was too disoriented to answer. "I...I don't know how to scuba dive," she finally managed to stammer. She kept her eyes on the glass she was scrubbing. "I've never tried it before."

"No problem. You're a quick study. It won't take me long to teach you."

The idea had appeal but she didn't quite trust Travis. Yet his voice was friendly, even coaxing, and when she darted a cautious look over her shoulder, to her surprise, she encountered only the most pleasant of smiles. "I, uh...I don't want to be any trouble."

"Hey! No trouble. I want to teach you. It'll be fun. And maybe, if we have time, we might catch a few redfish. They're plentiful out around the reef that surrounds the island."

Drying her hands on a towel, Rebecca turned to face him. As hard as she searched, she could find nothing in his face but open friendliness.

She twisted the towel. Part of her wanted to say yes, wanted his company, wanted this rare opportunity to spend some time with him without the old hostility and tension that had always marked their relationship. Another part of her—the wary part, the part that had been hurt too many times—cautioned against it.

"C'mon, Rebecca. It'll be fun. Whaddaya say?"

"I... All right. I'll give it a try."

"Great."

Travis slid out of the small dining booth and stood up. The action brought him to within inches of Rebecca, so close that she sucked in her breath and pressed back against the sink. Her eyes widened when, instead of moving past her as she expected, he raised his hand and cupped her face.

"Rebecca," he said hesitantly, and her breath caught. "Look, I . . . I'm glad you told me what you did. I just wish we'd had that conversation years ago."

"Would it have made any difference?"

"Maybe." He grimaced. "I don't know. Hell, I like to think so, anyway."

Neither said anything for a moment. In his eyes she saw compassion and regret, but there were reservations, too. Rebecca sensed that he was having trouble adjusting his image of her.

His gaze lowered to her mouth. Slowly, he swept his thumb over her lower lip, and Rebecca's heart banged against her ribs.

As though suddenly becoming aware of the action, he dropped his hand and stepped back. "I'll, uh . . . I'll go weigh anchor and crank up the engines. It'll take us about an hour to get to that island."

She stared after him. Unconsciously, she raised her hand and touched the tips of three fingers to her lips. After a moment a bemused smile blossomed there.

An hour later, after changing into a one-piece swimsuit, Rebecca stepped up onto the main deck, feeling horribly self-conscious. She hadn't appeared before Travis in a swimsuit since she'd been a skinny fifteen-year-old. The look in his eyes when he spotted her did nothing to alleviate her shyness. Neither did his own attire.

The swath of ruby red spandex that hugged his hips was barely three inches wide and left little doubt as to his maleness. His body was sleek and hard and tanned to the color of caramel, and pale gold hair dusted his chest, arms and legs. Not the slightest hint of lighter flesh was visible around those tight little trunks, and Rebecca suddenly had the startling thought that maybe he had done a lot of his fishing and sunbathing in the nude. He'd probably strolled around the house and deck that way, too, before her arrival on Rincon Island.

Travis watched her approach. Beneath slumberous lids, his silvery eyes darkened to the color of smoke. He looked her over, taking his time about it, his gaze sliding from her pink toenails, up over the long curves of her legs, settling for a moment at the top of her thighs where the shimmering sapphire maillot was cut up over her hipbones. He continued his appraisal over her flat abdomen and small waist, lingering again on her breasts before traveling up over chest and neck to finally meet her eyes. Rebecca felt that look all the way to the marrow of her bones, and her blush deepened.

Unexpectedly, Travis cut loose with a long, low wolf whistle and followed it up with a grin—a devilish grin that was a flash of white teeth and a twinkle in his eyes, the kind of grin that Rebecca had never thought to receive from him. Suddenly, absurdly perhaps, she felt on top of the world.

"I take it you approve," she said, chuckling at his foolishness.

"Oh, yeah. I definitely approve." The words rumbled out of him in a low, sexy growl that sent a wave of gooseflesh rippling over Rebecca's skin, but the little thrill that shot through her was short-lived.

No sooner had he spoken than he sobered, as though he had suddenly recalled to whom he was speaking and wasn't quite comfortable with their banter.

His manner immediately became impersonal. Rebecca felt a stab of disappointment, but she stifled it. She could live with impersonal. It was, after all, a vast improvement over his previous treatment of her.

Travis fitted her with scuba gear and patiently explained the procedure and the rules of safety. The brush of his fingers against her bare skin caused a fluttery sensation in the pit of Rebecca's stomach. Gritting her teeth, she scolded herself for the foolish reaction and concentrated for all she was worth on his instructions.

When at last he was done, she clomped to the side in the awkward flippers. Behind her, Travis made a sound that was suspiciously like a snort, and she felt a pang of disappointment. She turned to face him, braced for criticism or ridicule, but encountered instead an amused smile and laughing eyes that invited her to share the fun.

"What?"

"Oh, nothing. It's just that you look like a duck walking through molasses."

Her heart gave a little flip. Teasing came as naturally to Travis as breathing, but he'd never bothered to kid around with her before. "Is that so?" she parried, feeling almost giddy. "Well, you don't exactly move like Rudolf Nureyev yourself, you know."

"Tell me about it," he groaned, and high-stepped toward her, his flippers slapping the deck with the resounding "splat-splat" of a clapping seal. "But the difference is, I didn't think anything could make you look clumsy."

Bemused, Rebecca could only gawk at him. She could hardly believe her ears. It was a backhanded compliment, to be sure. But it *was* a compliment.

Another first.

All afternoon it was the same story. Most of the undercurrents of hostility and tension were gone, and once in a while Travis's natural mischievous nature slipped through and he teased her or flashed his devastating grin, but mostly his manner remained merely polite and pleasant, always falling just short of true friendliness.

At first, Rebecca found his attitude disconcerting. However, once they were in the water, swimming side by side in the calm cove, she scarcely noticed.

As she propelled herself through the crystal clear waters, every last bit of lingering tension in her body faded away. All she could think about was the incredible beauty she was viewing. In less than five minutes, she was thoroughly hooked on the sport of scuba diving.

Enthralled, Rebecca gazed through the glass plate of her mask at the many plants, undulating sinuously in the gentle currents, the fragile-looking coral formations that sheltered a multitude of underwater creatures. She saw starfish and abalone, crabs scuttling along the sandy bottom, tiny creatures that darted back into their shells or burrowed into the sand at her approach. She swam through myriad schools of fish of every shape, size and color—some silver and bulletlike, some flat and round as a pancake, some piteously plain and unremarkable, others striped or dotted and sporting extravagant translucent fins that fluttered with all the coy flirtatiousness of a fan dancer.

Rebecca darted from place to place, her excitement and delight at each new discovery firing her with energy. She was so caught up in the eerie beauty of the underwater world, she was hardly aware of anything else. Except for those times when Travis touched her arm to warn her against getting too close to the razor-sharp coral or to guide her around a less-than-friendly undersea creature, she scarcely noticed that he was around.

Time had little meaning in the quiet splendor of the underwater world. It seemed to Rebecca that they had been swimming for only a few minutes when Travis nudged her and signaled that it was time to quit.

The instant they broke the surface, Rebecca shook back her hair and pulled the mouthpiece out of her mouth. "Why are we stopping so soon?" she demanded. "We were just getting started."

Travis grinned and tapped his watch. "Wrong. We've been swimming for almost two hours."

"Two hours! It seems like only a few minutes."

"I'm glad you were enjoying yourself, but it's time to head for the *Freewind*."

"But I'm not in the least tired," she protested.

"Well I am. And you will be, too, when your adrenaline high wears off. Plus, we don't want to risk getting cramps. So c'mon."

"Why do I have to quit just because you're tired?"

"Because it's safer to swim in pairs, that's why."

"But—"

"Forget it, sweetheart," he said amiably enough, but there was a touch of pure steel in his lazy drawl. "Haul that cute little butt back into the boat. Right now."

Rebecca struck out for the *Freewind* without another word, conscious, in a way that she hadn't been while they were exploring the underwater life of the cove, of Travis cleaving through the water right beside her.

Once back on board she discovered that he was right. She was suddenly so exhausted it was all she could do to stand. Gripping the side rail for support, she hung her head and gasped for air, her chest heaving.

"You okay?"

"Ye-yes. I'm fine. I'm just more tired than I thought."

"Why don't you go below and shower and take a nap?"

She gave a weak laugh. "I'll take you up on that shower later. Right now I don't have the energy. If it's all right with you, I think I'll just crawl up on the foredeck and sunbathe for a while first."

"Suit yourself."

He loped down the steps and disappeared below deck. Groaning, Rebecca hauled herself up onto the *Freewind*'s foredeck and stretched out on her stomach on a towel. Two seconds after her cheek settled onto her stacked hands, she was asleep.

It seemed like only a minute later when something nudged her in the side. "C'mon. Wake up."

Rebecca shifted and made an irritated sound, but the nudge came again, harder. She opened her eyes a slit and saw a bare foot poking her ribs. Lifting her eyelids a fraction more, she encountered a hairy leg and followed it upward to the frayed edge of a pair of cutoffs. Above the denim shorts was a corrugated belly and a broad chest covered with a pelt of golden hair. Above that, Travis's face loomed, looking concerned.

"C'mon. Wake up sleepyhead."

"Go away," Rebecca mumbled.

Travis squatted on his haunches beside her. His voice softened with a trace of amusement, and this time he shook her shoulder gently. "C'mon Rebecca. You've been out here almost an hour. You're going to burn to a crisp if you don't get out of the sun."

"S'okay," she mumbled sleepily. "I used a sunscreen earlier."

"And most of it washed off in the water."

Rebecca sighed. He was right. Though her hair was a dark mahogany color, her skin was fair. Without gobs of strong sunblock she burned, and with it she barely tanned. Despite the past couple of weeks of swimming and sunbathing, her skin had taken on only a slight peach tint.

"Your back is looking pink alrea... Hey. What the devil is this?"

Rebecca felt his finger trail over her lower back, and she came awake instantly. When she'd put on the low-cut maillot she'd forgotten about those tiny raised nubs of flesh. She sat up, twisting around to face him and shielding her back from his view. "It's nothing," she said quickly.

"Nothing? Those look like scars to me."

"They are. Old ones. They're from an accident I had when I was a child."

Travis's eyes narrowed. "What kind of accident?"

All day he'd treated her with the politeness of a stranger, but there was nothing in the least impersonal or distant in his manner now. His gaze bore into her as though he was determined to see into her soul.

"I fell off my bike."

"You get scrapes from falling off a bike, not pea-size welts."

"That depends on what you land on. Don't you remember? The curved driveway in front of our house was made of white gravel. One day after a storm, before the yardman had had a chance to fill them in, I hit a pothole with the front wheel of my bike and went flying up into the air and landed flat on my back."

"Then why are the scars only along your waist?"

"Why... actually, you see, I landed at the edge of the drive. The upper part of my body hit the grass."

Travis studied her with unnerving directness. "I don't remember you taking a bad spill or getting hurt, other than an occasional scraped knee or elbow."

"Heaven's, Travis. What is this? An inquisition?" She gave a nervous laugh and shook her head. "A lot of things have happened to me that you know nothing about.

"Now, if you'll excuse me, I'm going to take that shower." She reached for the towel and started to stand, but Travis stopped her with a hand on her forearm while she was still on her knees. He searched her face, and Rebecca's heart thumped painfully.

Only inches separated them. She could feel his breath feather across her cheek, see each one of his ridiculously long lashes, the tiny chips of charcoal that seemed to float in the silvery irises. The scent of soap and clean male drifted to her, and she realized that Travis had showered while she slept. She felt each hard finger wrapped around her forearm, the heat emanating from him.

Her attention settled on his chiseled lips, so serious now, and she found herself wondering things she hadn't given a thought to in years.

To Rebecca's horror, her heartbeat doubled and she felt a shameful quickening at the heart of her femininity.

"Rebecca."

He said her name softly, still she started, her pupils dilating when her gaze jerked up to meet his.

"Just tell me one thing?"

"Wh-what?"

"Those women who looked after you as a child. Did any of them abuse you?"

She blinked, too astonished to answer for a second. Releasing a long breath, she chuckled, all the tension going out of her. "No, of course not."

"If so, you can tell me, you know."

"Travis, I swear to you, none of our housekeepers ever abused me in any way." Her hand covered his where it gripped her forearm, and she smiled and added softly, "But I do appreciate your concern."

Once again they looked at each other in silence. Rebecca's smile faded as the seconds ticked by. Travis's gaze dropped to her lips, and her heartbeat slowed to a heavy thud.

They were too close, only inches apart. She told herself to move, to get up and go below. She couldn't.

Travis's silvery gaze flickered to hers, then lowered again to her mouth. Slowly, his head tipped to one side and descended. Rebecca's breathing shuddered to a stop. Her eyelids drifted shut.

His lips settled softly on hers. They moved in a warm caress that was scarcely more than the brush of flesh against flesh. The whispery touch sent a flood of shimmering sparks cascading through Rebecca's body.

Her nipples puckered against the satiny cloth of her swimsuit. Buried within its folds, her fingers clutched the towel in a death grip.

There was nothing threatening about the unhurried kiss. It tested and tasted and invited her to do the same. Ever so softly, his lips rubbed and nibbled, while his agile tongue stroked and swirled with gentle persuasion, effortlessly gaining entry into her mouth and engaging hers in a tantalizing dance of discovery.

Rebecca felt on fire and shaken as the sweetest pleasure she had ever known showered through her.

The kiss ended as gently as it began. Travis raised his head, drawing his lips from hers slowly, coming back for a lingering last nibble, then easing away again. Rebecca opened her eyes and looked into his. They were the color of slate, watching her, waiting, questioning. Neither of them moved.

"Why did you do that?" she whispered.

Travis raised his eyebrows, pursed his lips, and, after a moment's consideration, shrugged. "It seemed right."

She laughed. She couldn't help it. The nonchalant answer was so typically Travis. "Right? How do you figure that?"

"Well...how about...you'd hurt yourself, so I kissed it better?"

The corners of his mouth lifted, and a mischievous twinkle entered his eyes. Rebecca had to struggle to keep her own grin under control. She was still shaken from the kiss, but when Travis turned on the teasing charm he was irresistible. "That was years ago, Travis. It's a little late for that, don't you think?"

"But I didn't know about it then."

She gave him a dry look. "You'll have to do better than that."

"Okay. How about...you looked pretty and kissable, so I kissed you."

"I see. So you make a habit of kissing women whenever the mood strikes, do you?"

"Hell, no. Do I look crazy to you? I'd get my head knocked off." He leaned closer and grinned. "But in this case I was curious. Haven't you wondered what it would be like between us, after all these years?"

"I...no, of course not," she lied in a flustered rush. "Why would I? You've always made it perfectly clear that you couldn't stand me. Anyway, you've already kissed me once. At Pepe's. Remember?"

"That doesn't count. I didn't know then that you had a crush on me."

Rebecca rolled her eyes and groaned. "I knew it was a mistake to tell you. I knew it. You're never going to let me forget that, are you?"

"Maybe," he replied cheerfully, and stood up. Grinning at her over his shoulder, he walked around the sidedeck and jumped down to the cockpit. "Then again, maybe not."

She scrambled to her feet and hurried after him. "The operative phrase there is 'had a crush.' *Had*, Travis. H-A-D, had."

This time his grin was wicked. Sticking his fingertips in the back pockets of his cutoffs, he sauntered to the stern to check his fishing line, whistling a jaunty tune between his teeth.

Torn between outrage and laughter, Rebecca stared at his broad back. In the end, laughter won, but she managed to storm below deck in a credible imitation of a woman in a huff before giving in to it.

"Travis McCall, you are an incorrigible flirt." The pronouncement bounced back at her off the fiberglass walls of the tiny bathroom. Fighting back a grin, she turned her face up to the warm shower spray. He was also, and always had been, an irrepressible, shamelessly appealing, charming devil. Try as she might, she couldn't be angry with him; it felt too good to be on the receiving end of his teasing banter for once.

Besides, for all his maddening devil-may-care ways and his past overt dislike of her, he was a kind man. He'd not only seen to it that she didn't spend her birthday alone, he'd made it memorable. He'd taught her to fish and to scuba dive. He'd made her laugh. He'd made her feel happy and alive—really alive—for the first time in years. Because of him, for a few hours she'd been able to forget about the past and the worrisome uncertainty of what lay ahead. How could she be angry with a man like that?

The kiss on the bow of the *Freewind* seemed to mark the beginning of change between them. It was nothing major, and they weren't exactly friends yet, but with each passing hour they grew more at ease with each other. For the remainder of the afternoon they fished off the back of the boat, exchanging only an occasional word or comment, but those held none of the stiff politeness of the morning, and the prolonged periods of silence were now companionable.

For Rebecca's part, she was aware of an underlying hum of excitement deep inside, but she wasn't concerned. After all, in many ways the day had been the fulfillment of an old, hopeless fantasy, just as that surprising kiss had been. A little excitement was surely a normal reaction. After she'd given the matter some thought, deep down she was even relieved to know that she could still respond to a man on a physical level.

None of it meant anything, of course. Rebecca didn't kid herself about that. This was just a space out of time. Tomorrow, when their truce ended, things would be as they'd always been between them. In the meantime, she would enjoy his company and the lovely day.

"Looks like rain," Travis said, breaking into her thoughts.

Following the direction of his gaze, Rebecca saw that dark clouds had begun to form on the horizon.

"Do you think it's heading this way?"

"I don't know. Those clouds are too far away to tell. But to be on the safe side, we'd better pack up and head for home. It'll be getting dark in a couple of hours anyway."

Rebecca's spirits drooped. She hated for the day to end, but she obediently followed Travis's example and reeled in her line. She helped him stow their gear and toss the remainder of the bait overboard. When everything was battened down and they were ready to get underway, she climbed up onto the flying bridge with him.

Standing next to Travis at the control console, Rebecca took one last wistful look around the quiet cove. It was so tranquil there, so beautiful, with the green island rising to the rear, the headlands curving around on either side like sheltering arms and the sapphire gulf stretching out beyond. She wished they could stay forever.

A sputter, followed by a labored mechanical whine, broke the peaceful silence when Travis pressed the starter, but the engine did not start. Rebecca glanced at him, but he appeared unconcerned. He tried the starter again, several more times, but the result was the same.

Worriedly, she watched him check dials and gauges. "What's wrong?" she ventured.

"Who knows." He pushed the button again with no luck. "She was running like a top all morning." He looked at Rebecca and patted her cheek. "Don't fret, sweetheart. We're not marooned yet. There's not an engine made that I can't fix. I'll go below and check it out."

Surprisingly, Rebecca wasn't worried. Somehow—she wasn't quite sure why—she had complete confidence in Travis. Maybe because he always seemed to have such complete confidence in himself. Also, she remembered the countless hours that he and his brothers, Ryan and Reilly, and his cousin David had spent working on cars back in Crockett. They'd spent half their teenage years covered with grease.

Curious, Rebecca followed Travis down the ladder to the main deck. When he removed the cover from the engine well and lowered himself into the dark compartment, she knelt beside the opening. "Is there anything I can do to help?"

"Yeah. See if you can find me a flashlight."

She scrambled to her feet and ran below. A quick search of the storage cabinets turned up a high-powered battery-operated lantern. She raced back up on deck and handed it down to him. "Anything else you need?"

"Get David's tool kit, willya. It's in the locked cabinet beside the live-bait well. The key's in the drawer of the nightstand beside the bed."

Rebecca darted below deck again and returned in less than a minute with the key. She quickly unlocked the cabinet and dragged the heavy tool kit over to the engine well.

For the next hour she sat cross-legged beside the opening, handing tools down to Travis whenever he asked for them. Amidst the banging and pounding and occasional grunts emerging from the engine well, they carried on a sporadic but amiable conversation.

Once, a loud "Ow!" erupted from below and was immediately followed by a string of colorful curses. Rebecca peered over the edge of the opening and saw Travis sucking on the knuckles of his right hand. She opened her eyes wide and fought back a grin. "Is there a problem?"

His eyes narrowed on her innocent expression. "You're enjoying this, aren't you?" he accused, but he couldn't hold on to the gruff demeanor, and a reluctant smile twitched his mouth.

"Of course. Why not? I'm having a great time."

He stood up and traded one wrench for another. Wiping it with a cloth, he tipped his head to one side and studied her curiously. "You're a surprising woman, Rebecca Quinn," he said softly. Smiling, he touched the tip of her nose with a greasy finger, then quickly squatted back down, chuckling at her sputtering outrage as she scrubbed the spot with a rag.

Less than a half hour later, the wind kicked up suddenly and rocked the boat. Standing up, Travis poked his head and shoulders through the opening and squinted at the sky. "Those clouds are rolling in fast. Soon it'll be too dark to work." He switched his attention to Rebecca, his gaze steady on her face, gauging her reaction. "This lantern isn't enough. I need natural light, too."

She looked up. Livid thunderheads were beginning to boil over them. Already an unnatural, greenish purple darkness had begun to descend. "What do we do now?"

"Well . . ." He braced his forearms flat on the deck along the edge of the opening and surveyed the sky again. "We've got two options. I can radio the Mexican Coast Guard for help or . . ." His gaze sought and held hers. ". . . we can stay here and I'll finish the repairs in the morning. I'll leave it up to you."

"Can you fix whatever is wrong?"

"Yeah, I can fix it. Given time."

She glanced at the angry sky. "Do you think it's going to storm?"

"Probably. But we're sheltered here. We'll be safe." He cocked one eyebrow. "So what's it gonna be? Do I radio for help, or do we stay?"

"What would you do if you were alone?"

"I'd stay."

"That settles it then," she stated with emphatic matter-of-factness. "We stay."

Tipping his head to one side, Travis studied her, his expression bemused. "You sure are taking this calmly. You're not scared, or even a little upset?"

"Why should I be upset? I have complete faith in you. If you say we'll be safe, then I know we will be. We have plenty of food and water and a comfortable shelter from the storm. And after all, there's really no urgent reason why either of us has to return to Rincon Island tonight."

Actually, Rebecca wasn't at all disturbed about the turn of events. Today was the first time she'd been happy in years, the first time she'd laughed in years, and she had been dreading it ending. The delay would simply extend the pleasant interlude for a few more hours.

"That's true. But before you make a final decision, there is one thing that you may have overlooked that I feel I should point out to you."

"What is that?"

Travis's mouth twitched. "There's only one bed on this boat."

Chapter Seven

Rebecca experienced a flash of alarm, like a tiny explosion in her chest. It stole all the oxygen from her lungs and sent aftershocks quivering through her. Somehow, though, except for the tiniest of starts, she managed to control her reaction.

She *had* overlooked that particular detail, but she wasn't about to let Travis see how much it unnerved her. Ignoring his twinkling eyes and twitching mouth, she pursed her lips and stared into the distance. "Mmm. You're right, I had forgotten about that. But I still think we should stay."

"You do, huh? Then you don't have a problem with sharing the bed with me? Because I warn you right now, no way am I sleeping on the deck."

Rebecca could not control the blush that crept up her neck, but she strove to ignore it. "I didn't say that, exactly. It will be awkward, of course, but I'm sure we can manage. It's a big bed. And we're both adults. After all, it's not as though I have to be concerned about my virtue with you."

"Hey!" Travis barked, giving her an affronted look. "What kind of crack is that?"

"Oh, for heaven's sake, Travis! I'm not attacking your virility. I simply meant that I know you aren't interested in me that way. You said yourself, you've detested me for years. I'm certainly not worried that you'll be overcome with lust."

Anxious to end the uncomfortable conversation, Rebecca clambered to her feet and brushed off the seat of her shorts. "Now that we've settled that, I think I'll go start dinner."

Before Travis could reply, a gust of wind rocked the boat, bringing with it the smell of rain. Lightning arced across the sky, followed seconds later by a deafening clap of thunder. Rebecca's hair whipped around her head. She swiped away the strands stuck to her face and grabbed the rioting mane with both hands and, like Travis, squinted up at the boiling clouds.

"It's about to hit," he yelled over the howling wind. "You go on below. I'll be down as soon as I secure the hatch and put the tools away."

Still holding her hair, Rebecca nodded and scurried down the steps.

Travis watched her go, his expression nonplussed. Did she honestly believe what she'd just said?

He shook his head, and with a sigh hoisted himself up out of the engine well. He wished he could be as certain. A couple of days before—hell, twenty-four hours before—she would have been right. Things were different now, though. Didn't she realize that?

Rebecca had surprised him from the beginning of this outing. She was cooperative, restful, easy to get along with, and open to whatever he suggested. Hell, he might as well admit it; she was damned good company.

Then at lunch she'd let her guard down and given him a glimpse of what her life had really been, and of the lonely, vulnerable child who had been made to feel unloved and unlovable. He realized now that she had masked her pain

and loneliness with that controlled facade all those years. He
suspected that that hurt child was still there, behind that
beautiful, calm face.

Travis was barely aware of the buffeting wind that
whipped his hair or the lightning that forked through the
sky, or even the drunken pitch and roll of the *Freewind*.
Kneeling on the deck, he paused in the act of returning a
wrench to the tool kit and looked toward the cabin. He
thought about the things she had revealed over lunch, and
his face contorted. Listening to her, he had experienced a
confusing welter of emotions, one on top of the other:
shock, sympathy, anger at Richard Quinn. Most of all, he
had felt rotten. Guilt, remorse and shame had hit him like a
blow from a set of brass knuckles when he thought of how
he had treated her.

He hadn't wanted to believe her. He'd fought against it all
afternoon, even though he'd known in his heart that she had
told the truth. Only an idiot or a blind man could have
missed the desolation in her eyes when she'd talked of her
childhood. He might be the first—at least where Rebecca
was concerned—but there was nothing wrong with his eye-
sight.

It was funny how a little bit of knowledge could change
your image of a person. He had always been aware of Rebecca's beauty. Travis snorted and dropped a fist full of
sockets and screwdrivers into the box and slammed the lid
shut. Hell, even as an obnoxious seven-year-old he'd known
she was a knockout. With her dark hair and milky skin and
those soulful blue eyes, he'd secretly thought she looked like
the pictures of Sleeping Beauty in his little sister's book of
fairy tales.

Looking back, he could see now that his cousins had been
right; he had never bothered to get to know Rebecca. He
had seen her quiet composure and shyness as nothing more
than the snooty aloofness of a spoiled rich girl. Over the
years, those misconceptions had kept him from liking her.
Travis frowned. Or maybe he'd clung to them because he'd
been determined not to like her. Hell, he didn't know.

One way or the other, those obstacles were gone now and, no matter how uncomfortable it made him, he had to admit that he was attracted to Rebecca, physically as well as emotionally.

Travis slung the heavy toolbox into the storage compartment and slammed the door shut. Thunder cracked overhead. He looked up at the sky and felt the first fat raindrops splatter against his face and bare chest. Grinning, he loped down the steps. Apparently, he mused with ironic humor, that possibility hadn't yet occurred to Rebecca. If it had, she wouldn't so blithely assume that they could share a bed without sex becoming an issue.

Rebecca stood at the counter in the galley, her feet braced against the roll of the boat, slicing tomatoes into a salad. He turned from shutting the cabin door, and she looked at him over her shoulder. "Dinner will be ready in ten minutes."

"Great. I'll go wash up."

Minutes later, he stepped from the head into the galley to find the table set, the microwave humming and Rebecca bent over the broiler. His offer to help met with a polite refusal and the assurance that everything would be ready soon. Travis slid into the dining booth to get out of her way.

Turning sideways, he leaned back against the bulkhead, propped one foot on the vinyl bench seat, draped his wrist over his updrawn knee, and watched her.

She worked with an economy of movement that was both graceful and competent. She had pulled her heavy hair back in a banana clip, and it cascaded down the center of her back in a froth of rich mahogany curls. Totally absorbed in her task, she stood with her back to him, turned slightly in one quarter profile. Travis's gaze was drawn to the tender curve of her neck, to her ear, the delicate skin behind it, the soft baby curls along her hairline that clung to her nape.

His chest tightened. He drew a deep breath, his nostrils flaring. The urge to run his lips over that fragile flesh tormented him. He could almost taste her.

Cool it, McCall, he cautioned. Think of something else, before you lose it and pounce on the poor woman.

The image that thought created caused his grin to flicker. Rebecca would be shocked. No lust, huh? Yeah, right.

He forced his gaze lower, but the bareness of her shoulders and back was no less tempting. Mesmerized, he watched the supple movements of her shoulder blades above the camisole top, the stretch and shift of feminine muscles beneath peach-tinted flesh. She was slender, her body well toned and firm but softly curved in all the right places. His palms itched to touch her.

She turned with a smile and set the salads on the table. "I think everything is ready," she said, and as if on cue, the microwave dinged. Immediately, she drew on oven mits and bent from the waist to open the broiler, unwittingly presenting Travis with an eye-level view of her bottom.

He stared at that firm, rounded flesh for a full ten seconds, not daring to breathe. Then his gaze traveled down the backs of gorgeous, impossibly long legs. Travis closed his eyes and groaned.

Rebecca straightened with the broiler pan in her hands, and sent him a worried look. "Is something wrong?"

Hell yes, something's wrong. If you don't park that cute little rear I'm going to go quietly out of my mind. "No." He managed a half-hearted grin. "I'm just hungry, is all."

"Well, you don't have to wait any longer. Everything is ready."

Dinner turned out to be broiled redfish with a lemon/dill sauce, baked potatoes and salad. "It's not very fancy, I'm afraid." She set the plates on the table and slid onto the bench seat opposite him. "But under these conditions, it's the best I can do."

"Are you kidding? This is delicious."

The boat was rocking so much they dared not fill their wine glasses more than a quarter full. Travis had seen seasoned sailors get sick from less, but Rebecca didn't appear to notice the constant motion. He watched her dig into her meal with obvious enjoyment, his expression amused and curious.

"The boat rocking doesn't seem to bother you," he commented idly, and she looked up with a hesitant smile.

"No. I've never had a problem with motion sickness. When we were kids and a carnival came to town, the twins and I used to love to ride all the rides. The wilder the better. Elise, poor thing, could barely make it through one round of rides without turning green, and even Erin succumbed once in a while, but I never did." Amusement sparkled in her eyes. "That used to annoy Erin no end."

"I can imagine. She was always such a tough little nut. That you could weather punishment like that better than she could, probably drove her crazy."

Travis gazed at Rebecca's serene face, trying to imagine her screaming her lungs out on a roller coaster, but he couldn't picture it, not that quiet little girl he remembered.

He and his two brothers and David had attended all the carnivals and fairs that had come to Crockett. Where had he been when Rebecca and his cousins had been running around the carnival grounds like little hellions? Probably doing his best to hide out from them, he admitted ruefully.

Conversation flowed during dinner and over coffee afterward. They reminisced about their childhood in Crockett, about how different life was in the sleepy east Texas town compared to places like Dallas and Houston, about the high jinks that the Blaine and McCall kids had gotten into.

If anyone were listening they'd think we were the best of friends, Travis thought, as Rebecca related a tale about when she and the twins had been in the tenth grade, and Erin had persuaded her and Elise to help her smuggle a cow into the principal's office one night.

They talked about the town's characters, and wondered what had become of old friends neither had seen in years. They talked about their college days and the places they'd been, about some of Travis's more colorful cases with the FBI. They talked about everything, he noticed, but Rebecca's marriage.

Travis made several attempts to work the conversation around to the subject, but Rebecca neatly side-stepped it each time.

Because it took only a couple of sips to drain the wine from the partially filled glasses, it was difficult to keep up with how much you were consuming. Travis noticed that the more Rebecca drank, the more relaxed she became, and he made a point to replenish her glass each time she emptied it. By the time they reached the coffee stage she seemed completely at ease, and he decided to abandon subtlety in favor of the direct approach.

"While we're on the subject of the past," he said casually, watching her over the rim of his cup. "You never did say what went wrong in your marriage."

Whatever lassitude the wine had induced vanished. Rebecca's gaze flew to his face, and he saw the wariness enter her eyes like shields snapping into place. Exasperated, she shook her head.

"I swear, Travis. You haven't changed a bit. Even when we were kids, whenever your curiosity was aroused you were just like a badger. No matter how much a person tried to divert you, you just kept right on digging. You're still doing it. But then, I guess that's what makes you so good at your job."

Travis grinned. "So what happened?"

She rolled her eyes and groaned. Travis's grin grew wider.

"I really don't want to talk about it."

"C'mon, gimme a break. You can't expect me to ignore the most obvious topic of conversation. Besides, I've told you all about my life since I left Crockett. Now it's your turn."

Her droll look said she seriously doubted that. It also hid the panic she felt. Travis was going to keep right on probing and picking until he got an answer. To shut him up, she was going to have to tell him at least part of the truth.

With a sigh, she spread her hands wide. "We just didn't get along. So I decided to end it."

"You're the one who wanted the divorce?"

"Yes."

"Was there another woman?" he asked gently.

Surprised, Rebecca looked up. She expected derision but there was only kindness in his eyes. Smiling faintly, she shook her head. "No, nothing like that. As far as I know, Evan was faithful to me."

Rebecca almost wished that her husband had found someone else. Except . . . she couldn't, in good conscience, wish that fate on another woman.

"How did your father take it when he found out?"

A sad smile tugged at Rebecca's mouth. "You mean how did he feel about losing Evan Hall as a son-in-law? I wouldn't know. I haven't talked to him since I left. Actually, I'm not sure he even knows about it yet. He's sailing the Mediterranean on a friend's yacht."

"You said you divorced Evan two months ago. You mean, in all that time, you haven't called or written your father?"

The shock in Travis's voice was unmistakable. Everyone in Crockett and most people in their Dallas circle knew the store Richard Quinn set in her marriage. Rebecca looked down at her coffee cup and fingered the handle.

"No."

Travis gave a long, low whistle. "Man, I wouldn't want to be in your shoes when he finds out."

Rebecca answered with a wan smile and felt sick to her stomach. She didn't want to be in her shoes either, but there was no help for it. Sooner or later she was going to have to face the music.

"How about Evan?" Travis probed relentlessly. "What was his reaction when you asked for a divorce?"

She stood up abruptly. "Travis, I really don't want to talk about this anymore." Her voice broke at the end, and she began to stack the dishes with stiff, jerky movements. Keeping her gaze fixed on the task, she avoided Travis's eyes, but she felt them following her every move.

He didn't utter a word or move until the table was cleared. Then he joined her at the sink, picked up a dish towel and began drying the dishes. The air in the cabin vibrated with tension.

The boat rocked and creaked in the wind. Rain lashed the sides and the decks, and streamed down the high narrow windows on either side of the cabin. The only other sounds were the swish of the dishwater and the clink of china.

"I'm sorry, Rebecca," Travis said, breaking the silence. "I didn't realize that you were so torn up about the divorce."

She swallowed and kept her eyes on the mounds of soapsuds in the sink. "I'm not torn up. Not the way you mean, anyway."

"But the end of a marriage, no matter how bad, is hard to take. Right? That's the reason you came to Rincon, isn't it? To give yourself time to get over it."

The breakup of her marriage was not the source of her pain. Far from it. To admit that to Travis, however, would invite more questions. "You could say that, I guess," she hedged, swallowing her guilt at the half-truth.

The silence stretched out again. Rebecca held her breath and braced for more questions, but when Travis finally spoke, his voice held a teasing note.

"In that case, it's a good thing I was here."

She slanted him a cautious look out of the corner of her eye. "Oh? Why is that?"

"Because I'm great at cheering up despondent women. Especially beautiful ones." He wriggled his eyebrows at her, Groucho Marx style, and Rebecca couldn't help but laugh.

"Oh, you are, are you?" she said, trying to enter the spirit of the game. Rebecca was not accustomed to taking part in lighthearted banter. She felt awkward and self-conscious about it. Still, the harmless teasing was by far preferable to fending off his endless questions about her marriage.

"You bet. You might even say I'm an expert."

"Mmm. And what exactly is it that you do for these women?"

"I'm charming and witty. I keep them company, entertain them, provide stimulating conversation." He leaned his elbow on the counter until his eyes were level with hers and their faces were mere inches apart. "Most of all," he continued in a husky voice, "I give them lots of TLC."

"I see." She pulled the plug from the sink and pretended to consider the statement as she dried her hands on a towel. "The first part sounds good, but I'm not in the market for any TLC."

"Oh, I don't know about that," he drawled. He lifted his hand and stroked her cheek with his fingertips. The feather-light caress sent a shiver rippling through her. "You look to me exactly like a woman who could use some tender loving care," he murmured. "Lots of it."

Rebecca stared at him, her heart thumping. In a blink his demeanor had gone from teasing to seductive.

A smile still curved his beautiful mouth, but he regarded her with unblinking directness, his eyes glittering beneath half-closed lids, hot and intent. He was so close she could feel his breath tickling her cheek.

He was serious, she realized, and shock sent another shiver skittering along her spine.

Rebecca drew in an unsteady breath and licked her lips. His silvery gaze zeroed in on the action, and his pupils expanded. The shiver spread over her back and up her nape, making the hairs there stand at attention.

"Travis, please," she pleaded in a voice just above a whisper. "You don't have to do this. Really."

"Do what?" His forefinger touched a soft curl at her hairline, the calloused tip grazing the fragile skin behind her ear. The touch left a trail of fire in its wake.

"Flirt with me."

"Is that what I'm doing?"

Instantly, doubt and acute embarrassment riddled Rebecca. Oh, Lord, had she read something into his actions that wasn't there? She risked another look at him, and uncertainty fled as fast as it had come. No, she hadn't been wrong. His slumberous gaze fairly sizzled.

"Aren't you?"

He appeared to give the question serious thought, then lifted one shoulder. "Yeah. I guess maybe I am."

The admission made her pulse leap, much to her disgust. *For heaven's sake, will you get a hold of yourself. You're not a silly teenager anymore,* she silently berated.

Gathering her composure, she slanted him what she hoped was a look of amused tolerance. "Look, Travis, I know that flirting is automatic with you, but in this case, don't you think it's...well...a bit ridiculous, given who we are?"

"At one time it would've been, but I've changed my mind about you."

"Oh. Well...that's good to hear, of course. I'm glad we're not enemies anymore. But that doesn't mean that we should be...uh..."

"Lovers?" he supplied for her.

"Yes." She struggled to ignore the hot tide of color that flooded her neck and face, and Travis's unholy grin. "It isn't an either/or situation, you know. There is a middle ground. Under the circumstances, that would be more appropriate."

His hand stilled on her neck. He studied her earnest expression, and after a while dropped his hand to his side. Straightening, he crossed his arms over his chest, leaned back and braced his hips against the counter. One side of his mouth kicked up in a wry, half smile. "Yeah, maybe you're right."

She smiled back, feeling both relieved and curiously disappointed.

Rebecca turned to hang the towel on the rack beside the sink. At the same moment, the boat went into a pitching roll and sent her stumbling right into the solid wall of Travis's chest.

Off balance, she clung to him as his arms closed around her and he settled her snugly between his thighs. Gasping, she looked up and encountered his amused, blatantly sensual gaze.

"But then again, maybe not," he drawled, and lowered his mouth to hers.

Rebecca clutched his shoulders, her fingers digging deep into the tanned bare flesh. She moaned. Between the rocking boat and the drugging kiss her head was spinning.

The gentle, tentative kiss they had shared earlier had no resemblance to this bold assault on her senses. This was deep, devouring, avid and unabashedly passionate. Taking advantage of her open-mouthed shock, Travis slipped his tongue inside to engage hers in an erotic duel. His hands stroked over her with brazen self-assurance and a familiarity that stole her breath away, gliding over her back and shoulders, slipping between their bodies to seek out her breasts, her abdomen, returning to boldly cup her buttocks and the backs of her thighs, lifting her against his arousal.

She felt a burning deep inside her femininity and moaned. Travis made a sound low in his throat—a purely masculine sound of triumph, of pleasure, of scorching desire.

Rebecca felt as if she were drowning in sensations—the incredible heat and hardness of his body, the manly smell that invaded her being with each shallow breath, the taste of him on her tongue, the raspy sound of his breathing, its warm moistness eddying against her cheek. The silky softness of his beard caressed the skin around her mouth with a feathery touch that made her shiver. Her heart was beating so hard and so fast it was almost suffocating her.

Pleasure swirled through her in waves, a sweet, honeyed pleasure that she hadn't known existed pounded, hot and thick, through her veins and seemed to settle in a throbbing ache at the apex of her thighs. Flattened against his chest, her breasts swelled, the nipples tightening into hard nubs, achingly tight and tender. Above the camisole top she felt the tickling brush of his chest hairs against her skin.

The oscillating motion of the boat rocked their bodies together with a shocking intimacy that pulled a long, throaty moan from Rebecca. Her knees had long since turned to putty, and all she could do was cling to Travis for support.

Eerie flashes illuminated the cabin as lightning arced and sizzled through the angry sky. Seconds later, thunder clapped and rolled and the wind howled. Neither of them noticed.

Travis broke off the kiss, and she gasped, but he immediately slanted his head at a different angle and reclaimed her mouth. With hot, open-mouthed kisses and the bold touch of his hands and body, he held her enthralled. For an endless time she half lay against him, while the boat rode the heaving swells and the heavens rumbled and the rain drummed overhead.

Sanity returned with a rude start when Rebecca's straw purse slid off the ledge where she'd stowed it and struck the backs of her legs. She yelped and jerked free of the kiss, but when she tried to step out of the embrace, Travis's arms tightened around her.

"Take it easy, sweetheart. It's okay," he soothed.

Dazed, Rebecca looked up into his smiling face, and her heart speeded up. Fear gripped her, warring with the excitement that pounded through her. Good, Lord. What was she doing? This was madness.

Trembling, she stood between Travis's legs within the circle of his arms, that part of her that ached and throbbed pressed tight against the unmistakable bulge at the juncture of his thighs. His crooked smile and sensual gaze reeked of predatory male. The sight sent an icy trickle down her spine.

His gaze dropped to her kiss-swollen mouth, and his head began a slow descent. With a quick catch of her breath, Rebecca pushed against his chest and leaned back, turning her head aside to evade his lips. "No, Travis. Don't. We must stop this."

He chuckled and settled for a nibble on her ear. "Now, why would we want to to that? We were starting to make sparks."

Hot breath dewed her skin, and Rebecca shuddered as he kissed and licked his way down the side of her neck. The reaction was due in part to excitement and in part to fright. She wasn't sure which was stronger.

"Oh, baby, baby," he murmured, his voice thick with passion. "You taste so good. So damned good."

Clenching her jaw against the delicious sensations spilling through her, and the debilitating terror that threatened to buckle her knees, she braced her forearms against his chest and pushed with all her strength. "No, Travis. Don't. I can't . . . I don't want this! Stop! Oh, please stop!"

The panicky note in her voice got through to him, and he stilled. He leaned back, keeping his arms around her, and studied her face. A slight frown formed between his eyebrows. "You're serious, aren't you?"

At her quick nod, his scowl deepened. "Why? The attraction between us is strong. And I know damned well that it's mutual. I didn't imagine your response just now, Rebecca."

"I don't deny that," she managed shakily. "But it was a mistake. It should never have happened. A, uh . . . a romantic relationship between us would just complicate things, and my life is complicated enough as it is."

"Maybe a love affair is just what you need to take your mind off your problems."

"No, Travis."

"Then tell me why? After all, we're both consenting adults. We're both single. So what's the problem? If you're worried about protection, I have it with me. And I've been tested—"

"It's not that." Blushing furiously, Rebecca searched for a way to explain without revealing too much. "Travis, I'm just not cut out for a casual affair. I've never had one. Evan . . . Evan is the only man I've ever been intimate with."

Travis's eyebrows shot skyward. Then his expression softened. "Rebecca, honey. I understand. Really, I do. A part of me is even glad that you're inexperienced. But don't you think it's time y—"

She stopped him by placing four fingers over his mouth. "No. Listen to me, Travis. I can't handle an intimate relationship right now, casual or otherwise. I . . . I don't want to get involved with you that way. It just wouldn't work."

He grinned and captured her hand. "Oh, I don't know about that. You told me yourself that you wanted me once. Judging by the way you kissed me back just now, I think I could make you want me again."

"Oh, Travis." The look she gave him was sad and mildly reproving. "I'll admit that you could probably stir the embers of that old crush back to life, if you tried. But if your feelings about me really have changed, as you say, you won't do that." Her eyes pleaded with him, and her voice came out quavery and earnest. "I don't need a lover, Travis. What I need at this point in my life is a friend."

Travis stared down into those soft blue eyes and felt a peculiar tightening in his chest. Misty and soulful, they silently implored. In the crystal depths he saw a naked, soul-deep sadness that tugged at his heart, but what bothered him most was the fear that she could not hide.

What had put it there? Good Lord, was she afraid of him? Had years of being subjected to his antagonism done that? The appalling thought tightened his chest even more, to the point of pain.

He knew a sudden urge to erase that look, to see her smile at him freely, happily, with no haunting shadows and no holding back, no nervous skittering away.

Still, his aroused body ached and demanded. He wanted her, dammit. He wanted to bury himself in her softness, wanted to feel her beneath him, going wild, that impassive expression banished, her face flushed and blurry with passion. For him.

For several seconds a battle waged inside Travis between raw desire and his more noble instincts. Finally he sighed, and his mouth twisted. "Friends, huh?"

Rebecca nodded. He let loose another long-suffering sigh and released her. Bracing the heels of his hands against the edge of the counter on either side of his hips, he watched her back away and had to consciously work at holding on to his amused expression.

"Aw, what the heck. Friends it is."

"Are you sure? I mean, I know that this is a big change for you. If you'd rather not be friends, I'll underst—"

"Hey, no problem. I'm fine with this. Actually…it ought to be interesting." His mouth widened in a slow, wicked grin, and he winked. "This'll be a first for me. I've never been just friends with a woman before. At least, not with one who turns me on."

She looked stunned, as though she didn't quite know how to take that, but after a quick search of his face, she relaxed and her mouth began to twitch. "I'll bet," she returned, somewhere between cheeky and embarrassed.

"Hey, I'm serious. I don't think you realize what a sacrifice I'm making for you. If this ever gets out, my reputation will be shot to hell and gone."

As he had hoped it would, his foolishness loosened her up even more. He watched the tension gradually drain from her and a hesitant light of mischief enter her eyes.

"Poor baby. If it will help, why don't you look at this as a character-developing exercise?"

"Yeah. Right." He assumed a pained expression, and a giggle broke from Rebecca.

With exaggerated martyrdom, Travis rolled his eyes and made a face. "Aw, what the hell. Since I'm being so noble and self-sacrificing, I'll even give you first dibs on the bathroom. If you want, you can borrow one of Abigail's nightgowns. I'm sure she won't mind."

While Rebecca disappeared into the forward cabin in search of sleepwear, Travis took a beer from the refrigerator and made himself comfortable at the table, sitting sideways on the bench seat with his back against the bulkhead. He'd no sooner settled back than Rebecca returned with a minuscule swath of pink cotton draped over one arm. Taking a long pull of beer, he watched her dig through her purse and take out a small plastic cylinder.

"What's that?"

"A toothbrush. I always carry a spare. You never know when you'll need to brush your teeth."

"You women and your purses. It's amazing what you lug around with you in those things." He shook his head, the picture of a bewildered male. Recalling the monstrous canvas tote that David's bride, Abigail, carried and the astounding assortment of stuff it contained, he chuckled.

"Laugh if you want," Rebecca returned with mock hauteur. "But you're the one who'll have to make do with a dab of toothpaste on a washcloth."

Acknowledging the sally, Travis grinned and lifted the beer can in a silent salute. His amused expression gave way to somber thoughtfulness the minute Rebecca stepped into the head.

He stared at the closed door, aware of the strange tightness in his chest. Why the hell did he feel so disappointed?

She was probably right. A romance between them would never work. There were too many things against it. For one, their lives were just too closely intertwined. With Rebecca being Erin and Elise's best friend, it would be awkward when their affair ended, no matter how amiably they parted. They were bound to run into each other now and then at his cousins' homes, or maybe even in Crockett, if she returned there to live.

Then there was the matter of Rebecca's inexperience. That, coupled with her background, was enough to tell him that she wasn't equipped to handle an affair. She was an emotionally fragile woman, and as strange as it seemed, given their history, the last thing he wanted was to hurt her.

Anyway, it was ludicrous for two people who had known each other practically all their lives to suddenly become lovers.

What the hell. If friendship was what she wanted from him, then that's what she'd get. It was the least he could do after the way he'd treated her all those years.

The winds had died down and the rain had lessened to a monotonous downpour. The steady drumming blended with the sound of the shower, drawing Travis's attention. Immediately an image formed in his mind of Rebecca standing naked beneath the spray, her pale skin rosy from the hot water, mounds of lather slithering down over her breasts and abdomen, the long curving length of her legs.

Heat surged into his loins, and Travis groaned. His grip tightened, crushing the aluminum beer can, and the foaming brew spewed onto the table like a small geyser.

"Aw, man. Get a grip, willya," he spat in utter disgust, and bolted out of the booth. He snatched up a dishcloth and mopped up the mess, muttering under his breath the whole while. "For Pete's sake. You're not a randy teenager anymore. So you find the woman attractive and sexy. So what? If you're going to make this friendship thing work, you've got to put those kinds of thoughts right out of your mind."

By the time Rebecca stepped out of the head, he had his wayward body under control and had convinced himself that he could deal with the situation. One look at Rebecca proved him wrong on both counts.

The pink cotton nightie barely skimmed the tops of her thighs and beneath the ruffled hem peeked the edge of a pair of matching panties. The gown hung from her shoulders by two tiny straps, exposing an expanse of creamy skin, tinted the slightest peach by the day in the sun.

This was Abigail's nightgown? Until that moment, Travis hadn't had any idea that his cousin's prim little wife even owned such a provocative garment.

Rebecca's face was scrubbed clean of makeup and shining, and her hair tumbled about her shoulders in a glorious mass of dark gleaming curls. Warm moist air roiled from the head, carrying the smells of minty toothpaste and women's toiletries—floral soap and talc and lotion. The exquisitely feminine scents made Travis's head spin and his heart pound and his body harden all over again.

"The bathroom is all yours." The hesitancy in her voice and the way she kept tugging at the bottom of the nightie betrayed her nervousness. Travis knew that the rosy glow of her skin owed its origin to more than exposure to the sun and a hot shower. Strangely, he found her embarrassment endearing.

"Great." He forced a casual smile and had to grit his teeth to keep it in place as she scurried past him and went into the forward stateroom.

"Oh, yeah. Just great," he muttered, closing the head door behind him.

Though he'd taken a shower earlier, he took another one. A cold one. A *long* cold one.

Thirty minutes later, when he stepped from the head, the lights were out in the forward cabin. Dressed in only his underwear, Travis turned off the lights in the galley, groped his way through the darkness and slipped into bed beside Rebecca.

She lay stiff as a poker, not moving so much as a muscle. He guessed that she wanted him to think she was asleep. He knew that she wasn't.

Rain pattered on the foredeck above them, and the boat rocked gently. The darkness thrummed with a heavy quiet and tension vibrated the air like the soft, silent beat of a predator's wings.

Travis turned on his side, and Rebecca jumped.

He laughed; it was either that or groan. "Relax, honey. I'm not going to bite you."

"I know that."

"Oh, yeah? Then what are you braced for?" He raised up on one elbow and peered at her through the darkness. "I'm not going to jump your bones the minute you fall asleep, Rebecca." He paused a beat before adding wickedly, "I'm going to wait an hour or two and catch you by surprise."

"Oh, Travis, you idiot." She laughed, as he had intended, and gave his shoulder a playful sock.

Though he could make out only her vague outline, he could feel the tension seep out of her and her body slowly relax beside him. After a moment he asked, "Feel better now?"

"Yes. Much. Thank you, Travis."

"Hey. That's what friends are for. Now go to sleep."

He lay back and turned over, facing away from her. Rebecca shifted positions and punched her pillow.

"Good night, Travis," she murmured softly.

"'Night."

The silence stretched out again. The rain pattered. The boat rocked. Water slapped the hull.

"Travis?"

"Mmm?"

"I'm glad we're friends."

"Yeah. Me too."

She exhaled a contented sigh and wriggled around, finally snuggling into a comfortable position. The smell of floral talc and warm woman drifted to him through the darkness. Travis gritted his teeth.

He *was* glad, dammit. The problem was, his body wanted a helluva lot more.

Rebecca awoke to find herself enveloped by Travis. His arm lay draped across her waist, and his muscular leg was hooked over both of hers. Along her backside, from shoulder to toes, his body heat warmed her like a blast from a furnace.

Glancing over her shoulder, Rebecca eyed him warily, grasped his wrist between her thumb and forefinger and removed it from her waist. Then, just as carefully, she began to work her legs from beneath his. When at last she was free, she inched to the foot of the bed and climbed out. She retrieved her clothes and started to leave the stateroom, but at the head of the bed she paused and looked down at Travis.

Asleep and rumpled, he should have looked vulnerable, less appealing, but he didn't. He looked every bit as sexy and devilish as he did awake.

Those impossible lashes lay against his cheeks like feathery fans, their blackness a startling contrast to the long blond hair spread across his pillow. Her gaze was drawn to his mouth. His lips were open partway, revealing the edge of perfect while teeth. Rebecca stared, recalling how those chiseled lips had felt against hers, the passion that had exploded between them. Unconsciously she touched her own mouth with her fingertips.

It had come as a surprise to discover that she was still attracted to Travis—even if it was only on a physical level. That's all it was, of course. That's all it could possibly be.

All the reasons she had given Travis were valid. Her life was a mess right now; she had no business starting any sort of relationship with another man until the past was truly behind her. Her emotions were too raw and battered. After Evan, she no longer trusted her own judgment where men were concerned.

She couldn't—she *wouldn't*—let herself be drawn into a temporary summer affair that would only hurt her in the end, all because her heart persisted in hanging on to the remnant of a foolish, teenage crush that had ended years ago.

Her mouth set in a determined line, and she slipped out of the room into the galley.

Thirty minutes later, when Travis joined her, she was topside, standing at the rail, sipping her second cup of coffee and watching the rising sun paint the glassy waters of the cove a vivid flamingo pink.

"Are you always such an early bird?" he asked, and Rebecca turned to find him standing at the top of the companionway steps, yawning and scratching his furry chest.

"Mmm. I like to get up and watch the sunrise."

She smiled and took another sip of coffee to hide her disquiet at his appearance. He had obviously just stepped into his disreputable cutoffs, but he hadn't bothered with a shirt or shoes, or even to comb his hair. His cheeks, above the beginning beard, still bore the marks of sleep and his eyes were drowsy. And sexy as all get out. Rebecca was quite sure he knew it, too.

He gave her a heavy-lidded look and ambled closer. "Shoot, I can think of a lot better reasons to stay in bed. You sure you don't want to drop this 'friendship' nonsense and let me demonstrate one or two?" he asked with an outrageous leer.

Rebecca experienced a flash of panic until she looked into his eyes and saw that he was teasing. Fighting a grin, she lifted her chin and tried for a stern look. "No, I most certainly do not. You promised you'd be my friend and I'm going to hold you to it."

Travis rolled his eyes mournfully and sighed. "Somehow, I knew you were going to say that."

She laughed at his woebegone expression and skirted around him. "I'm going below to cook breakfast. In the meantime, since you're not interested in the sunrise, why don't you have another look at the engine."

"Jeez, what a slave driver."

That first encounter set the tone for the rest of the day. Travis teased Rebecca every chance he got, his silvery eyes dancing with wicked delight at her blushes and valiant parries.

Gone was the surly antagonist she had encountered all her life. Gone, too, was the quiet, watchful companion of the day before. This devilish, sexy flirt was the Travis the rest of the world had always known. Though she privately chided herself for letting it matter, Rebecca was thrilled at last to be on the receiving end of his charm.

Between preparing breakfast and lunch and doing the dishes, she spent the day sitting beside the engine well, talking to Travis and handing him tools when he asked for them, reveling in the easy companionship that was growing between them.

By late afternoon Travis had the boat running again and they headed back to Alhaja Verde. Rebecca had enjoyed herself so much she hated for the outing to end.

In San Cristobal Travis described the trouble they'd had with the *Freewind* to the mechanics at the boatyard and turned the craft over to them with instructions to give it another thorough going-over. Weary and anxious now to return home, they headed for Rincon Island in the speedboat.

They had no sooner docked the boat and headed up the pier than they were greeted by the incessant shrilling of the telephone. Exchanging a surprised look, they hurried to the house and let themselves in.

"I'll get it," Travis said, dumping his fishing gear in the middle of the living room floor. He strode over to the wide counter that divided the kitchen and living room, snatched up the receiver and barked an impatient, "Hello."

"Travis McCall, you rat!" Erin screeched right back at him. "Why the devil didn't you let us know that you and Rebecca were engaged?"

Chapter Eight

"Engaged!" Travis chuckled. "Good, Lord, Erin! What the devil are you talk—"

He halted as his gaze met Rebecca's and their eyes widened simultaneously. A look of horror came over her face.

"Oh, my word! We forgot to explain to Pepe!"

"Aw, sh—"

"I'm talking about your engagement to our best friend," Erin snapped, cutting of the crude expletive. "I've always known you were a devil with the ladies, but this is working a bit fast isn't it, even for you?"

"Erin's right," Elise chimed in, and Travis groaned.

He should have known she would be on the line, too. They always acted as a pair. Arguing with them was like arguing with a stereo; they came at you from two directions at one time.

"Rebecca is vulnerable right now," the gentler of the twins continued in a softly accusing voice. "I'd hate to think that you took advantage of her, Travis."

"Now, Elise, sugar, you know I wouldn't—"

"Elise has a point. Rebecca is in no shape to be making such a serious commitment. And another thing. I am very disappointed in you, cousin. I figured you for a lot of things, but never a sneak."

"Whoa! Now wait just a minute, Cuz. I am no sneak."

"Oh, no? What about all those years of you claiming not to like Rebecca? Huh? What about that? And all that ranting and raving you did just a few weeks ago about having to share the beach house with her? Why, only yesterday morning you were still pretending not to like her. And all the while you were taking unfair advantage of her emotional state. You ought to be ashamed of yourself, Travis McCall, rushing poor Rebecca that way."

"Hold on. I haven't—"

"Not that we don't think you and Rebecca would make a good match, you understand," Elise inserted quickly, trying, as always, to pour oil over troubled waters. "We do. It's just that we think Rebecca needs more time to recover before she gets serious about another man."

Travis made an exasperated sound and cupped his forehead with his palm, his thumb and first two fingers moving in a rotating massage against his temples. David was right; his sisters could drive a saint crazy.

Agitated, Rebecca stood beside him, wringing her hands and shifting from one foot to the other. "What are they saying? Are they upset? Oh, dear. Maybe I should talk to them."

Before Travis could answer, Erin jumped in again.

"And since when have you been in such an all-fired hurry to get married, I'd just like to know? You've always been as slippery as an eel whenever a woman even mentioned commitment."

"Now look—"

"She didn't mean that the way it sounded, Travis. She's just concerned. We both are. We've been so worried about you and Rebecca."

"That's right. And while we're on the subject of worry, where the devil have you two been? When we called Rebecca back last night to wish her a happy birthday, there was no answer. We called all night long. By dawn we had begun to imagine all sorts of horrible things. That's when we telephoned Pepe and Constanza to see if they had heard from you.''

''Ahhh, I see. And of course they just had to blab that Rebecca and I were engaged.'' Travis's drawl held wry amusement, but Rebecca gave a distressed moan.

''You really should have told us yourself, Travis. Do you have any idea how much it hurt to hear news like that from a third party?''

''Elise, sweetheart, please believe me. I didn't tell you because there's nothing to tell.''

''Then you didn't tell Pepe and Constanza that you were engaged?'' Erin demanded.

''Well . . . yeah, we did. That is, I did.''

''So you are engaged?''

''No!''

''Then why in heaven's name did you let the Moralleses think that you were?''

''If you'll shut up for thirty seconds I'll tell you,'' he said between clenched teeth, his much-acclaimed insouciance strained to the limit.

''Really, Travis, there's no need to get testy,'' Erin drawled. ''That's precisely what we've been trying to get you to do for the past five minutes.''

The sound that came from Travis's throat was somewhere between a growl and groan. He gritted his teeth and tried to count to ten, but on four he thrust the receiver at Rebecca. ''Here. I give up. They're your friends. You deal with them.''

''Hi, it's me,'' Rebecca said cautiously into the receiver, watching Travis stroll away into the kitchen and open the refrigerator.

''Rebecca!'' the twins exclaimed in unison, and both began talking at once, peppering her with questions.

''Where were you and Travis last night?''

''What's this business about being engaged?''

"Are you all right? That cousin of ours isn't giving you a hard time, is he?"

"Do you want us to come down there and set him straight?"

Rebecca opened and closed her mouth several times, but she couldn't get a word in edgewise. Finally she gave up.

Travis turned from the refrigerator with a frosty can of beer in his hand. Holding it aloft, he looked at Rebecca and mouthed, "You want one?" She shook her head, hitched herself up on a bar stool and settled down to wait for the excited pair to wind down.

Finally a lull occurred in the babble, followed by an uncertain, "Rebecca? Are you there?"

"Yes, I'm here. If the two of you are finished, I'll answer your questions. First of all, I'm sorry I missed your call last night. But before I get into that, let me explain this business about an engagement."

As calmly and concisely as possible, she gave them an expurgated version of what had happened, leaving out any mention of that stunning kiss in the middle of Pepe's cantina. She did her best to make light of the incident and pass the whole thing off as a joke. "So you see, it was all just a harmless ruse."

"Humph. Sounds to me like our dear cousin used you to get himself out of a sticky situation."

"Well . . . maybe. But I didn't mind."

"Nevertheless, Travis should not have put you in such an embarrassing position," Elise declared. "What I don't understand, though, is why you didn't explain the whole thing to the Moralleses?"

"We meant to, but yesterday morning, when we reached Alhaja Verde, we were in such a hurry to stock the boat with supplies so we could start our fishing trip, that we forgot." She glanced at Travis, and added, "It was as much my fault as it was Travis's."

"Wait a minute. Are you saying that he took you fishing on your birthday? Voluntarily?"

Rebecca laughed at the surprise in Erin's voice. "Yes. Wasn't that nice of him?"

Smiling at Travis's sardonic expression, she quickly told them about the fishing trip on David's boat, and what an enjoyable day she'd had. Then she explained about the engine trouble and the storm, and their decision to remain in the cove and ride it out.

"Travis spent today working on the engine. When he got it running again, we headed back to the marina in San Cristobal and left the *Freewind* at the boat yard. We just arrived back here."

Silence followed. Finally Erin, her voice low and incredulous, said slowly, "You mean you slept with Travis?"

"No! Of course not. That is . . ."

"Rebecca. There's only one bed on the *Freewind*. Travis is a gentleman, but with a storm raging outside I doubt that even he would sleep up on deck."

"He didn't. That is . . . Oh, all right, yes. I did sleep with him. I mean, I didn't *sleep* with him, of course," she said in a rush, blushing scarlet.

Travis wasn't helping matters any. Sitting on the stool next to hers, he lounged back against the bar, grinning, and observed her discomfort with an unholy twinkle in his eyes.

"What I mean is, we shared the bed, but nothing happened. It was all perfectly platonic."

Travis snorted, and his eyebrows shot skyward. His mocking look challenged her claim and made her squirm. Rebecca tried to ignore him but she felt heat spread over her neck and face as her blush deepened.

"Uh-huh. Travis McCall, the sexiest hunk to ever fill a pair of jeans, lies side by side with a beautiful woman all night without laying a finger on her. Yeah, sure. I buy that," Erin drawled. "And donkeys fly."

"Now, Erin. If Rebecca says—"

"I'm telling you, nothing happened. I swear it."

Travis leaned forward and yelled into the receiver, "Don't you believe it. We made mad, passionate love all night long."

"*Travis!*" Rebecca slapped at his shoulder and tried to push him away but he laughingly fended her off and kept right on.

"It was fantastic. The sex was so hot we nearly set the boat on fire."

"Ohhh! You...you..." Words failed her, and finally, in desperation, she twisted around on the stool, turning her back on him, and cradled the receiver between her ear and her hunched shoulder. "Don't pay any attention to him. He's teasing. You know Travis."

"Yes, we certainly do," Erin concurred. "I'd like to speak to him, please, Rebecca."

"Oh, but—"

"Don't worry. We believe you. Travis is not the kind to brag. If he had made love to you he'd be as closed-mouthed about it as a clam. I just want to have a word with him is all."

Relieved, Rebecca swiveled back around and handed him the receiver. "They want to talk to you."

Travis's teasing had created an unsettled feeling in the pit of her stomach. Needing to put distance between them, she slid off the stool with all the nonchalance she could muster and went to one of the rattan sofas, curling up in the corner with her feet tucked under her.

Grinning, Travis watched her and leaned back, elbows propped on the counter. "Yeah, Cuz. Shoot."

"Don't tempt me, Travis," Erin warned.

"Hey! Lighten up, willya? It was a joke."

"Yeah, well you take care with Rebecca. You hear me?"

"You can quit worrying on that score. You'll be happy to know that Rebecca and I have finally cleared things up between us. We're friends now."

The statement met dead silence at the other end of the line. Finally, in a pleasant voice laced with steel, Erin drawled, "As I said, dear cousin. You take care with Rebecca."

"Meaning?"

"That we know you, Travis. There isn't a snowball's chance in hell of you remaining 'just good friends' with someone like Rebecca. Before you start something, you'd better think it over carefully. We don't want her to end up as your latest 'girlfriend of the month.'"

"Hey! I resent that."

"Tough."

"Erin's right, Travis. If all you want is a lighthearted affair, then leave her alone. Rebecca has been hurt enough."

The real concern in their voices sobered Travis. He knew that divorce was always painful, but this sounded like more than just incompatibility or irreconcilable differences.

"Would you mind explaining that?"

"We already told you, Travis, we can't betray her confidence. Just remember what we said and take care with Rebecca."

The warning came through loud and clear, and aroused his curiosity all the more. Travis glanced at Rebecca. In the past, the twins' fiercely protective attitude toward her had always baffled and angered him, but after spending the past two days in her company he understood it. There was something about Rebecca that inspired protectiveness. She put up a good front, but under that calm control there was something fragile about her. Something sad and wounded. Like a baby bird with a broken wing.

"Oh, all right," he agreed finally. "I swear, you don't have a thing to worry about on that score. Now, tell me..."

Listening to Travis cajole his cousins out of their ire, Rebecca looked on in amazement and reluctant admiration. Through all the years she had known him—as a barefoot, sweaty-faced little boy, a gangly adolescent, a cocky teenage heartbreaker, and now as a mature man in his prime—he had used that easygoing charm and devil-may-care self-confidence to his advantage. It had disarmed teachers and adults, endeared him to other males, captivated old ladies and enslaved young ones. No doubt, it had gotten him out of many a tight situation during his years as an agent, as well.

His appeal was magnetic and potent and thoroughly disarming. The man ought to be required by law to wear a warning label stamped on his forehead, Rebecca mused wryly. *Beware, may be hazardous to female hearts.*

Travis hung up the telephone and turned to her with a self-satisfied air. "That was a close one, but I think the terrible twosome is off our backs. For a while anyway."

"No thanks to you," she said tartly, but her voice lacked heat and she knew it. It was difficult to be angry when faced with dancing gray eyes and that outrageous grin. She, it seemed, was no more immune to his allure than any other female. "Honestly, Travis. Whatever possessed you to say those things?"

"Hey, I was just trying to help." Unrepentant, he sauntered toward her with that hip-rolling gait, and Rebecca's mouth went dry. He bent down, bracing his hands along the back and arm of the sofa. "With every word you were digging yourself in deeper. I gotta tell you, sweetheart, you don't lie worth spit."

"I didn't lie!"

Those chiseled lips tilted up in an outrageously sexy smile. From beneath heavy lids, his glittering eyes mocked her. "Honey, we may not have made love," he murmured in a raspy voice. "But to claim that nothing happened between us is a bald-faced lie. You know it and I know it. And I'm pretty sure, from the way you were babbling, that Erin and Elise know it now, too."

"Travis, you promised—"

"That I'd be your friend. Yeah, I know. And I will. But, honey, there are all kinds of friendships. And the feelings that you and I spark off each other are anything but platonic." His hot gaze roamed her face, inspecting each individual feature before settling on her mouth. Rebecca watched his pupils expand, his nostrils flare, and her heart lurched. "You wanna know the truth, I don't think they ever have been," he whispered.

Rebecca could not have moved or said a word had her life depended on it. Their faces were only inches apart. She could feel his breath feathering over her cheek. Trembling, she stared at his eyes, half-concealed behind those incredibly long lashes, watching him watch her.

At last, with apparent effort, he tore his gaze from her mouth and looked into her eyes, and she felt a bolt of white hot fire sizzle through her.

Rebecca's heart pounded like a wild thing in her chest. She had only to lean forward a couple of inches and their lips would touch.

She was tempted. Travis McCall was the embodiment of every girlish dream she'd ever had about love and romance, and though she knew it was foolish, a part of her still clung to those fantasies. Even so, life had taught her harsh reality. Caution had become an ingrained response, fear instinctive.

For a short while—a few hours or days or weeks, maybe even for the rest of the summer—if she let him, Travis could make her forget, could blot out the rest of the world and the troubles of the past and the ones that waited. She could indulge herself and wallow in a sizzling summer affair with the man who had unknowingly held her heart for most of her life. It would be wonderful, she knew, a dream come true, a balm for her shattered soul. Except . . . Rebecca suspected that when it ended she would be worse off than she was now.

Caution and fear won out, and she leaned back. Trying for a light touch, she made a face. "Travis, for heaven's sake. This is absurd. You can't just go from feeling antagonistic to . . . to amorous in the space of just a few hours."

"You wouldn't think so, would you? But there it is. Go figure." He leaned closer and she jerked back.

"Travis!" she warned, fixing him with a stern look.

"Oh, all right, spoilsport. Have it your way." His eyes glinted with mischief and sensuous heat. Before she realized his intent, he hooked his hand around her nape, pulled her to him and planted a quick kiss on her parted lips.

Rebecca came up sputtering. "Travis McCall! You cheat. You promised to behave yourself," she accused, but he had already sprung away and the remarks were addressed to his bare back as he sauntered around the counter into the kitchen.

He shot an innocent look over his shoulder. "That wasn't cheating. Good friends kiss and hug all the time." He winked. "I'm a demonstrative guy, so you'd better get used to it."

Blinking, Rebecca stared at him, not quite sure how to respond.

Travis opened the refrigerator and bent over to inspect the contents. "I don't know about you, but I'm starving," he said, changing the subject with an ease that confounded her even more.

The comment hung in the air, unanswered. Rebecca felt suddenly awkward and uncertain. It occurred to her that she had no idea where they went from there. She and Travis were on friendlier terms now, but that didn't necessarily negate the rules they had mapped out the first day.

On the boat they'd had no choice but to share meals, but things were different on shore. Travis had made it clear from the beginning that he liked his privacy.

Deciding that the safest approach would be to abide by their arrangement, Rebecca stood, murmured a quiet goodnight and headed for her room.

It was his night to use the living room. By rights, she was supposed to have first turn in the kitchen, but she felt awkward about pointing that out. Besides, she wasn't all that hungry. She could come back for a late snack when he'd gone to bed.

"Hey! Where're you going?" Travis demanded before she'd taken three steps.

Pausing, she turned and gestured feebly toward the right wing. "I, uh…thought I'd turn in. I mean…since it is your night to use the living ro—"

"Forget those rules. Good grief, Rebecca, how could you possibly think they still applied? If we're gonna be buddies, you're gonna have to loosen up a little, babe."

"Travis," she began hesitantly. "I'm glad that you've changed your mind about me. Really, I am. But…

well . . . that doesn't mean I expect you to put up with my company all the time. I don't want to impose."

"Sweetheart, believe me, you won't. If anything, I intend to take advantage of you."

Rebecca started, and Travis grinned at her suddenly wary look. "You see, I can't cook for sour apples, and since you can, I was sorta hoping we could work out a new arrangement."

Relaxing, she tipped her head to one side and looked at him askance, getting into the spirit of the exchange. "Oh, really? And just what did you have in mind?"

"Simple. We share all meals. You do the cooking, and I clean up afterward."

"Wash and dry?"

"Yeah, sure. No problem."

A smile hovered around Rebecca's mouth. She was tempted to point out that with a dishwasher, cleanup was hardly onerous, especially since she was a cook who usually washed up as she went along, but she held her tongue. She truly enjoyed cooking, and the prospect of having Travis's company at every meal was a pleasant one. It wouldn't do, though, to let him know that. "Well . . . I suppose we can try it for a while."

"Great." Travis rubbed his palms together, his expression comically expectant. "What's for dinner?"

Mealtimes were far from the only occasions Rebecca was treated to Travis's company. After the fishing trip, he seemed to take it for granted that they would spend their days together.

The prospect held enormous appeal for Rebecca, perhaps too much so. For that reason, she at first attempted to demur, but Travis blithely brushed aside all her excuses. Before she knew it, her halfhearted defenses crumbled and she let herself be swept along by his teasing charm. After the first few days she gave up even the pretense of resisting his suggestions.

As the summer days rolled on in lazy succession, she and
Travis savored each one to the hilt, doing whatever struck
their fancies. They swam and snorkeled in the turquoise
waters, they picnicked on the beach, they went sailboard-
ing and they water-skied and surfed. A whole day was spent
circling the island on Erin's dune buggy, investigating all the
coves and beaches.

One day, on Alhaja Verde, Travis talked Rebecca into
going up in a hang glider pulled by a speedboat. The ride
turned out to be the most thrilling and heartstopping experience of her life, and the most embarrassing, given that she
landed smack-dab in the middle of a beach volleyball game.
She bowled over a half-dozen people, upset their net and
became so entangled in the webbing it took half an hour to
extricate her. Travis, of course, found the whole episode
vastly amusing.

Together, she and Travis strolled through the market in
San Cristobal, visited the ancient ruins of a bygone civili-
zation and the island's new undersea aquarium. When they
had sampled all that Alhaja Verde had to offer, they toured
other, less developed islands in the chain.

One day when a rainstorm kept them indoors, they played
endless games of gin rummy and Scrabble, and Rebecca
discovered that Travis's easygoing air hid a competitive
streak a mile wide. They argued like children and taunted
one another unmercifully, crowing over victories and pooh-
poohing defeats as intentional or insignificant.

Travis was good company. He was always pleasant and,
in his own teasing way, even gallant. In deference to her, he
had even shaved off the scruffy beard. "Can't have that
pretty skin of yours marked up with whisker burn," he had
quipped by way of explanation.

He was an outrageous flirt and, as he had warned, completely uninhibited about expressing his feelings. In passing, he often gave her shoulder a squeeze or touched her
hair, and when they walked together, he casually held her
hand or draped his arm over her shoulders. Often, while she
was cooking, he would come up behind her and smell her

hair or make growling noises while he pretended to bite her neck. He thought nothing of giving her an affectionate hug or kiss whenever the spirit moved him, whether they were alone or out in public. However, though he often gave her searing looks and made suggestive remarks, he never followed through on them.

If at times, in response, Rebecca's heart skipped a beat or she got that crazy woozy feeling in her stomach, she ignored it. Travis was a charmer, but a woman would be a fool to take him seriously. Besides, she was enjoying herself too much to let anything spoil the the enchanted interlude.

He was good for her, she realized with a faint sense of shock. Her worries about facing Evan and her father were never far from her mind, but with Travis she could push them aside for short periods and relax.

Around him she could just be herself and not worry about having to please someone else. She didn't have to watch every word she said or walk on eggshells for fear of setting him off. He was undemanding and funny and affectionate, and just being around him was healing. He made her laugh, he made her enjoy life, he made her content. He made her happy.

Of course, it couldn't last. This was just an idyll, a space out of time, and when summer ended they would go their separate ways. Rebecca accepted that. In the meantime, however, she was determined to live every moment to the fullest.

Accordingly, she pushed aside the occasional fleeting thought that perhaps it was unwise to spend too much time in close company with Travis and entered wholeheartedly into whatever activity he suggested.

One morning after a leisurely, late breakfast he proposed that they spend the day exploring the interior of the island. Rebecca thought it sounded like fun and agreed without hesitation.

Hours later she found herself struggling up a narrow animal trail, huffing and puffing and mentally lambasting herself.

I must've been out of my mind to let him talk me into this, she groused silently. Although, she supposed she should have been prepared. In the past two weeks she had learned that for all his lazy, laid-back air, the more strenuous or exciting or difficult an activity was, the more Travis liked it.

They had been climbing the forested mountain for over four hours, and her calf muscles were beginning to cramp. She was tired, she was thirsty, she was hungry, she was sweaty and grubby, *and* she was fairly certain that she had blisters on both feet.

Much to her annoyance, a few yards ahead, Travis marched along as though he were out for a leisurely stroll. Rebecca glared at his broad back with something close to active dislike. It wasn't fair; he wasn't even breathing hard.

Glancing back, he paused and held out his hand to her, his expression one of amused indulgence. "C'mon, slow-poke. We're never going to get anywhere at this rate. You're gonna have to hustle it, woman."

"Hu-hustle my...f-foot." She stumbled a few feet closer and accepted his assistance, letting him pull her up the rest of the way. "Tra-Travis. I have to re-rest a while."

"Rest! C'mon, sugar. Why, we haven't covered but four or five miles. That's just a good stretch of the legs."

"On the be-beach, maybe. Cli-climbing a mountain, it's pure tor...tor...torture. Travis, I—"

"Shhh. Listen," he said, cutting her off abruptly. Alert, he stood perfectly still. "Do you hear that?"

"Wh-What?" Rebecca tried, but all she could hear was the rasp of her labored breathing and her own heartbeat booming in her ears.

"It's a waterfall. Don't you hear it? It's..." He cocked his ear, then pointed straight ahead. "...that way. C'mon."

He tugged on her hand and pulled her along the path. Rebecca didn't argue. The mere word waterfall conjured up an image of a sylvan glade with a crystal pool, a tranquil place where she could lay back and soak her aching feet.

Thirty or so feet ahead, the animal trail leveled out. From there they followed its winding path for another fifty yards through a thick stand of trees. With each step the sound of rushing water grew louder, until finally they stepped into a small clearing and came to a halt. The idyllic setting that Rebecca had imagined paled in comparison to the scene before them.

"Oh, my," she murmured.

"Yeah," Travis agreed with something akin to reverence.

At the northern end of the clearing a plume of sparkling water plunged thirty feet or so down a rocky cliff face. Bubbling foam, like a froth of white lace, spread out from where the cascade struck the pool at its base and mist rose in a cloud. The sun striking the gauzy vapor created twin rainbows that arched across the clearing and disappeared over the trees.

The rock-lined pool was about twenty feet wide and twice that long. At the end opposite the fall, water spilled over boulders into a smaller pool a few feet farther down the side of the mountain, and from there into yet another, even smaller pool.

Ferns lined the far bank and on the near side the glade was carpeted with lush green grass and clumps of wildflowers.

The instant Rebecca reached the bank, she dropped down and stripped off her shoes and socks. Plunging her feet into the water, she sighed and leaned back on her elbows, closing her eyes in ecstasy. "Ahhh, that feels heavenly."

"I don't know about you," Travis said, eyeing the pool with relish. "But I'm ready for a swim."

"Mmm, me too, but we can't. We didn't bring our swimsuits."

"So? Who needs suits?"

Rebecca's eyes popped open. "Travis! You're not suggesting... We can't..."

"Sure we can. Back when we were in school a lot of us went skinny-dipping in the river all the time."

"Well, *I* certainly never did." Rebecca's gaze narrowed. "Does your mother know about that?"

Travis stripped off his shirt and sat down to go to work on his shoes and socks. "Are you kidding? She would've skinned me alive." He winked and added wickedly, "Especially if she had known that Barbara Buford was usually one of the group."

"No doubt," Rebecca agreed dryly.

The girl in question had been known around school as Backseat Babs, and if rumor was correct, the nickname had been well earned. The image of Travis and the girl together brought on an unexpected and unwelcome surge of jealousy, which Rebecca immediately squashed. However Travis had sewn his wild oats as a teenager, it was none of her business, she told herself sternly.

"Ah, the things that girl taught me while we were swimming." Travis sighed, rolling his eyes. "Thanks to her I learned—"

"Travis, I really don't care to know," Rebecca snapped.

"—to tread water," he finished with exaggerated innocence. He grinned at Rebecca's blush and tweaked the end of her nose. "What's the matter, Quinn? Got your mind in the gutter?"

"No, I do not. But neither am I naive enough to believe that was all you learned from Backseat Babs Buford."

He laughed and tugged on the knot in his left shoelace. "I'll never tell. Now, quit stalling and strip."

"Travis, I am *not* going to swim with you in the nude."

"Why not? So it's a little naughty. So what? There's no one here but us. It's an incredible sensation. Trust me, you'll love it. And just think," he added with a leer. "As an added bonus, you'll get a peek at my bod."

Rebecca snorted. "What on earth makes you think *that* is an inducement?"

"C'mon, Rebecca, don't tell me you're not curious." Eyes twinkling, he nudged her ribs with his elbow. "Fess up. I'll bet that back when you had a crush on me you used to dream about how I looked..." Pausing, he wiggled his eyebrows at her and whispered, "You know...buck *nekked.*"

"I did no such thing!" She gave his shoulder a punch, laughing and blushing all at the same time. "Travis Mc-Call, you're terrible!"

"Maybe. But you know you love it." Catching her by surprise, he cupped the back of her head and brought her close for a hard, hot kiss that made her head spin.

Before Rebecca could react, it ended, and he sprang to his feet. Dazed, she watched him unsnap his jeans and lower the zipper, but when he hooked his thumbs beneath the waistband, she gasped and turned her face aside. A moment later, from the corner of her eye she saw a blur of motion and heard a jubilant shout. Immediately a tremendous splash followed, and a spray of cold water splattered the front of her body.

She shrieked, and Travis laughed. When she opened her eyes he was grinning at her from the middle of the pool, only his head and the tops of his shoulders visible above the water. "Oh, man, this is great. C'mon, honey, forget your modesty and join me."

"No, thank you. I'm fine just as I am."

"What's the matter? You chicken?" Tucking his thumbs in his armpits, he flapped his arms and made clucking noises.

Rebecca chucked a pebble at him. When it missed by a foot, he laughed and she stuck out her tongue. "Very funny, but I'm still not going to disrobe for you, so forget it."

"Not even if I promise not to watch?"

"No. I don't trust you."

"Okay. How about if you just strip down to your undies? Hell, they can't be any more revealing than a bikini."

He had a point. The panties and bra she had on were navy blue and made of opaque satin. If anything, except for the lacy inserts on each side of the panties and along the top of the bra cups, they were far more modest than most bikinis. Except, of course, she never wore bikinis because of the scars on her lower back. But then, Travis had already seen those. And she was hot and sweaty and the water did look inviting.

"C'mon, sweetheart," Travis urged in his most seductive voice. "Live dangerously for once. You know you want to."

"All right, but you turn the other way. And no peeking. You have to promise to keep your distance."

"I will. Scout's honor. See, I'm turning around."

Keeping a cautious eye on Travis's back, Rebecca stood up, and with quick, jerky movements stripped off her shirt. As quickly as she could, she shimmied out of her jeans, kicked them aside and leapt, feet first into the pool.

The shock of the deliciously cool water against her skin was pure heaven. As it closed over her head, she shut her eyes and savored the sensation. The pool was deeper than she had thought; before her feet touched bottom she began to drift back up. Giving a kick, she shot upward toward the glow of sunshine and broke the surface with an exultant gasp.

Laughing and swiping water from her eyes, she looked around for Travis, but he was nowhere in sight. She treaded water and started turning in a slow circle, but before she made half a revolution, sinewy arms closed around her waist.

Her instinctive shriek turned to a "glub, glub" when water closed over her head. Outraged, Rebecca pounded at Travis's chest and shoulders, but he merely grinned and pulled her close, and with a powerful kick sent them shooting back up.

They broke the surface amid laughter from Travis and coughs and sputters of outrage from Rebecca.

"You cheat! You promised!"

"I lied."

"What about Scout's honor?"

He shrugged and flashed an unrepentant grin. "I was never a Scout. So sue me. By the way, I like those lacy strips down the sides of your panties."

"Why, you!" She tried to shove him away, and in the attempt her hand grazed his hip. Her eyes widened.

"You . . . you're wearing your briefs! You rat! You let me think you were naked!"

Releasing her, he backed away and held his hands up. "Hey, I was just trying to protect your modesty."

"Ha! You just wanted to make me look ridiculous. I'll get you for that, McCall," she shrieked, making a lunge for him.

Laughing, Travis dodged the attack and struck out for the falls, and the battle was on. For almost an hour they chased each other nonstop around the pool, dunking and splashing and launching sneak attacks under the surface. Several times Travis tossed Rebecca up in the air. She retaliated by attacking his ticklish spot.

Finally, her energy flagging, Rebecca tried to call a King's Ex, but Travis was having none of it.

"Oh, no, you don't. No time-outs allowed. This is a fight to the finish." Catching her around the waist, he hauled her up against his chest, his steely arms holding her prisoner.

"*Traa-vis!* I'm exhausted. I need a rest."

"Fine. All you have to do is admit defeat."

"You are so competitive," she accused, scowling.

"Uh-huh. You give?"

Rebecca sighed and rolled her eyes. "Oh, all right. You win. I surrender."

The last came out on a breathless sigh, but the soft sound seemed to electrify the very air around them.

Travis tensed. Their gazes met and held, and Rebecca's heart took a leap right up into her throat. Fascinated, frightened, she watched the fire ignite in his silvery eyes.

Muscle by muscle, his face tightened into a look of raw passion. Suddenly all was quiet, the only sounds the roar and splash of the waterfall, the only movement the instinctive swirl of their legs beneath the water. Even the birds had ceased their twittering.

In those few tense seconds, tiny, inconsequential things imprinted themselves on her consciousness: the incredible beauty of his spiked lashes, the throbbing pulse at the base of his neck, the slow swing of the saber earring dangling from his left ear, the smell of the water clinging to his skin, the way his pale hair lay sleeked back from his face, the random fall of droplets from the sodden tendrils.

A bead of water trickled down from his temple. Rebecca tracked its erratic path along the ridge of his cheekbone to his nose, then down the crease line to the corner of his mouth, where it clung. She stared at the drop, and unconsciously the tip of her tongue sneaked out to touch the corner of her own mouth.

Travis's gaze homed in on the action. His pupils expanded. His nostrils flared and whitened.

Rebecca couldn't breathe.

Mesmerized, she watched his sculpted lips part, his eyelids drift downward and his head begin a slow descent.

Every instinct screamed that this kiss would not be a teasing smooch or an affectionate peck like those he had bestowed on her during the past two weeks. She knew she should protest, but she couldn't seem to move, or even utter a sound. Her throat tightened and her heart pounded painfully in her breast, and as his warm breath touched her face and his features began to blur, her eyelids fluttered shut, and she released a shuddering sigh.

His mouth closed over hers with the devouring hunger of a starving man. Without hesitation or any hint of enticement, he deepened the kiss, his tongue plunging and swirling with rapacious demand.

The kiss should have sparked revulsion and terror, anger at the very least, but it didn't. Excitement and need pounded through Rebecca. Of their own volition, her arms slid up over his slick shoulders and tightened around his neck. She wanted, needed, to meld with him, to crawl right into his body until you could not tell where she left off and he began. She pressed closer, but it wasn't enough, and a moan tore from her throat.

Travis captured the sound with his mouth and answered it with a groan of his own. Sliding his hands down her back, he cupped her bottom and pulled her hard against him. His arousal pressed against that part of her that ached for him.

Her swollen breasts were flattened against his chest, the fine hair covering it tickling the lush swells spilling over the tops of the bra cups. Only his briefs and two lacy straps of satin separated their bodies. The flimsy barrier was at once both enticing and frustrating.

Desperately they clung to each other, their mouths fused in a hot, wet, endless kiss, their yearning bodies straining. So complete was their absorption, both forgot where they were and the need to stay afloat, and as their legs entangled, they slowly sank below the surface of the pond.

Even then neither noticed. Turning in graceful slow motion, they spiraled downward, sinking lower and lower, locked together in passion. Not until their starving lungs finally demanded oxygen did full awareness strike.

For Rebecca, panic followed hot on its heels. Stunned and horrified by what was happening, by her own behavior, she frantically tore herself from Travis's embrace and struck out for the surface. She shot through the water like a bullet, kicking as hard as she could, uneasily aware of him right beside her.

They reached the top at the same time and exploded up into the air, gasping. When they were once again treading water, only a couple of feet separated them. Breathing hard, they struggled to catch their breath and looked at each other warily.

"Rebecca—"

"Why did you—"

They spoke at once, and both immediately fell silent.

Travis looked away at the waterfall, then looked back at her. He sighed and raked a hand through his wet hair. Desire still simmered in his eyes but the muscle twitching in his cheek and his clenched jaw told her he was fighting it. "Look...Rebecca...I'm sorry. That shouldn't have happened. I, uh...I guess I just got carried away."

It shouldn't have hurt. He was absolutely right. Hadn't she been about to blurt out the same thing?

So why did she have this terrible ache in her chest?

God knew, she couldn't afford to start anything with Travis. She didn't *want* to start anything with Travis. She had put all that foolishness behind her long ago.

Then why did you let him kiss you that way? her conscience prodded. *And why did you kiss him back?*

It occurred to her then that it was fortunate they had been in the water. If that sizzling kiss had occurred anywhere else they would be making love at that very moment, she realized with a fresh flutter of panic.

Pride came to her rescue, and she unconsciously fell back on the defense that had served her well all of her life. Her chin lifted a notch, and her face took on that carefully schooled look of polite neutrality. "We were both a bit carried away. It was just an extension of high spirits that got out of hand. That's all. Let's just forget it, shall we?"

Travis frowned. "Rebecca—"

"We'd better head back, don't you think, if we're going to make it home before dark." Without waiting for his reply, she started for the bank.

Treading water, Travis watched her climb from the pool and pick her way over the rocks. The skimpy panties clung to her firm bottom, and water sluiced down her back and those long gorgeous legs. The sight sent another surge of desire slamming through him.

Dammit, he still wanted her. He'd been wanting her for the past two weeks, and it was getting worse by the day. If she had been anyone else, he would have already made his move. But there was that damned promise he'd made Erin and Elise.

As bad as he hated to admit it, they were right; Rebecca wasn't a woman you took lightly. She was special. She was...hell, she was Rebecca. She was also easily hurt. Hadn't he just seen that flash of pain in her eyes when he'd given that clumsy explanation. He could have kicked himself.

She deserved more than a summer fling. She deserved a man who would love her, who would build a future with her, make babies with her.

The trouble was, he wasn't sure he was ready for that kind of commitment. Hell, he wasn't sure he ever would be. "Great. Just great. Until you are sure, you'd damned well better keep your hands off the woman," he muttered to himself as he stroked for the bank.

Neither spoke while they dressed and each took care not to glance at the other. For the most part, the awkward silence continued throughout the long trek back down the mountain. They spoke only when they had to, polite, monosyllabic phrases like, "watch your step" and "give me your hand" and "thank you," but the friendly, sometimes teasing badinage of the past two weeks was nonexistent. In its place was a polite stiffness.

Travis hated it, but he had no idea what to do to change it. By the time they reached the beach house, he had convinced himself that it was wisest not to try. Perhaps a little distance between them was what was needed.

The minute they entered the house, Rebecca went into the kitchen and started dinner. Travis flopped down on one of the sofas, picked up a magazine and started flipping through it, though he hadn't the slightest idea what he was looking at. The air practically pulsed with tension.

The firm knock on the door a moment later caught them by surprise and they both jumped as if they'd been shot.

"Who the hell—!"

Puzzled, they looked at one another. Darkness had fallen and neither had seen the lights of a boat approach the dock. "It's probably someone from the village. Or maybe one of the other summer residents," Travis said, heading for the door.

It was obvious, however, judging by his expensive suit, that the man standing on the deck was neither a fisherman nor a neighbor.

Stepping forward into the light, their visitor's eyes narrowed coldly on Travis, then looked past him to where Rebecca stood motionless in the middle of the living room.

"My name is Evan Hall. I've come to see my wife."

Chapter Nine

Stark terror grabbed Rebecca by the throat. She could not speak or move. Deep inside, in the very core of her being, an awful, uncontrollable quaking began. She was cold. So cold. Oh, God. How had he found her?

Travis glanced sharply at Rebecca, then back to Evan. "I believe you mean your ex-wife, don't you?"

Evan looked him over as though he were a particularly repulsive form of vermin, but he did not deign to answer. Instead he took a step forward, only to be brought to an abrupt halt when Travis shifted and grasped the door frame. The other man glanced pointedly at the arm stretched across the doorway, barring his entrance. "Do you mind?" he said with the cold hauteur of one who is accustomed to being obeyed.

"Me? Naw, I don't mind," Travis drawled, but Rebecca heard the steel in his voice. "But then, it's not up to me, is it?" He looked over his shoulder, one blond eyebrow cocked. "Rebecca?"

Yes! Yes, I mind!

Her every instinct screamed the answer. She had only to say the word and Travis would send him away. Evan wouldn't accept the decision gracefully—there might even be a physical clash—but she had every confidence that Travis would prevail. She pressed her lips together to stop them from quivering. Temptation clawed at her.

In her heart, though, she knew that that was the coward's way out. In any event, it would solve nothing. From the beginning she had known that she would eventually have to face Evan. But, heaven help her, she had hoped for more time.

The words almost choked her, but in an unsteady voice she finally managed to reply, "Th-That's all right, Travis. You may let him in."

With obvious reluctance, Travis removed his hand from the door frame and stepped inside.

Evan shot him a contemptuous look and walked past him into the living room. "How kind of you, darling. Seeing as how I've come all this way just to see you, I would have been...hurt...had you turned me away."

"Now there's a pity," Travis muttered.

Rebecca's heart skipped a beat. Subtle as it had been, she caught the threat in his words.

Despite the island breezes, not a strand of Evan's dark brown hair was out of place, nor did so much as a grain of sand cling to his handmade Italian shoes or his tailored suit. His silk tie, knotted to perfection, lay in precision alignment between the crisp collar points of his Egyptian cotton shirt. He appeared calm and unruffled, the picture of urban sophistication.

Rebecca shivered. She wasn't fooled; she knew that he was furious. Just as she knew what that cold smile and ultrapolite tone always presaged.

"I must say, though, I am surprised. I didn't expect to find you with another man. Surely this...this...*person* isn't the reason you left me so precipitously?"

"You know perfectly well why I left, Evan. And why I divorced you," she added in a shaky but determined voice.

She would not allow him to conveniently ignore that fact. "It had nothing to do with anyone else, so don't try to shift the blame."

"I don't mind," Travis interjected cheerfully, earning himself an irritated glance. Otherwise Evan ignored him.

"Oh, don't worry, my dear. I know precisely who is responsible for this unpleasant episode."

The words sent a trickle of ice down Rebecca's spine. "Why are you here, Evan?"

"If you don't mind, I'd rather discuss that in private," he said, glancing pointedly at Travis.

"Hey. Don't mind me."

"Tell him to leave, Rebecca."

Travis did not budge. He had taken up a position a few feet from Rebecca, propped negligently against the back of a sofa, his arms folded over his chest. Keeping his gaze fixed on her ex-husband, he said, "You don't have to be alone with this guy, sweetheart. I'll stay if you want me to."

"This doesn't concern you," Evan stated, addressing Travis directly for the first time since entering the house. His voice now had a definite edge to it, his controlled facade beginning to show the first signs of fraying.

"I think that's for Rebecca to decide."

Evan's irate gaze swung to her. "Who *is* this man?"

"My name is McCall. Travis McCall. I'm a friend of Rebecca's."

"One she's picked up in the last few months, I assume, since I don't recall ever having met you. Honestly, Rebecca. Have you sunk to associating with a degenerate beach bum?"

"Actually, I've known Rebecca since she was five years old. We grew up together."

"You're from Crockett?" Surprised, Evan looked Travis over, taking in the disreputable sneakers, the holey jeans, the faded chambray shirt that had never seen an iron, and lastly, the long hair and the dangling saber earring. "Amazing. And I thought that hick town only produced country bumpkins."

It was not a compliment, but Travis grinned. "Thanks. I've been working out of state since college. I guess I've picked up some polish during my travels."

Anger replaced cool condescension. Evan stabbed Rebecca with a sharp look. "We have to talk, Rebecca. Privately."

She looked at Travis and caught her lower lip between her teeth.

"Do you want me to stay, sweetheart?" he asked gently.

Yes! Oh, Lord, yes! Please don't leave me alone with him. The plea hovered on the tip of Rebecca's tongue, but she held it back. As much as she wanted Travis to stay, it wasn't fair or right to involve him in her problems. "Thank you, Travis, but I, uh . . . perhaps it would be best if I talked to Evan alone."

"You sure?"

No, I'm not sure. I'm not sure at all. But I have to do this. "Yes. I'll be fine. Don't worry."

Travis did not looked convinced. If anything, he looked disappointed—briefly, even a bit hurt—but he nodded and headed for the door. "I'll be down at the boathouse if you need me."

Through the glass panes of the French doors, Evan watched him cross the deck and lope down the steps. When he disappeared into the darkness, Rebecca's ex-husband turned back to her with a cold smile. "Very touching."

The quaking deep inside worsened. She felt as though she were about to fly apart at any second. Rebecca folded her arms across her midriff, holding herself tightly to control the trembling. She regretted the defensive posture, but she could not let Evan see how much he frightened her.

That was one of the things they had stressed at the crisis center. Never cower. Stand up for your rights. Refuse to be a victim. Bullies pick on those they think are weaker than they.

Swallowing the knot of fear in her throat, Rebecca lifted her chin. "How did you find me?"

"It wasn't easy." Evan's eyes narrowed, and she realized, too late, that it had been unwise to remind him of the trouble to which she had undoubtedly put him. "Your friends were most uncooperative. However, the detective I hired is the best in the business. From the beginning I knew you would turn to Erin and Elise for help when you got low on funds. It took my man a while, but he eventually learned about this place. I knew then that I'd find you here."

"Why did you bother? As I explained in my letter, the divorce is final, and I'm not asking anything from you, even though we both know that I could, since Texas is a community property state. All I want is my freedom, and the divorce granted me that. I can't see that we have anything to discuss."

"I didn't come here to talk. I came to take you home, where you belong."

Rebecca's eyes widened. The calm statement sent a fresh shaft of fear stabbing through her. She hugged her arms tighter and tried to battle against it.

Stay calm. Don't let him panic you. He has no power over you anymore.

"I'm not going anywhere with you, Evan. Didn't you hear a word I just said? The divorce is final. It's over between us. The marriage has ended."

He smiled and walked toward her. It took every ounce of will Rebecca possessed to quell the urge to back away. Fear shimmered through her like shards of ice. Her shaking was visible now, but she managed, somehow, to hold her ground.

"That can and will be remedied by a quick ceremony as soon as we return to the States. Though I must say, I find the necessity of doing so exceedingly annoying." He stopped in front of her and smiled cruelly. "You didn't honestly think I would let a piece of paper stand in my way, did you? You are my wife, and you will remain my wife."

"Why?" Rebecca asked desperately. "Why would you want a woman who doesn't want you? You don't even love me, so what possible reason could you have?"

"Because you're mine. And I hold on to what belongs to me. If our marriage ever ends it will be because *I* decide to end it, not you," he said in a feral snarl that made her jump.

Her reaction pleased him, and his cold smile returned. His tone became matter-of-fact, almost pleasant. "As it happens, at the moment the appearance of a stable marriage is important to my plans. You see, I've decided to run for Congress in the next election. A wife, particularly a beautiful, classy wife, is an asset when it comes to garnering votes. And make no mistake about it, I do intend to be the next Senator from Texas."

Every cell in Rebecca's body quivered. She was so frightened she could barely stand. As little as a year ago she would have crumbled under that veiled warning and hastened to agree with whatever he wanted. Anything to avert a violent explosion. The cowardly part of her was tempted to do so now, but she refused to give in to it.

Stand your ground. You're free of him. He can't make you return.

Her heart was beating so hard it was almost suffocating her. Her breathing was shallow and painful. "Whatever your political ambitions are, you'll have to manage them without me," she said with quavery determination. "I'm not coming back."

Evan's eyes narrowed. They glittered with rage. "Go pack you bags, Rebecca. *Now!*"

She jumped again. For an instant she thought she might faint, so great was her fright. Instead she drew a deep breath and did what a year ago would have been unthinkable; she defied him openly.

"No. No, I won't."

"You'll do as I say!"

Too late, Rebecca saw the blow coming. He raised his arm for a backhanded swing and brought it down with all his might. His hand struck the side of her face, the heavy diamond ring he wore smashed into the tender flesh at the corner of her eye. Pain exploded in her head.

The force of the powerful clout knocked her head to the side and sent her staggering backward. She slammed against the counter that divided the living room and kitchen, catching the edge in her ribs, but she didn't even feel the agonizing impact.

Whimpering, she put one hand over her injured face and clutched the edge of the counter with the other, hunching over the surface. Red-hot fingers of pain streaked through her skull. Her eye stung and her head reeled. Blood trickled warmly down her face. Already she could feel her cheek swelling. She felt sick to her stomach.

Shock and humiliation washed through her. For all her uneasiness and fear, she had not really believed that Evan would strike her—not there, with Travis so close by. Oh, God, she felt like such a fool.

She cried out as a rough hand grabbed her arm and jerked her around. Evan snatched her close and brought his nose down to within an inch of hers. The handsome, debonair man was gone. His eyes glittered viciously and his face was contorted and ugly with rage. "Maybe that will teach you to do as I say," he snarled. "You've got exactly ten minutes to get your things together. Otherwise, you'll get more of the same."

He shoved her away, sending her slamming back into the counter again. He looked coldly at her shattered expression, his own radiating cruelty and utter confidence.

Breathing hard, Rebecca steadied herself against the bar, and stared back at him. She thought of the nightmare that her six-year marriage had been. She thought of the courage and effort and careful planning it had taken to escape and end it. She thought of the counseling she'd received from the doctors at the crisis center, the support from the other women there who were struggling to regain their dignity and put their lives back together. Had it all been for nothing?

No! Fight back! Don't let him do this to you anymore! You don't have to take it!

Her head moved slowly from side to side. "No, I won't."

Black fury screwed up Evan's face again, but before he could move, Rebecca darted around the end of the counter and into the kitchen. He was after her in a flash, but she snatched a wicked-looking butcher knife from a drawer and whirled to face him. "Stay back, Evan! Stay back! Or so help me, I'll use this."

He pulled up short, his expression shocked. It would have been almost comical had the situation not been so serious.

Recovering himself quickly, he sneered. "Oh, please. You don't actually expect me to believe you'd use that on me. You wouldn't dare." He took another step, but stopped abruptly when she jabbed the knife toward him.

"Oh-yes-I-would," she said between gritted teeth, in a voice that left not one doubt that she meant it. "You can count on it." She stood slightly crouched, tensed and ready, the knife gripped tightly in her hand and held in front of her, the picture of a desperate woman who had been pushed too far.

"For years I've taken your abuse, but no more. *No more!* Do you hear me? I am no longer your wife. You have no hold over me. No right to even touch me. I promise you, if you try to hurt me again I'm going to hurt you back. So help me I will. Now, get out of here, Evan. And don't you ever, *ever,* come near me again."

She knew the exact moment when he decided to try a different tack. His expression softened, and he smiled beguilingly and extended his hand to her.

"Come on, darling. You know that I don't enjoy hurting you," he said in his most coaxing voice, but when he moved toward her she made another feint with the knife, slashing it through the air on a level with his belly.

"I said get out! Now!"

Evan sucked in his stomach and jumped back. "All right! All right, I'm going," he yelped, all trace of tenderness vanishing from his face. "Just take it easy with that thing." Holding his hands out in front of him, he backed away until the counter was between them, then he whirled around and strode for the door.

Rebecca remained where she was and watched him every step of the way, her braced posture never easing.

He paused by the open French door to glare back at her. "This isn't the end of it, you know. You're going to pay for this little stunt."

"I've already paid. For six years I've paid. But all that's behind me now. If you come near me again I'll charge you with assault. We'll see what kind of effect that has on your political chances. Now, get out, Evan. And don't come back."

After one last enraged glare, he stomped out.

No sooner had he disappeared from sight than her nerve deserted her. The adrenaline that had carried her that far suddenly dissipated like smoke in the wind, leaving her weak. She began to shake violently.

The knife clattered against the surface of the counter. With a soft cry, she sagged against the cabinet and covered her face with both hands.

Standing on the deck of the *Juanita,* thumbs hooked in his front pockets, feet crossed at the ankles, Travis leaned back against the rail and pretended interest in the tale that Raphael Gomez was spinning. The tough little Mexican, one of Pepe's many cousins, was a commercial fisherman working out of San Cristobal on Alhaja Verde. Being an enterprising soul, however, he was not averse to earning an extra peso or two, and had gladly agreed to ferry Evan Hall to Rincon... for a price. Travis fervently hoped that he'd soaked the arrogant jerk good.

He was still upset and chagrined that he had not noticed the boat docked at the end of the pier earlier, when he and Rebecca returned. Some hotshot FBI agent you are, he told himself scathingly, while giving a sage nod to something Raphael said. If you'd been on a case, a mistake like that could have cost you your life.

His only excuse was that it had been dusk, and difficult to see. That... and his mind had been occupied with thoughts of Rebecca and the uncomfortable constraint that had developed between them after that kiss in the mountain pool.

"...and the marlin there! Ai yi yi!" Raphael laid his hand over his heart. "I tell you Señor, they were *gigante.*"

"Mmm. Sounds great, Raphael. Rebecca and I will have to take David's boat out tomorrow and give that area a try."

That is, if she was still there.

Travis frowned. Dammit, what had brought Evan Hall to Rincon? The divorce was final, so the property settlement had already been hammered out. They had no children to form a common bond between them or to squabble over. He couldn't think of a single reason why the guy had sought her out.

Unless he wants her back.

Shifting uneasily, Travis glared at the house. Light spilled from the double set of French doors in the living room and illuminated the deck, but from where he was, he couldn't see what was going on inside. Surely Rebecca wouldn't go back to that cold bastard.

She had sidestepped all his attempts to find out what had gone wrong in the marriage, but it stood to reason that things must have been pretty bad for her to divorce Evan. She'd claimed that he hadn't been unfaithful, but that could have been face-saving on her part.

Pursing his lips, Travis mulled the thought over. Naw. It was more likely, given what a cold fish the guy was, that he'd neglected her. For someone like Rebecca, who had been starved for love all of her life, that would have been devastating.

He was probably worrying for nothing. Rebecca was a smart woman. Hall could sweet-talk her all he wanted to, but she had to know that nothing had changed.

Jerking his thumbs out of his pockets, Travis gripped the rail on either side of his hips. His hands squeezed the cold metal, relaxed, then squeezed again. Why the devil should it matter to him, anyway? Hell, just a little over two weeks ago, he would've been happy to be rid of her.

If she went back to the guy, so what? It was no skin off his nose. He'd just finish out the summer alone, as he'd planned. That way he'd have plenty of time to think over his options and come to a decision about his future. He probably wouldn't even miss her.

Yeah. Sure. Travis sighed. Who the hell was he kidding? He'd miss her all right, and for more than just her cooking. He'd miss her laughter and her soft smiles, her gentleness and patience, her sweet, undemanding companionship. Hell, the plain truth was, he liked being with her. He liked her.

He sighed again, no longer even hearing Raphael's chatter. Face it; he more than liked her.

And he hated the very thought of her returning to that arrogant bastard she'd married.

In the past two weeks he'd come to care for Rebecca in ways that he'd never dreamed of before. One corner of Travis's mouth twitched. Hell, he'd been so sure that they could be friends. And they *were*. However, the feelings between them were developing into much more than that. What, exactly, he wasn't certain—he wasn't even sure he wanted to find out—but he knew that she felt it, too.

So why hadn't she let him stay? If she wanted to discourage the guy, then what better way?

Jaw set, Travis glared at the house again. How long did it take to tell a guy to get lost, for Pete's sake? He sure as hell wasn't going to stay out here all night, cooling his heels. One more minute—that was all he'd give them. Then, like it or not, he was going back inside.

The silent threat had no sooner formed than Evan Hall appeared at one of the French doors. He paused briefly with his hand on the knob, then strode out. Against the light spilling from the house he was just a black silhouette, but that was all it took to read his mood. He marched across the deck and stomped down the steps, each stiff, jerky movement radiating anger.

The sight cheered Travis immensely, and he came away from the rail grinning. So, Rebecca had sent him away with a flea in his ear, had she. Good for her.

"Sorry, *mi amigo*," he said, interrupting Raphael's long discourse on the correct bait to use for catching swordfish. "But it looks like your passenger is ready to shove off. I'd better get going. See you around. Tell Pepe and Constanza that Rebecca and I will be over in a day or so," he added as he hopped onto the pier.

Evan Hall strode toward the *Juanita* so fast the two men drew even before Travis had covered a quarter of the pier. Travis cocked his eyebrows and grinned. "What? Leaving so soon?"

The other man shot him a furious glare and brushed past without bothering to answer.

Travis chuckled. Whistling a jaunty tune, he stuck his fingertips into the back pockets of his jeans and sauntered toward the house. Hot damn, he felt good.

When he stepped through the French doors, Rebecca was in the kitchen, standing at the sink with her back to him. Some of his cocky elation drained away when he noted the hunch of her shoulders and her utter stillness. Ah, hell. Had she *wanted* to reconcile with that jerk? Was it possible that she still loved the guy?

The thought did not set well with Travis, and his features fell even more. He stepped farther into the room and stopped. All of a sudden, he didn't know what to say. "Well, uh...how did it go? Did you get everything settled?"

Rebecca jumped at the sound of his voice, and hastily tossed something into the sink. Travis frowned. He watched her shoulders square and her head come up.

"Yes. I...I think we came to an understanding."

"I see. Good. Good." He waited, hoping she would elaborate, but she remained silent, her back ramrod straight and stiff. He shifted his weight to one hip and hooked his thumbs into his belt loops. "Umm...do you think he'll be back?"

A visible shudder rippled through her, and his mood immediately brightened again.

"No... that is... I don't know. I hope not."

"Look. If you don't want to see the guy again, you don't have to, you know. If he comes back I'll get rid of him for you."

"That's sweet of you, Travis. But I can't involve you in my problems."

"Hey, it'd be my pleasure," he said with gleeful relish. "No offense, but to tell you the truth, sweetheart, something about your ex rubs me the wrong way. Kinda makes me question your taste in men, too, if you know what I mean."

Though the first was true, he had added the last to tease her and lighten the mood. He waited for her to laugh, or to retaliate with one of her sputtering comebacks, but she didn't make a sound. She simply stood there.

Travis frowned at her stiff back. What the devil was wrong with her? The least she could do was turn around and look at him.

He rounded the end of the counter and came up behind her on her left side. "Rebecca? What's wrong?" he said gently, laying his hand on her shoulder.

She jumped at the contact and turned her face away. "Nothing," she denied quickly. "Nothing at all."

"Then why won't you look at me?" He tried to turn her to face him, but she resisted and craned her head even farther around the other way. "Rebecca, sweetheart, are—?"

Whatever question he had been about to ask shot right out of his mind when he spotted bloodied paper towel lying in the bottom of the sink. "What the—?"

His gaze snapped to Rebecca, but all he could see of her averted face was a thin sliver of her jaw and temple, right in front of her ear. His heart began to slam against his chest.

"Rebecca, look at me," he ordered, but when he tried to turn her again, she gripped the edge of the sink.

"No. Please, no. Just leave me alone."

The pathetic plea came out in a whimper that tore at him. No power on earth could have made him do as she asked. Reaching around in front of her, he caught the tip of her chin between his thumb and forefinger and urged it toward him.

"No. Oh, please don't," Rebecca begged tearfully, grabbing his wrist.

She fought against the inexorable pull, but her strength was no match for Travis. Slowly, her profile came into view. Her lips were pressed tightly together to stop their trembling. Tears seeped from beneath the fan of lashes that lay against her left cheek, and under his fingers her chin wobbled pathetically.

"C'mon, sweetheart," he urged, turning her face slowly but surely. "Let me look at—"

Travis sucked in his breath. "Good . . . God!"

He stared at her, and felt as though he'd received a blow from a sledgehammer right in his solar plexus.

The entire right side of Rebecca's face was swollen, and already her creamy skin showed a purple discoloration. A cut at the corner of her right eye oozed blood and the lid was so puffy she could not open the eye but a slit. Already an angry, dark red ring surrounded it. By tomorrow it would turn purplish black.

"That bastard did this to you?" Travis snarled. "He *hit* you?"

Rebecca pressed her lips together tighter and nodded, but she still did not open her eyes.

"Why that sorry, son-of-a—" His head snapped toward the French doors. He took an instinctive half-step in that direction before he realized the futility of the action. The *Juanita* was already far out to sea, her running lights only a faint glow in the distance.

Travis let loose a string of vivid curses. Rebecca whimpered and turned her head aside again.

"Oh, God, sweetheart, I'm sorry. I'm so sorry," he said fervently when he became aware of her distress. "If I could get my hands on that bastard I'd kill him. I swear I would."

When he tried to pull Rebecca into his embrace, she resisted, but Travis was having none of that. He wrapped his arms around her and with gentle but firm pressure settled the uninjured side of her face against his chest. He held it there with his big hand cupping the back of her head, his splayed fingers buried deep in the glossy curls. "Shh. Shh. Take it easy. Don't fight me, sweetheart."

Though she stopped struggling, she stood stiff and unyielding within his embrace. He felt the awful trembling that seemed to come from her soul, the choppy sobs that shook her chest, which she fought so hard to hold back. Travis's own chest felt as though it were being squeezed in a vise.

A sob broke free, and then another, little choking sounds that tore from her throat.

"Go ahead and let it out, sweetheart," he crooned. "It's okay. God knows, you've got a right to cry."

Her whole body jerked as, one after another, three more sobs burst forth, each stronger and less controlled than the one that had preceded it.

"That's it. That's the way. Come on, baby, let go. You'll feel better when you do."

The soft coaxing rent asunder her already cracked defenses. Like water bursting forth through a collapsing dam, the tears she had been holding back erupted. She sagged against him, her hands clutching fistfuls of his wrinkled chambray shirt as though it were a lifeline. Great racking sobs poured from her, raw, raspy cries that shook her whole body and were terrible to hear. Her tears flowed freely, the warm wetness soaking the front of his shirt and melding it to his hairy chest.

Travis laid his cheek against her crown and rocked her gently. The hand not cupping her head rubbed up and down her back as the agonizing cries went on and on. The vise around Travis's heart tightened. He swallowed hard. His eyes began to burn. His nose stung.

Rebecca clung to him and cried until there were no tears left. When her sobs had tapered off to shuddering sighs and occasional watery hiccups, Travis put his finger beneath her chin with the intention of lifting her face.

At the first touch she stiffened and tried to pull away, taking a half step back before he caught her arms and stopped her.

"No, don't look at me. Please." She hunched her shoulders, and pulled against his hold. Turning her face to the side, she closed her eyes and caught her lower lip between her teeth.

"Rebecca? Honey, come on—"

"No, please don't look at me. Please don't. I can't stand it."

Travis stared at her profile. Her spiked lashes lay against her pale left cheek like a wet fan. Fresh tears seeped from beneath them, and despite her efforts to hold them still, her lips quivered uncontrollably. Utter misery stamped her features—misery and, he realized with astonishment, humiliation.

"Sweetheart, listen to me." He cupped her chin in the V between his thumb and fingers and firmly turned her face around. "You have absolutely no reason to be embarrassed. Hurt? Sure. Angry? Hell, yes. But not embarrassed. You haven't done anything wrong, and you have nothing to be ashamed of."

Her lashes lifted slowly and she looked at him with desolate, tear-drenched eyes. "You don't understand—"

"That's right. I don't," he agreed, brusquely cutting her off. An unaccustomed anger consumed him. It swelled inside his chest and spread, filling every cell in his body, making him want to lash out at something, but for the moment, for Rebecca's sake, he knew he had to subdue it. "I'd be happy for you to explain it to me later, but right now I'm putting you to bed." Before she could respond, he swooped her up in his arms and headed for her room.

He ignored her protests. In her room, he laid her down on the bed, issued instructions for her to stay put, and disappeared into the bathroom. Minutes later, he returned with a pan of water, a washcloth and a first-aid kit.

"Travis, you don't have to do this."

He sat down on the bed and, without a word, tenderly bathed her swollen face and the cut at the corner of her eye. Every time she flinched, he felt as if someone were twisting a knife in his gut. Throughout the ordeal, whenever their gazes met, Rebecca's immediately skittered away. The sadness and defeat in her eyes filled him with savage fury.

When he finished bathing her face he smeared antibiotic cream on the cut. "I don't think it needs any stitches, but I'll take you to San Cristobal to see a doctor if you want."

"Thank you, no. I'm sure it'll be fine," she said in a meek voice that made him grind his teeth.

He firmed his mouth and held on to his temper. Barely. He wanted to beat the living hell out of Evan Hall.

He had to get away from her—at least for a few minutes—before he vented his wrath by putting his fist through the wall, and scared her even more.

"I'll be right back," he muttered, and stomped into the bathroom. When he'd emptied the pan of water and returned the first-aid kit to the cabinet, he prowled the small room, fists clenched, jaw clenched, his face contorted.

A red rage engulfed him and ate at his soul like corrosive acid. He felt violent. He, who rarely got angry over anything, who most people swore hadn't a nerve in his body, who let all the ugliness and brutality in the world, all of mankind's greed and vice and viciousness, roll off him like water off a duck's back, wanted to commit murder.

The emotions that roiled through him were stronger than anything he'd ever experienced. He hadn't known it was possible to feel something to that degree and not explode. The thought of that son-of-a-bitch hitting Rebecca was almost more than he could bear.

Glancing toward the bedroom, he raked a hand through his hair and sighed. Somehow, though, he was going to have to get a grip on his fury. There was nothing he could do about Evan at the moment, and Rebecca needed him.

After rummaging through the cabinets for a moment, he returned to the bedroom and handed Rebecca a glass of water. "Here, take these," he said, and shook two aspirin into her palm. She started to protest, but Travis forestalled her with a gruff, "And don't tell me you don't need them. I've been in enough fights to know that your cheek and eye have got to hurt like hell."

Unable to meet his stare, Rebecca nodded meekly, tossed back the painkiller and settled back on the pillow.

"Here. I couldn't find an icebag, but this will help." Travis laid a cold wet washcloth against her swollen cheek, and Rebecca made a sound somewhere between a sigh and a groan.

Travis sat down on the bed again, facing her. For a moment he didn't speak but merely watched her adjust the cloth to her satisfaction, and try to avoid his gaze. "How long has this been going on?"

She flinched and shot him a stricken look, her one good eye widening. She looked down at her hands. "Almost from the beginning of our marriage."

"Six years? My, God, Rebecca. Why? Why didn't you leave the bastard a long time ago? No, wait. Don't answer that." Shaking his head, he held his hands up, palms out. "I promised myself that I wouldn't badger you. You're in no shape for an inquisition. Tonight what you need is rest and care." He stood abruptly and stalked across the room to the dresser and began to rummage through the drawers.

"Th-thank you, Travis."

Pausing, he shot her a level look over his shoulder. "Don't thank me too soon, Rebecca. Tomorrow morning you and I are going to have a long talk."

He went back to pawing through her things and finally pulled out a teal silk nightgown with small puffed sleeves. Holding it aloft, hooked on one finger, he surveyed the garment with disgust. "Don't you have anything more substantial than this to sleep in?" On one level, he was aware that at almost any other time the mere thought of Rebecca's delectable body swathed in the wisp of silk and lace would have turned him on, but at the moment all he could think about was making her warm and comfortable.

"N-n-no. I don-don't th-th-think so."

The broken reply brought his head snapping around. He frowned when he saw that she was shaking so hard her teeth were chattering.

Delayed shock. After what she'd been through, he wasn't surprised. Cursing, he dropped the nightgown back in the drawer. "Hold on just a bit longer, sweetheart. I'll be back in thirty seconds," he told her, and dashed out the door.

He was back in ten with the top half of his fleece-lined sweats. "Here, let's get you out of these clothes and into something warm and comfortable." By the time he got the words out, he had unbuttoned her shirt, unsnapped her jeans and was peeling both off of her.

"Tra-Tra-vis, wha-what are y-you...st-st-stop tha-that."

"Don't fret, sugar. Trust me, I know what's best for you." He brushed her hands aside, effortlessly fending off her feeble attempts to stop him. Shoes, jeans and shirt were quickly stripped away and flung aside. With practiced ease, he dealt with the clasp on her bra and sent it sailing after the other items of clothing, leaving her clad in only the tiny navy blue panties and white cotton socks.

Rebecca's hands came up to shield her bare breasts, but her embarrassed moan was quickly muffled by folds of fleecy knit when he dropped the sweatshirt over her head. With gentle but firm efficiency, as though dealing with a sick child, he stuffed her arms through the sleeves, tugged the banded edge down until it almost reached her knees. Lifting her with one arm, he whipped back the covers and tucked her beneath them.

She lay stiff, gazing hopefully up at him with her one good eye, shaking so hard the covers quivered. Her teeth chattered like castanets. "Be right back," Travis said, and hurried out again.

He quickly turned out the rest of the lights in the house and sprinted back, bringing with him the afghan from off the back of one of the living room sofas. After spreading it over her, he stepped out of his shoes, unsnapped his jeans and lowered the zipper.

"Wha-what are you d-d-doing?"

"Just what it looks like. I'm getting ready for bed." He hooked his thumbs beneath the waistband of his jeans and shoved them down. In seconds he had shucked pants, shirt and socks. Wearing only his white knit briefs, he calmly lifted the corner of the covers and slid into bed beside Rebecca.

"Tr-Tra-vis, you can't—"

"Shh." Wrapping his arms around her, he gathered her close and firmly settled her head against his shoulder. "Don't be frightened, sweetheart. I'm just going to hold you."

"Bu-but—"

"Shh. I'm not going anywhere, Rebecca, so you might as well save your breath. You shouldn't be by yourself tonight. Just relax and go to sleep and let me take care of you."

Travis didn't think Evan would have the nerve to come back, but just in case, he wasn't about to leave her alone. Beyond that, he *needed* to hold her. And he was certain that—whether she admitted it or not—she needed him, too. She was fragile and hurting, and no power on earth could have driven him from her side; certainly not Rebecca's feeble protests.

She ceased struggling, but lay stiff within his embrace. He nuzzled his cheek against the top of her head and felt her silky hair catch in his whisker stubble. In a slow, mesmerizing rhythm, he rubbed his hand up and down her back and held her close, absorbing her shivers, imparting his heat, giving the comfort and solace of his nearness and caring.

Gradually, she stopped shaking and relaxed, muscle by muscle. After a while her breathing grew slow and even. Travis smiled and kissed her forehead, but still he held her close against his heart.

For hours he lay awake, staring at the shadowy ceiling, his thoughts and emotions in chaos. He felt...weird. His chest was tight with feelings that were new and a bit scary—a murderous fury that still simmered beneath the surface of his control, disbelief, horror, a gut-wrenching concern. Most of all, he felt a fierce protectiveness toward the woman who slept in his arms.

There had been many women in his life—pretty ones, plain ones, smart ones, dippy ones. He'd liked and enjoyed every one of them. Some he'd even been fond of, but he'd never been possessive of a woman before. Yet the thought of any man raising a hand to Rebecca, or hurting her in any way, made him feel savage, like a primitive man defending his mate.

He tried to shut it out, but the memory of her battered face and the shattered look in her eyes tormented him. He had the uneasy feeling that it always would.

Travis's arms tightened around Rebecca, and he sighed as there in the darkness, with her sweet woman scent all around him and her soft body pressed to his, he realized that he never wanted to let her go.

Chapter Ten

Rebecca surfaced slowly from the deepest sleep she had enjoyed in years. The feeling of complete security was so deliciously addictive she did not want to let it go. Refusing to open her eyes, she made a blissful sound and snuggled deeper beneath the cover.

Something tickled the end of her nose. Sniffing, she scrunched up the tip and wiggled it. When that didn't help, she tried to bat the irritant away, only to have her fingers encounter a pelt of hair. Rebecca frowned. Incredibly, her nose seemed to be buried in the silky stuff.

It was then that she became aware of the firm but resilient cushion beneath her cheek and the wonderful warmth that surrounded her. She blinked slowly, once, twice, then again. When things came into focus, she was looking at a muscled chest covered with a forest of golden blond hair.

"Morning. How do you feel?"

The deep rumble jerked Rebecca awake and sent her gaze shooting upward. Flustered, she found herself staring into Travis's concerned gray eyes, just inches from her own.

It took an instant for her to remember the events of the previous night, but even when she recalled how she had come to be in bed with Travis, her overwhelming reaction was embarrassment. They had lost the impersonal cover of darkness, and she was suddenly conscious of the intimacy of their situation.

Warm and rumpled from sleep, she lay cuddled against him, her head on his shoulder, her breasts nestled against his side. The neck of the enormous sweatshirt she wore draped off her shoulder halfway to her elbow, exposing one white globe almost to the nipple. Sometime during the night the banded hem of the knit top had rucked up above her waist. Below it, her only covering was a minuscule scrap of silk and lace and their bare, intimately entwined legs.

"I—I'm fine," she said, and jerked her attention back down to his chest.

"Are you?" Cupping her chin, he lifted her face for his inspection, his narrow gaze minutely scanning each feature and probing the condition of her injury. Rebecca's heart began to slam against her ribs. His taut face and the fire that simmered in his gray eyes somehow managed to radiate both tenderness and fury.

With a feather-light touch, he ran his fingertips down her injured cheek, his eyes darkening as they followed the action. "If I could have gotten my hands on your ex-husband last night, I would have killed him," he said with such quiet intensity that Rebecca's eyes widened. His gaze lifted from her mouth and fixed on her eyes. "I still could."

A thrill of fear and something else trickled down Rebecca's spine. The old, teasing Travis was nowhere in sight. Set and serious, his handsome face looked carved from granite. Only intense emotion glittered in the gray eyes that trailed over her as though he were searching out her soul.

Not knowing what to say, Rebecca could only stare at him, her heart doing a crazy dance in her chest.

With his fingertips he caressed her temple and the side of her neck, the rim of her ear. His thumb smoothed over a silky eyebrow, her bottom lip. "A woman like you was meant to be cherished,'' he murmured in a mesmerizing voice. Lowering his head, he placed the softest of kisses on the spot between her eyebrows, another on her nose, another on the corner of her mouth.

Rebecca's breath caught, and her throat tightened. A shiver rippled through her. His tenderness was devastating. She felt as though she were coming apart on the inside.

Shifting, he gently rolled her to her back and braced over her. Her hands spread against his taut chest, unconsciously flexing. ''The thought of anyone hurting you makes me crazy,'' he whispered. Travis's open mouth skidded across her cheek, his breath leaving a warm trail of dew on her skin. He buried his face in the side of her neck and nuzzled.

Rebecca's breathing was reduced to short pants. Her eyes drifted shut. She needed this, she realized with a fatalistic acceptance. Affection, tenderness, a loving touch, the warmth and closeness, the thrill of being desired—they were all things that had been missing from her life, things that her soul cried out for . . . the only things that could blot out the fear and ugliness she had lived with for so long. The pain.

She craved what Travis was offering—needed it—the way a desert craved rain.

Deep down, though, she knew there was more to it than that. If it had been anyone but Travis offering the solace she so desperately desired she could have resisted. But it wasn't anyone else. This was Travis . . . and her heart remembered.

She owed this to herself, she thought, shivering to the feel of his tongue's wet caress. All of her life, in a secret part of her heart, she'd wanted this man, wondered what it would be like to be loved by him. Now was her chance.

It would just be a lighthearted summer fling; she knew that. Travis was not the type to settle down. But, surely if she went into it with her eyes wide open, she could handle a brief affair. Even if she ended up with more heartache, it would be worth it. It had to be, because she hadn't the strength or the will to call a halt. At the moment the affection and tenderness that Travis offered were as necessary to her survival as air to breathe.

In mindless absorption Rebecca closed her eyes and slowly tipped her head back, offering up her arched throat to his lips and tongue and nipping teeth.

He accepted the invitation, strewing the white column with kisses and love bites, mouthing the tender skin beneath her jaw.

Fire tingled along Rebecca's nerve endings. She was awash with feelings, bombarded with sensations. Rational thought and reason fled. Pain and terror ceased to be. For that moment in time nothing existed for her but this lush swell of feelings. She became a purely sensual creature, and all that mattered in the world, all that was real, all that had meaning, was the exquisite pleasure he bestowed on her, the alluring warmth and closeness of their straining bodies.

She shifted restlessly, her arms sliding around him. "Travis," she whispered. "Travis."

His lips touched hers, a brush of fire that scorched her right down to her toes. A small moan seeped from her throat, and she started to tighten her embrace, but before she could, he jerked away.

"No, I can't do this. I won't," he gasped in a rough voice.

"Travis . . . ?"

"We have to talk, Rebecca."

Jackknifing into a sitting position, he tossed back the cover and threw his legs over the side of the bed.

The stunning rejection rendered Rebecca immobile. Hurting too much to cry, or even to speak, she watched him snatch up his jeans, step into them and yank up the zipper. He stuffed his bare feet into his shoes and scooped up his shirt on the way to the door.

"I'll go make coffee," he said, glancing at her over his shoulder. "When you're ready, join me in the living room."

For several minutes after he had gone, Rebecca gazed at the empty doorway. Pain radiated outward from the tight knot in her chest, suffusing every cell in her body. She could barely breathe.

Finally, moving like an old lady, she climbed from the bed. On the first step her foot encountered something soft, and she looked down at one of Travis's crumpled white socks. She had to bite her lip to stifle a moan. Holding herself erect, she headed for the bathroom, each jerky movement slow and careful. She felt fragile—brittle inside—as though the least wrong move would cause her to shatter into a million pieces.

The reflection that greeted her in the bathroom mirror drew an anguished sound. She leaned close to the glass and inspected the damage, probing the puffy flesh gently with her fingertips. The swelling had gone down somewhat but the area around her eye and cheek and down the side of her jaw was a livid purple. Experience told her that in a day or so it would turn greenish black and yellow and look even worse.

No wonder Travis had pulled away. She looked hideous. Rebecca closed her eyes and sighed. What man wanted a woman who had been abused and degraded?

No! No, she wouldn't think that way, she scolded her reflection. Not anymore. She was a person of worth and dignity. She would *not* let Evan's brutality devalue her humanity. If Travis or anyone else thought otherwise, that was their problem.

Pride lifted her chin, and she turned away from the unsightly reflection. After adjusting the faucets, she stripped off the sweatshirt and panties, stepped into the shower and turned her face up to the spray, wincing as the water hit her face. Clenching her jaws, she willed away the tears that threatened. She had survived without Travis all these years; she would continue to survive without him.

Half an hour later, Rebecca entered the living room. Spying Travis taking mugs down from the cabinet, she paused and bit her lower lip. She dreaded facing him, answering his questions, but she had no choice. After last night she owed him an explanation.

Turning, he saw her, and Rebecca took a fortifying breath and started forward. He slid a steaming mug of coffee onto the counter when she seated herself on a bar stool.

"Thank you," she murmured, not quite meeting his gaze. Grateful for something on which to focus, she picked up the mug in both hands and sipped the scalding liquid.

"Sure." Travis poured a mug for himself and joined her. Swiveling sideways, he sat facing her, knees spread wide, feet hooked over the bottom rung of the bar stool. He propped his elbow on the counter and studied her somberly through the steam rising from his mug.

Acutely conscious of his scrutiny and her appearance, Rebecca cupped the mug of coffee in her hands and stared down at the shiny surface. She scarcely noticed the blistering heat against her palms. She had combed her hair back from her face and the thick mane hung down below her shoulder blades in a tumble of wet curls, soaking the back of her yellow sundress. Other than applying a bit of moisturizer, she hadn't bothered with makeup or beauty aids. What was the use?

Travis had used the time to clean up as well. The smell of soap and shampoo and shaving cream drifted to her across the small distance that separated them. Once again he wore his favorite attire, which consisted of threadbare but clean cutoffs and nothing else. His shiny hair still bore the brush marks of a recent blow-dry.

"There was no bike accident when you were a kid, was there?" Travis said, breaking the strained silence. "Those marks on your back... your ex-husband put them there, didn't he?"

Rebecca fingered the handle of her mug. She considered lying, but after a second's hesitation, she nodded.

"And that scar at your temple?"

She started, and shot him a look, her eyes wide.

"You didn't think I'd noticed that one, did you?" Smiling sadly, he reached out and smoothed his fingertips over the hair that hid the thin white line.

"No."

"I notice everything about you," he said, so softly that Rebecca experienced a strange stab of panic and quickly looked back down at her coffee.

When she did not reply, he stroked the back of his forefinger down her jaw, beneath the injury. "I still can't believe that you put up with this kind of treatment for six years. Why, Rebecca? Why didn't you just leave the bastard?"

She looked at him then, and despite all she could do, her eyes filled with tears and her lips quivered. "It's difficult to explain," she said in a small, aching voice.

"Try."

"At first I...I kept hoping things would change. Get better. Instead they just kept getting worse. There were periods when Evan was pleasant, even affectionate, and on the surface things were fine. Those times always followed a beating. They lasted days, sometimes even weeks." Rebecca's mouth twitched. "In counseling I learned that it's called the 'honeymoon period,' and it's part of the cycle of abuse. After a while, though, the tension begins to build again and inevitably erupts in violence."

"When I met Evan, I thought that I'd finally found someone to love who would love me back. I wanted that so much." Her voice broke on the last word, and her chin started to wobble. She looked up at the ceiling and widened her eyes to hold back the tears. They spilled over anyway, and she wiped them away with her fingertips.

"And then there was...there was my father," she went on doggedly. "Evan was the son he'd always wanted. Daddy never quite forgave me for being born female, you know, instead of the son and heir that he'd wanted. The only time I ever truly pleased him was when I married Evan. I couldn't quite bring myself to face his wrath if I ended the marriage."

She took a sip of coffee and fought for control. After a moment, she waved one hand. "Anyway, abusive husbands tend to keep their wives on such a tight leash and so totally dependent on them for everything that leaving is al-

most impossible. Evan kept a close, constant check on me—
where I went, who I saw, how long I stayed. He made sure
that I had no close friends in Dallas, so that I would have no
one to turn to for help. He doled out money to me in small
amounts, as though I were a child. And of course he
wouldn't hear of me having a job. I had charge accounts at
all the best stores, but getting my hands on enough cash to
even purchase a bus ticket out of town was almost impossible.''

"Yet in the end you did leave. How did you manage it?''

"Things got so terrible I had no choice. I had to get away.
So I pawned some jewelry and . . . I, uh . . . I returned something of value—a gift from Evan, actually—for cash. I used
the money to get out of the state and file for divorce. For
two months before I came here, while I waited for the final
decree, I lived in Reno in a shelter for abused women. I
knew that Evan would be searching for me. All I could do
was pray that he wouldn't find me until I was free.''

"Good grief, Rebecca.'' Travis's gut clenched at the
thought of Rebecca hiding out in one of those places, scared
and alone, among strangers in a strange town.

Something of his thoughts must have shown on his face.
Briefly, Rebecca's gaze met his, then skittered away. She
pressed her lips together and stared down at the cooling mug
of coffee.

"Don't look so horrified, Travis,'' she said, and the defensive edge to her voice made him wince. "It wasn't a bad
place. I got a lot of help there—from the counselors and
from the other women. Their support and encouragement
gave me the courage to examine the past and come to terms
with it and get on with my life.''

"Look, I'm not bad-mouthing women's shelters. I know
they fill a need and that they do good work, but why did you
have to go to one? Good grief, Rebecca, you have friends
who care about you. Why didn't you just turn to Erin and
Elise from the start?''

His jaw clenched when once again her gaze flickered to
him, then darted away. Ah, man . . . he *hated* it when she did

that. He always had. When they were growing up, it had irritated the living hell out of him when she wouldn't meet his
eyes. He'd thought they were beyond that. God knew, she
hadn't been this skittish around him since the night she arrived. Dammit, look at me, he raged silently.

"I couldn't ask Erin and Elise for help. I . . ." She bit her
bottom lip and stared at her hands. "I just couldn't. Not
then."

"Why not?"

"I . . . I was too ashamed."

She spoke so softly, at first Travis thought he had misunderstood, until he took a good look at her downcast profile. "Ashamed!" He spewed out a string of blue language
before regaining his much-lauded control. "That's just
about the most foolish thing I've ever heard you say. Now
you listen to me, Rebecca Quinn. You haven't done anything wrong. The one—the *only* one in all this—who should
feel shame is that sorry ex-husband of yours! Not you! You
got that?"

She flinched at his outburst but managed a wan smile. It
didn't quite reach her eyes, Travis noticed. "Yes, I know
that now. Intellectually, I always have. But what you don't
understand, Travis, is it does something to you. . ." She put
her hand over her heart and patted her chest. ". . . in here,
on the inside, to be abused. You feel so . . . so worthless, so
guilty. So ashamed," she added in a painful whisper. "You
keep thinking that you must have done something wrong, or
that you must be a terrible person to deserve that kind of
treatment. It's humiliating and degrading. You don't want
anyone to know, least of all your family and friends."

Travis gritted his teeth. He knew all that, dammit. Back
in college, when he'd studied for a career in law enforce-
ment, he'd read profiles on abused women. Typically, they
were gentle women, shy and often insecure. Most, for one
reason or another, desperately needed love.

He knew the scenario of dominance she described was
typical, also. Given what he had learned of Rebecca's

childhood, she had undoubtedly been ripe for a sadistic bastard like Evan Hall.

However, the case histories he'd studied in college had been nameless, faceless women. Strangers. They hadn't been Rebecca. The very thought of her husband, the man who was supposed to have loved and cherished her, brutalizing her made his stomach churn and his blood boil.

He raked a hand through his hair and struggled for calm. "All right. I suppose I can understand why you feel that way. But, honey, believe me, no one's going to think any less of you for what he's done."

She looked at him then, her eyes full of irony. "Oh no?" Her small, mirthless chuckle made his gut clench. "Now who's being foolish? There are people who think that if a woman gets slapped around she must've been asking for it. Which, of course, must mean that there's something wrong with her." He started to speak, but she cut him off with a raised hand. "Oh, I'll admit, they might feel sorry for her, in an abstract, condescending way, but God forbid they should get too close."

"C'mon, Rebecca. You don't really believe that, do you?"

"Oh, Travis," she said sadly, shaking her head. "Even you pulled away after you learned what my marriage had been like."

"*Me!* The hell I did!"

"Do you honestly expect me to believe that you called a halt this morning because you were honoring our friendship agreement?"

"This morning? That's it? That's what this is about?" Travis gaped at her. He could not have been more shocked if she had hauled off and slapped him. "Woman, are you crazy?"

He slid off his stool and spun hers around until her back was to the counter. Hooking his hands behind her knees, he spread her legs and stepped between them, leaning in close so that their bodies touched intimately.

"Travis!" Rebecca gasped. Eyes wide, she strained back against the edge of the counter, but when she tried to scoot off the back of the stool he jerked her forward again. Clamping his hands to the bar on either side of her, he enclosed her within the prison of his arms. "Travis, stop this."

"Damn you, Rebecca," he growled, ignoring her protest. "Never—not once in my life—have I been as angry with a woman as I am with you at this moment. How could you think, even for an instant, that I called a halt because I didn't want to become involved with you? That I thought you weren't good enough? How, dammit?" he barked, and Rebecca jumped.

"Travis, I—"

"Shut your mouth and listen."

Her eyes dilated. Swallowing hard, she nodded and pressed back so hard the counter gouged into her back.

"You're right about one thing. I wasn't trying to preserve this so-called friendship of ours. Baby, you should have known that was doomed from the start. Sparks have flown between the two of us since the day we met. The feelings we stir in each other are, and always have been, too strong for anything as bland as mere friendship. For the past weeks I've just been biding my time, waiting for you to realize that." He leaned closer and his voice dropped to a sensual growl. "Whenever I so much as get near you all I can think about is being inside you, making love to you until neither of us can move."

Hot color blossomed in Rebecca's face, but she struggled to ignore it. "Then why did you stop this morning? You must have known that I was willing."

"Oh yeah. I knew." Passion roughened his voice to a raspy murmur. Beneath heavy eyelids, his slumberous gaze drifted down to her mouth. "Pulling back was the hardest damn thing I've ever done. But I knew you were still shaken and raw from Evan's attack. Sweetheart, it's only natural that you'd crave affection and tenderness after what you'd just suffered. But what kind of man would I be if I took advantage of that?"

He exhaled a long sigh, and all the anger drained out of him. Touching her cheek with his fingertips, he smiled tenderly. "When you and I make love—and make no mistake about it, sweetheart, we will—I don't want you to regret it later."

Mere inches separated them. She searched his face, feature by feature, her eyes wide and misty. "Do you mean that?" she asked in a quavering whisper.

"Every word," he whispered back. "I've been fighting it since I was seven years old, but something tells me that you and I have always been each other's destiny."

Her eyes grew luminous and her lips quivered. "Oh, Travis." Looping her arms around his neck, she gave him a melting look. "You really didn't have to stop this morning." Her fingers threaded through his long hair, her nails lightly scoring his nape. "To tell the truth...I wish you hadn't."

The sultry, aching softness of her voice feathered over his skin, making every nerve ending in his body tingle. He shuddered. "Rebecca...honey. After what you went through, you need to be pampered and cared for, not seduced. Later, when you've—"

"No, don't leave me," she said quickly, and looped her legs around the backs of his knees when he would have backed away.

"Rebecca..."

"No, Travis, listen to me. The injury isn't that bad. I've had much worse," she insisted, and he felt a fresh spurt of rage rise up inside him. "Regardless of what Evan did, I know what I want. And believe me, no matter what happens, I know I'll never regret making love with you."

Travis's heart began to boom like a kettledrum. Desire surged through him. "Sweetheart...you don't know what you're saying. You're still strung out and upset from last night. I can't take advantage of you, Rebecca."

The slow smile that tilted her lips was pure provocation. A quick toss of each foot sent her sandals tumbling to the floor. Slowly, she rubbed her soles down the backs of his calves. "Actually, I'd be taking advantage of you. You are exactly what I need, Travis. Don't you see? Not just because of what happened last night, but because of my whole barren life. I need your warmth, Travis, your passion. I need to feel a special closeness with a caring man. I need to feel desired . . . wanted. I need it all," she whispered. "Very badly."

She sifted her fingers through his long hair and her gaze roamed his face, her eyes awash with longing. "You're a very special man, Travis McCall. You like women—really like them—and it shows. I think that was what drew me to you all those years ago. Even when you were a teenager you had a knack for making girls feel special. Pretty or plain, fat, skinny or shapely, prom queen or wallflower, it didn't matter. You were charming to them all. Except to me, of course," she added with a wry grimace that sent a stab of guilt through him. "Even so, your natural warmth and caring drew me like a moth to a flame. It still does." She leaned forward and brushed his mouth with hers. Pulling back just inches, she looked into his eyes, her own soft with entreaty. "Please, Travis," she whispered. "Don't deny me this."

Travis's heart clubbed his ribs. He stared in those limpid blue eyes. His gaze dropped to her lips. He tried to swallow, but his throat felt as though it had an iron wedge stuck crossways in it.

What the hell was he going to do? He wanted her. More than he'd ever wanted any woman. More than he wanted anything on earth. More, heaven help him, than he wanted his next breath.

But, dammit, he also wanted what was best for her. Was it possible . . . ? Could the two really be one and the same? Or did he simply want to believe so?

Rebecca leaned forward to kiss him again, but Travis grasped her shoulders and held her away. She looked at him somberly, her blue eyes swimming with hurt. "Please, Travis," she pleaded. "Make love to me. If you care for me at all . . . make love to me."

The raw emotion in her voice, in her face, tore at his heart. Pride and passion, hope and uncertainty, longing and despair—they all mingled there. He could see how much it had cost her to ask. Travis felt humbled. Protective. Touched to his soul.

Right or wrong, wise or foolish—it no longer mattered. He could not deny her. He could not deny them.

He gazed into her upturned face, so open, so vulnerable, so incredibly lovely, and felt his heart turn over. Tenderly, as though she would break at the slightest touch, he cupped his hand to the uninjured side of her face. "Oh, sweetheart," he murmured in a voice that shook with the force of his feelings. "Sweetheart."

Slowly, savoring the moment, he drew her closer. Travis's head descended. Rebecca's lifted. Her eyes fluttered shut, and as their lips met a sigh shuddered through hers. Travis felt the soft eddy of breath feather against his mouth, and his chest tightened.

From the first touch the kiss was heated and hungry. Travis wrapped his arms around her and pulled her close. He drank from her mouth as though he would devour her. Rebecca made an eager sound, and her arms tightened around his neck.

Shafts of sunshine penetrated the skylights, and dust motes floated like specks of gold in the shimmering beams. In the kitchen, the refrigerator hummed and the coffee-maker made a gurgling sound. The rich smell of fresh-ground coffee beans hung in the air.

Neither noticed. Mouths fused, they clung together in a paroxysm of need and want, straining to get closer, as though each sought to absorb the other. Small frantic sounds and frustrated moans issued from the pair.

Travis placed his palms against the sides of her breasts, alternately pressing the soft globes and rotating the heels of his hands against them. Rebecca gasped and broke off the kiss. "Travis. Oh, Lord, Travis!" Unconsciously she tightened her legs around him, bringing his aroused body tighter against that part of her that throbbed and burned for him.

Travis growled deep in his throat. With an urgency that bordered on desperation, his hands roamed her back and hips, her shoulders, tunneled beneath the fall of damp curls and explored her bare back above the cotton sundress.

Rebecca clutched and kneaded the hard muscles of his waist and back, skimmed her small hands up and down his sides, finally working one between their bodies to stroke his taut belly.

He stilled abruptly, his stomach muscles clenching. "Ahhh, sweetheart, yes. Yes!" he ground out in a pained voice.

He jerked, and his breath hissed through his teeth when her finger delved into his navel.

The tiny caress snapped his control, and with a frustrated sound, he curled his hands around the straps on her sundress and yanked. Threads popped, and the thin spaghetti straps tore free.

Taking a half step back, he hooked both thumbs under the elasticized top of the dress and shoved it down to her waist. His withdrawal drew a small sound of protest from Rebecca, but before she could pull him back, Travis filled his palms with her breasts. She stilled, her breath catching.

He stared at the lush mounds. The thunderous pounding of his heart reverberated in his ears. His loins grew hotter, heavier. Her pale skin had a pearly tone, and just beneath the surface ran a delicate tracery of blue veins. Small, dusty pink areolas, velvety as rose petals, crowned each uptilted globe, their centers pointy and straining.

Mesmerized, he watched his thumbs sweep across her nipples. The already aroused peaks puckered into pebble hardness. "Lovely," he murmured. "So lovely."

Rebecca made a keening sound and arched her back. Her hands tightened on his shoulders, her fingernails digging into his flesh. Slowly, his gaze lifted, and he froze.

Rebecca sat absolutely rigid with her head thrown back, her eyes squeezed shut, that lovely face taut with agonizing passion. She was so erotically beautiful, just looking at her made him hurt all over. Perched there on the stool like a pagan offering, bare from the waist up, her body flushed and trembling in the throes of passion, she was the most exquisite, most desirable woman he had ever seen.

The last vestige of Travis's control snapped. With a growl, he snatched Rebecca back into his arms and fastened his mouth on hers. Her breasts flattened against him, the turgid little nipples thrusting through his chest hair to rub erotically against his skin, and Rebecca moaned. He caught the sound in his mouth, devouring it and her lips with the avidity of a starving man at a banquet.

His hands ran over her bare flesh with unmistakable urgency. "Ah, sweet . . . I can't . . . I've got to . . ."

His panted cries drove Rebecca to even greater frenzy. She clung to him, scattering kisses over his neck and shoulders, the underside of his jaw, his chest. "Yes. Yes. Hurry, Travis. Oh, please, hurry," she gasped, when he tossed the skirt of her sundress up and hooked his fingers in the top of her panties. At his urging, she lifted up, and he stepped back far enough to whisk the undies down her legs and toss them aside. Before the scrap of silk and lace hit the floor, she popped the snap on his cutoffs and shoved them and his briefs down over his hips. The garments fell around his ankles and he kicked them aside, and reached for her.

Caught in the maelstrom, they gasped and moaned and snatched desperately at one another, out of control, their hands bold and seeking, their trembling bodies on fire. Neither gave a thought to where they were or to the incongruity of making love in the living room when there were a half dozen beds in the house. Nothing mattered, nothing existed but the burning desire that drove them.

Cupping her hips with his broad palms, Travis pulled Rebecca forward until her body balanced on the edge of the stool. She gave a little whimper of pleasure and her eyes glazed when he nudged the moist petals of her womanhood.

Travis set his jaw, and in one smooth motion he slid his hands down her thighs, lifted her legs around his waist and thrust his hips forward. Rebecca gasped, and Travis said her name in a guttural voice.

He pressed deep and stilled, his teeth clenched. For a moment only the harsh rasp of their breathing sounded.

Then they began to move.

The hunger that had been building in both of them rose to the surface, voracious and consuming, setting a frantic pace. In silence, they clung together tightly and loved each other. With each rock of his hips, Travis's movements grew stronger, faster. Rebecca's legs tightened around him, her hips rising in a powerful undulation to meet each thrust.

Urgency drove them. Glorious, consuming urgency. It was a race to the summit. Neither could hold back. Neither wanted to. Within seconds Travis felt Rebecca's body tense, felt the first pulsing spasms overtake her.

"Yes. Yes! Oh, Lord, sweetheart! *Yes!*"

"Oh! Oh! *Traa . . . vis!*"

Together they reached the top and went sailing out into space, carried on an explosion of purest ecstasy, their hoarse cries of completion echoing through the firmament.

Later—he had no idea how much later—Travis gradually became aware that he had collapsed against Rebecca. His legs seemed to have turned to mush and the weight of his torso had pushed her back against the counter, which seemed to be the only thing holding them upright.

She was draped around him like a wet towel, her head on his shoulder, arms dangling over his, legs looped limply around his thighs. Their lungs were working like smithies' bellows, but except for the heaving of their chests, neither of them moved. Travis made a gasping attempt at a chuckle and wondered if they could.

Finally, when he'd caught his breath and he trusted his legs to support him, he straightened, easing back from Rebecca. As he disentangled them, she stirred.

Lifting her head from his shoulder, she gave him a fluttering smile and a sleepy-eyed look. "Mmm, hi," she mumbled.

"Hi, yourself," he replied, gazing tenderly down at her. A fraction of a second later, Travis saw the first flicker of awareness enter her eyes. A wicked smile tugged at his mouth, but before embarrassment could set in, he scooped her up in his arms and headed for her bedroom.

"What—Travis! Where are you taking me?"

"Back to bed. I don't know about you, but I'm exhausted. Besides, the next time we make love I want it to be somewhere comfortable, where we can take it slow and easy."

Hot color flooded Rebecca's chest and neck and surged up into her face, but she ignored it. Looping her arms around his neck, she peered at him uncertainly and chewed at her lower lip. "Travis . . . about what happened—"

He stopped her with a kiss, a long, thorough kiss that made her go limp again and lasted until her back sank into the mattress.

"Travis, I don't want you to think—"

"You know what I think?" He stretched out beside her and firmly gathered her close. "I think what happened out there was the hottest, sweetest, most earth-shattering, mind-boggling, heart-stopping loving I've ever experienced. I think it was fantastic." He dropped another kiss on her mouth. "I think you're fantastic. Now, quit talking, woman, and let me hold you while we both get some rest. I need a nap."

Brooking no argument, he tucked her head into the hollow of his shoulder. With a sigh, Rebecca snuggled against his side. At the small sound of acquiescence, Travis grinned and added wickedly, "Otherwise, you're liable to kill me the next time."

"Travis!"

She punched his chest and tried to jerk out of his arms, but he held her tight and laughed. "Ah, sweetheart, I'm sorry. But you're such a delight to tease I just couldn't resist." He squeezed her tight and nuzzled the top of her head with his chin.

"You're impossible," she grumbled against his collar-bone, and tweaked a tuft of chest hair for good measure.

Travis grunted. Laughing, he captured her hand and brought it to his mouth before she could inflict more damage. "Yeah, but you know you love me," he teased, alternately nipping and kissing the end of each finger.

She tipped her head up and smiled sweetly. Using the other hand, she grabbed a hunk of flesh along his side and gave it a hard twist. Travis jumped as though he'd received a jolt of electricity.

"Ow! Ow, that hurts!"

"Serves you right, you conceited oaf," she charged, but amused exasperation robbed her voice of heat. "That was just a childish crush and you know it. Ooooh, I knew it was a mistake to tell you about it. I'll show you love, you—"

She reached for another hunk of flesh, and Travis yelped and jerked away. Squealing in mock outrage when he grabbed her hand, Rebecca bucked and pitched and struggled against his hold.

"Pinch me, will you? You little devil."

"If you don't quit throwing that confession up in my face I'll do more than that, you jerk!"

Travis laughed and wrapped both arms around her, trapping her hands between their bodies, and they rolled together back and forth across the king-size bed amid whoops and grunts and giggles and shouts. Soon they were both convulsed with laughter, but as they came to an exhausted stop, their eyes met and held, and the laughter faded away. In its place was a thick silence, pulsing with sensual awareness.

In an instant of panicked hindsight, Travis questioned the wisdom of allowing the teasing to turn into a wrestling match. The last thing he wanted to do was frighten Rebecca. To his relief, there was no sign of horror or fear in her eyes.

Lying perfectly still, her dark hair spread out around her head in glorious disarray, she stared up at him with wide, overly bright eyes. Her breasts heaved, and her breath hissed through her parted lips with each gasping pant. He felt the soft gusts against his collarbone, and his own chest swelled in rhythm against hers as he sucked deep draughts of air into his lungs.

Rebecca's tongue peeked out, and Travis's gaze dropped to watch the moist tip sweep over her lips. His body quickened. When he looked back into her eyes, they were slumberous and glazed with passion.

He smiled. "On second thought, maybe we can skip that nap," he murmured, and lowered his head.

Chapter Eleven

"I've got you now, you little devil!"

Travis lunged and made a grab for Rebecca. She cut loose with an ear-piercing squeal and dodged, and he hit the water face first. Rebecca whirled and splashed toward the beach as fast as she could run through the shallow waves.

Travis was after her in a flash, and her peeling laughter increased in pitch and volume, the musical sounds trailing behind her. She pelted across the sand but he caught her a step before she reached the blanket they'd spread on the beach.

"No fair! No fair! I'd already won!" she squealed. Hand in hand, they sank to their knees, laughing and gasping for breath.

"In a pi... pig's eye! You owe me a for... for... forfeit, woman." Dripping water, his chest heaving, Travis hooked his hand around the back of her neck and planted a salty kiss on her lips.

Rebecca did not resist but they were both too breathless to sustain the kiss long, and when it ended they collapsed, sprawling facedown onto the blanket. Boneless as a jelly-fish, Rebecca lay in blissful exhaustion.

After a while, drifting somewhere between sleep and wakefulness, she became distantly aware of Travis rousing himself. At the sound of ice cubes rattling, she opened one eye a slit and saw him rummaging through the cooler, cursing under his breath.

A sharp rap on her behind popped Rebecca's eyes open wide. Travis sat back on his heels with his hands braced on his thighs, grinning down at her. "We're out of beer *and* soft drinks. I'm gonna run up to the house for some more. You want something?"

She smiled sleepily and nodded. "A ginger ale would be heaven."

"Be right back." He sprang to his feet and trotted away with what Rebecca thought to be amazing vigor, considering how sapped she felt.

Raising up on her elbows, she watched him go. Her gaze ran greedily over him, taking in the long, muscular legs, lightly dusted with golden hair, the narrow hips and tight buttocks covered by a tiny swath of blue spandex, the tapered waist above it. With each long lope and swing of his arms, muscles bunched and rippled across his back.

Rebecca felt a warm glow inside. He really was a beautifully made man, she mused, smiling dreamily. Everything about him was uncompromisingly masculine...except, perhaps, those luscious eyelashes, and they merely served as a sharp contrast to his potent maleness. The way he walked, the way he talked, those chiseled features, the devil-may-care gleam in his eyes, even his long lion's mane of blond hair, proclaimed him to be all man.

He fairly oozed sex appeal from every pore in his body. That devilish grin alone was enough to make a woman go weak in the knees. And a lusty look from those gray eyes, or a glimpse of that loose-limbed, hip-rolling saunter could turn any female's thoughts to cool sheets and hot skin and whispered words in the darkness.

Travis jogged up the steps of the deck and disappeared into the house. With a sigh, Rebecca rested her cheek on her crossed hands and closed her eyes again. Being with Travis this way was the perfect medicine for her right now. He was like an antidote to an insidious poison that had been slowly killing her.

In Travis's undemanding company she could relax and be herself, without worrying about every word she said, or that something she did would set off a violent reaction. The plain truth was, she felt safe and at ease around Travis. Which, considering their past relationship, was really weird, but there it was.

Travis was always cheerful and amusing, his lighthearted affection in no way threatening or suffocating. In the ten days since Evan's attack he had spoiled her shamelessly, showering her with attention and tenderness and pampering her as though she were made of fragile glass. He went out of his way to entertain her and make her laugh. It was his way, Rebecca knew, of taking her mind off the pain and ugliness of the past, particularly that last clash with Evan. In his laconic, laid-back fashion, Travis was a thoughtful, very sweet man.

He was also a wonderful lover.

The thought made Rebecca's nipples tighten and started a fire low in her belly. She blushed just thinking about all the times and ways and places they had made love.

Travis was a sensual man and he made love with an uninhibited ardor that made her tremble. In the last ten days he'd taught her things she had never even imagined, aroused feelings and responses she hadn't known existed, or dreamed that she was capable of experiencing. She had never been so thoroughly loved, nor felt so thoroughly satisfied. If she were a cat she would purr.

Of course, all the old feelings she'd once had for Travis had returned, she admitted with a fatalistic sigh. She supposed it had been inevitable. At times she wondered if they had ever really left her, or if she had just buried them deep— one less hopeless dream for which to yearn.

It was still a hopeless dream. This was just an interlude. She knew that. It was going to hurt when the affair ended, but she couldn't regret that she'd let it happen. She loved Travis, and she was going to enjoy every moment of this time with him. At least when they parted she would have a wonderful memory. That was more than she'd had before.

Something icy touched the small of Rebecca's back, and she screamed. "Travis! You beast! That's cold!" she screeched, and scrambled to a sitting position in time to see him plop down on the blanket beside her.

"Here, catch." Grinning unrepentantly, he tossed her a frosty can of ginger ale, then tipped his head back and took a pull from a long-neck bottle of beer.

Tiny chunks of ice slithered down the outside of the can and melted on Rebecca's fingers, but she barely noticed. She stared, fascinated, at the rhythmic movements of Travis's throat. From there her gaze slid across his shoulder and zeroed in on the tuft of hair under his raised arm, and she felt a flutter in her stomach.

Lowering the bottle, Travis made an appreciative sound, leaned back on one palm and draped his other hand over his raised knee, the neck of the bottle hooked loosely between his thumb and forefinger. "Man, this is the life," he commented, gazing out at the blue waters of the Gulf. "Nothing but sun and sea and sand and plenty of time to enjoy it."

"Yes." Rebecca popped the tab on the ginger ale can, and took a sip. "I've gotten spoiled in the last few weeks. I'm going to miss the sybaritic life when I leave here."

For just an instant, the hand holding the beer bottle halted in midair before continuing on to his mouth. When he'd taken another healthy swig, Travis resumed his casual pose. "When do you think that might be?"

The question took Rebecca by surprise. For the past ten days, by silent, mutual consent, they had avoided any mention of the future—perhaps, she thought sadly, because they both knew they would not have one together. They had spent their time reveling in the physical pleasure they shared and talking of casual, inconsequential things while skirting serious issues. It was as though, by ignoring the future, they could hold it at bay.

"I, uh... I had originally intended to hide out here until late August. But now that Evan knows I'm here, I suppose I could leave at any time."

Holding her breath, she watched him out of the corner of her eye and waited for his reaction.

Travis stared out at the water, his mouth pursed. Finally he shrugged. "I think you should stay. It'll give Evan more time to cool off. Besides, you ought to take advantage of the chance to relax and recuperate before rejoining the rat race."

Rebecca almost sagged with relief. The last thing she wanted was to leave. Keeping her expression carefully neutral, she nodded. "You're right. I think I will."

With her fingertip, she drew patterns in the condensation on the ginger ale can. "Is that what you're doing here? Escaping the rat race?"

Travis looked surprised. "Me? Naw. Well... yes and no. I took a leave of absence to do some thinking and try to figure out what I want."

"I thought you decided that years ago when you joined the FBI."

"Yeah, so did I. But lately... I don't know, I've been feeling antsy." He took another swallow of beer, then stared at the remains as he swirled them in the brown bottle. "When David recruited me into the Bureau I was young and wild and feeling my oats and doing undercover work seemed exciting. Lately, though, it has lost some of its glamour." He gave a snorting laugh. "Somehow, when you're twenty-four, risking your life is a helluva lot more fun than when you're thirty-one."

Rebecca's gaze went to the puckered scar on his right thigh. She wondered if he realized he was massaging it with his thumb. A part of her wanted to ask how he'd gotten it, but she was afraid to find out.

"So anyway, I came here to think things over and try to decide if I want to stay with the Bureau or take David up on his job offer."

"David offered you a job?"

"I didn't tell you that?"

Rebecca shook her head. No, they'd been too busy taking each day as it came and living for the moment.

"Now that David is married he wants to cut back on the amount of traveling he does. Where security is concerned, he has carte blanche at Telecom International. He's moving into a more executive position, and he wants me to take over most of his current duties, especially the globe-hopping."

"I see. It sounds like a golden opportunity."

"It is. The pay is great and the work is interesting. I'd get to travel all over the world." He shot her a crooked grin. "*Without* putting my neck on the line. The trouble is, I'm just not sure it's the job for me."

That he would even consider leaving the FBI surprised Rebecca. He was ideally suited to the work.

Travis had always been restless and hungry to taste life, to experience the world outside their sleepy east Texas town. She had not been at all surprised when, on getting his law degree, he had become an agent. For all his indolent air, he thrived on excitement and challenge—things he would never find in Crockett...or in the ordinary, comfortable existence for which she longed.

For several minutes, they discussed the pros and cons of the job with Telecom. If Travis decided to take a job in the private sector, Rebecca doubted he'd find one to which he was better suited. Traveling the globe, dealing with security problems at the worldwide electronics firm's many plants, was definitely a job for a footloose single man. Which was precisely why David was looking for someone to take it over. Newly married, he naturally wanted to spend more time with his wife.

The discussion saddened Rebecca, though she hid her feelings behind a carefully neutral expression. Whether he stayed with the Bureau or took David up on his offer would not change a thing between them. However, the very fact that Travis was considering the position underscored for her just how impermanent their relationship was.

"So what are you saying? That I should take the job?" Travis looked at her expectantly, his whole body tense, as though her answer were of vital importance to his future.

"I'm merely saying that you're well qualified and certainly suited to the job. The decision to take it or not is up to you."

He turned his head sharply and stared out over the water. Rebecca had the strange feeling that her answer had disappointed him for some reason.

"So...what are your plans when you leave here?" he asked after a while.

"I'm going back to Crockett."

Travis's head whipped around. "You're kidding."

"Not at all. While I was waiting for the divorce I contacted the school board about a teaching position. Don't look so surprised, Travis. I did major in education, you know. Unfortunately, all the permanent positions were taken, but they said I could substitute teach and wait for an opening. Finances will be tight, but I think I can get by with part-time work for a while, since I plan to live in my father's house."

"Get by? You mean you *have* to work?"

"Of course. I have to earn a living. What did you think?"

"I assumed that you'd gotten a hefty settlement out of the divorce. After all, in Texas you're entitled to half of everything."

Lowering her gaze, Rebecca picked up a handful of sand and let it trickle through her fingers. "I didn't ask for anything," she said in a subdued voice. "All I wanted was my freedom." The trickle of sand stopped, and she picked up another handful. "All my life I've been dependent on someone else for my happiness and well-being. It's time I took charge of my own life." She gave him a bright, brave smile and ignored the aching knot in her chest. "I'm looking forward to it, actually."

Travis clenched his teeth so hard his jaws ached. Well, McCall, now you know. It's pretty damned clear that she has her life all mapped out . . . and that there's no place in it for you. Satisfied?

He ground his teeth harder. He wished to hell he'd never brought the subject up.

He could feel Rebecca watching him. To cover his feelings, he picked up her bottle of sunscreen. "You'd better have another coat of this stuff before you start to broil. Lie down and I'll rub it on your back."

Rebecca sighed but obeyed, stretching out on her stomach and resting her cheek on her crossed arms. After unhooking her bikini top, he squeezed a squiggly line of the lotion along her spine from the shoulders to the tiny scrap of yellow knit cupping her bottom. She flinched at the coldness, but when his hands began a slow massage she moaned with pleasure.

"You know, I'm surprised that you would return to Crockett," he commented, keeping his voice casual. "You've lived in Dallas for six years. Won't you be bored?"

"Hardly. I learned in those six years that I prefer small-town living. I missed the slow pace and the friendliness and the old-fashioned values. I need... Mmm, that feels good," she purred when he worked his thumbs across her shoulders.

Chuckling, he placed a kiss on the back of her neck and whispered in her ear, "So you're a regular small-town girl, are you?"

"Uh hmm," she answered dreamily. "Besides, Crockett is my hometown. There are people there I've known all my life. Like Erin and Elise's parents. Dorothy and Joe Blaine are the closest I've ever come to having a real family."

Travis made an understanding sound and smoothed lotion over her waist and lower back, gritting his teeth when he felt the raised pebble scars against his palms. In the past ten days he'd become familiar with every inch of Rebecca's body, and in doing so had discovered more evidence of her ex-husband's brutality. The sight never failed to rouse him to a white-hot rage. The crafty bastard had been careful to inflict the damage where it wouldn't show.

Quelling his murderous feelings, Travis moved his hands down her body in slow, sensuous circles. Whenever he thought about how she had suffered his instinct was to comfort and caress her, to flood her senses with so much pleasure that the harrowing memories would be wiped away.

"It was either return to Crockett or move to Santa Fe to be near Erin and Elise," Rebecca continued in a drowsy mumble.

"So why didn't you choose Santa Fe?" He kneaded the upper curves of her hips, his thumbs pressing deep into the dimples on either side of her spine.

Travis felt a tremor quake through her and smiled. He scooted backward, squirted a large glob of lotion into his palm and began massaging it onto her thighs.

"No...even...even Santa Fe is too big and bustling. Mmm. Oh, yes, that's nice," she groaned. "The...the area is pretty, in its own way...but I...prefer the forests and lakes and rolling...hills of east Texas to...arid desert."

Slowly, Travis worked his way down, rubbing the oily white stuff into the backs of her knees, the firm, sweetly curved calves, circling her delicate ankles with his hands. By the time he reached the soles of her feet, she was trembling and he could barely draw breath. "Oh, Travis!" she gasped, when his broad palms smoothed back up her legs in one slow sweet sweep.

"Why don't we just get rid of this," he suggested in a rumbling voice, and hooked his fingers under the top edge of the yellow bikini bottom.

Obediently, Rebecca lifted her hips, and Travis smiled. That she allowed him to remove the garment in broad daylight on the beach was an indication of just how much she had loosened up in the past ten days. And of how much she trusted him.

Evan Hall had not only been a vicious bastard but a fool as well. The man had evidently made no effort to tap the deep well of sensuality beneath his wife's ladylike surface.

Until he and Rebecca had become lovers, she had never showered with a man, or gone skinny-dipping in the moonlight, or sunbathed in the nude. Nor, until now, had she made love on the beach in broad daylight.

"Mmm," she groaned, as he worked lotion over her buttocks. Taking his time, he smoothed his hands over the firm flesh, kneading and stroking in a sensuous rhythm. When done, he kissed each pale rounded mound, then grasped her hips and slowly rolled her over.

He feasted his eyes on her small, perfect breasts lifting from the cups of the bikini bra, rose-tipped and lush, their shape yielding to the tug of gravity, and felt a rush of heat to his loins.

She lay supine before him, longing and apprehension swirling in her glazed eyes. Slowly, his gaze wandered lower over her small waist, the slightly concave belly with its dainty navel, the sweet curves of hips and thighs, the glossy nest of mahogany curls at their apex. Her skin was silky smooth all over, like flawless porcelain, tinted a pale peach by their days in the sun.

Travis burned for her. He felt the fire from his toes to the roots of his hair. Like molten lava, his blood sizzled through his veins, settling hot and heavy in his loins.

His searing gaze lifted to hers, and he saw the flicker of uneasiness mixed with desire.

"Travis . . ."

"Shh. Just lie still," he ordered in a raspy whisper.

Sitting astraddle her thighs, he rubbed sunscreen between his palms and cupped them around her breasts. His hands moved in slow circles over the malleable flesh, squeezing gently, lifting, shaping, his lotion-slicked thumbs sweeping back and forth over the taut nipples.

Rebecca whimpered and arched her back, but when she reached for him, he pushed her hands away. "No, don't move. I'm not finished yet."

Staring straight into her eyes, he coated every inch of her body with lotion. His slick hands glided over her neck and shoulders, down her arms all the way to the tips of her fin-

gers. Chest, midriff, belly and legs received the same attention. Still holding her gaze, he moved back, lifted one of her
legs and braced her foot on his raised knee. With feathery
strokes, he smoothed sunscreen over the ankle, across the
delicate arch. Then, one by one, he coated each toe. By the
time he finished and reached for the other leg her eyes were
bright and feverish and her breath hissed through her parted
lips in erratic gasps.

When done, he stood abruptly and stripped off his
trunks. Rebecca swallowed.

"Travis, we can't," she protested faintly.

"Sure we can." He dropped down on the blanket and in
one fluid motion covered her body with his.

She gasped when their warm flesh met and melded. Travis
groaned and shuddered. Taking the weight of his upper
body on his forearms, he cupped the sides of her breasts and
nuzzled the silken valley between them, drawing her woman
smell, tinged with the floral scent of sunscreen, deep into his
lungs.

"Tra-Travis, it's... it's broad daylight."

"So?" He dragged his open mouth up over one lush globe
and took her nipple into his mouth. Rebecca cried out and
arched her back. She clutched his hair with both hands and
rolled her head from side to side.

"S-Someone might... see us."

"Don't worry. There's no one else on this side of the island," he muttered, mouthing the velvety areola. With the
tip of his tongue he flicked the engorged bud and tasted the
slight bitterness of sunscreen and the salty tang of seawa-
ter.

"But... wha-what if someone comes?"

"They won't." He caught her mouth with a hot, open
kiss. Rebecca gave a desperate little growl and dug her fingers into his back.

After that there was no need for words.

Occasional moans and sighs and pleasured gasps were the
only sounds from the entwined couple during the passion-
filled interval that followed. Overhead, sea gulls squawked

and tattered palm leaves stirred with a dry clatter. A playful breeze wafted over them, bringing with it the smells of sun and sand and salt air. It caressed their heated skin and toyed with the ends of their damp hair. A few feet away the gentle surf whispered against the shore, edging ever closer to their tangled limbs. The sun beat down on their sleek, undulating bodies as time drifted by, unnoticed, and the world beyond the gritty blanket ceased to be.

Sated and utterly spent, Travis kissed Rebecca's neck one more time and raised up on his forearms. Her eyelids lifted as though they were weighted with lead, and she gave him a slumberous smile. He felt a rush of fierce satisfaction. She had the look of a woman who had just been well loved.

Emotion flooded him. Love. Tenderness. A soul-deep contentment. Unable to speak, he cupped the side of her face with his hand. Sweeping his thumb back and forth over the hollow beneath her cheekbone, he studied her lovely face. The swelling was gone, thank heaven, and so were most of the bruises. The cut at the corner of her eye had healed to a thin pink line. Only there did her skin still have a faint yellowish tint, and that she was able to cover with makeup whenever they left the island.

"Rebecca. Sweetheart, I . . ."

He tensed as a faint sound registered. He raised his head and looked out over the water, squinting his eyes against the glare.

"What is it? What's wrong?"

Rolling off of Rebecca, Travis sat up and cupped a hand over his eyes, keeping them trained on the small dot approaching across the turquoise water. "You'd better get dressed. It looks like we're about to have company."

"What!" Rebecca jackknifed into a sitting position and snatched up her swimsuit. "I knew someone would come by. I just knew it."

"Take it easy, honey. They're still too far out to see anything. You've got plenty of time." Nevertheless, while they dressed, Travis positioned himself between her and the boat, shielding her from curious eyes with his body.

By the time the fishing boat reached the pier they had returned to the house and were standing on the deck waiting. Raphael waved to them from the deck of the *Juanita* before jumping onto the dock to secure the mooring lines. Travis frowned. For a moment he thought the little fisherman had brought Evan back, but the man who walked down the short gangplank had gray hair and weighed at least thirty pounds more than Rebecca's ex-husband.

He felt Rebecca tense beside him. He looked down at her pale, taut face and tightened his grip on her hand. "Is that who I think it is?"

She bit her lower lip, her gaze glued to the man striding up the pier toward them. "Yes. That's my father."

Dear Lord, Rebecca thought. I'm not ready for this.

In truth, she knew that she would never be ready for this meeting, but there was no way to avoid it. She drew a shaky breath and lifted her chin.

Her father had always intimidated her. One sharp word, one disapproving look from those hawkish eyes and she dissolved. But not this time, she told herself. No longer would she come to him as a supplicant, desperately seeking his love and approval.

Richard Quinn stormed toward them, his piercing stare locked on his daughter. Everything about him—the set of his jaw, his stiff carriage, his long stride—radiated anger.

A shiver rippled through Rebecca. Travis squeezed her hand again and murmured, "Easy, sweetheart. Easy."

Her father climbed the steps to the deck like a storm trooper. Coming to a halt, he fixed her with a furious glare, his lip curling disdainfully as he took in her attire. Rebecca did not think it was possible, but his eyes hardened even more when he noticed her hand clasped in Travis's.

"So it's true," he bit out. "Evan told me you were shacked up with some ne'er-do-well, but I didn't want to believe it."

"Hello, Father," Rebecca said with a trace of irony.

"Don't 'hello, Father' me. And don't use that tone, either. I had to cut short my cruise in the Mediterranean to fly back here and straighten out this mess, and I'm in no mood for your snippiness. How could you walk out on Evan and get some quickie divorce? And without so much as a word. Have you lost your mind, girl?"

"Father, please. Could we go inside and discuss this calmly?"

Her composure, fragile as it was, seemed to throw him, and his eyes narrowed. "Oh, very well. And for heaven's sake, put some clothes on. That bikini is indecent. You would not have dared to flaunt yourself that way when you were married to Evan. He wouldn't have allowed it."

Rebecca did not respond to the caustic comment. Gritting her teeth, she lead the way inside. Once there, she excused herself and hurried to her room to change.

Unburdened with an overabundance of modesty, Travis did not bother. Besides, he had no intention of leaving Richard Quinn alone, not even for the short time it would take him to change clothes. He didn't trust the man.

"Have a seat," he said, and when Richard sat down on one of the rattan sofas, Travis took the one across from him, slouching on his bowed spine. He propped his sandy feet on the coffee table, folded his hands across his bare abdomen, and met the older man's disapproving glare head on.

Richard squinted at Travis. "Don't I know you? You look familiar."

"The name's McCall. Travis McCall. I grew up in Crockett."

"McCall. McCall," Richard mused, giving Travis a steely look from beneath beetled brows. Travis recalled that the fierce stare was a tactic Richard Quinn often used to intimidate people. It worked on most, but Travis weathered the look with bland unconcern. "You Colin McCall's boy? That hotshot attorney back in Crockett? The one that married Margaret Monahan?"

"One of them."

"Humph! Never could figure out what Maggie saw in the man." To Travis's surprise, briefly, Richard got a faraway look in his eyes and his face softened. "She was a pretty little thing. I courted her myself. Would have married her, too, if that father of yours hadn't blown into town and swept her off her feet."

That bit of news came as a shock to Travis. His mother and Richard Quinn? He shuddered at the thought. He wondered if she knew what a narrow escape she'd had. By heaven, the next time he went home he was going to make a point of telling his dad how much he loved him.

Travis grinned at Richard. "Yeah, I've heard the story. Dad and my Uncle Joe were roommates in college. Uncle Joe was dating Aunt Dorothy at the time and when Dad came home with him one weekend, he fixed him up with her younger sister Margaret." Travis's grin grew, turning from smug to taunting. "The rest, as they say, is history."

Richard shot him an annoyed look and dismissed the matter with a disgruntled, "Humph!"

Silence followed. Travis, his expression mildly amused at the older man's obvious frustration, stretched hugely, then relaxed back into his lazy sprawl. Behind his insouciance, however, he was coldly watchful, his body taut with catlike alertness.

"When my daughter returns, I wish to speak to her in private," Richard blurted out angrily. "You'll have to leave."

Travis regarded him with a level stare. "Not a chance."

Accustomed to having his orders obeyed without question or pause, Richard was so stunned, for a second all he could do was goggle at Travis. "Now, see here," he blustered. "You listen to m—"

"No, you listen," Travis snapped, all trace of good humor gone. "The last time I left Rebecca alone with a visitor it was that ex-son-in-law you think so highly of, and the bastard beat her up. So save your breath. I'm staying."

"That's a black lie!" Richard roared.

"No, Father. It's true."

Rebecca walked into the room, wearing a thick terry cloth robe. She had taken time to rinse the salt water out of her hair and comb out the tangles, but she hadn't bothered to dress.

Travis subjected her to a narrow-eyed inspection, his keen gaze probing her face with concern. The brief respite had calmed her, he noted with relief. Her face was still taut and pale, and she still seemed fragile, but the look of panic had gone from her eyes.

"I don't believe you," Richard snarled. "You're lying to cover your own guilt. Anyway, even if he did slap you around a little, it's no more than you deserve. You can hardly blame a man for losing his temper when he discovers his wife has been cheating on him."

Rebecca sat down next to Travis, adjusted the folds of the long robe over her knees and looked steadily at her father.

"It isn't possible to cheat on an *ex*-husband, Father," she said with such admirable poise that Travis wanted to cheer. "Aside from that, Evan never needed an excuse to hit me... as I think you very well know."

"And just what do you mean by that?"

"I mean that Evan's abuse goes back almost to the beginning of our marriage, and if you didn't know, or at least suspect, it was because you didn't want to know."

"That's a lie!"

"Oh, Father." Rebecca shook her head sadly. "How could you not have known? Didn't you ever wonder, even once, why I had so many 'accidents' or how I got all the bruises and cuts? Or sometimes didn't you wonder why I was 'ill' so often and couldn't have visitors? Of course you did, but you chose to look the other way."

Richard's mouth compressed into a straight line. He almost vibrated with fury. After a taut moment he made a dismissive gesture and bellowed, "Why the devil are we even discussing this? It's not important. The point is, you married a rich, influential man. Someday soon he's going to be a U.S. senator. Maybe even president. Are you so stupid that you'd throw away all that over something so paltry as a slap or two?''

Rebecca flinched. If her father had struck her himself he could not have hurt her more. His callous disregard for her pain and her feelings told her louder than words ever could how little he valued her.

Travis's feet hit the floor. He bit out a curse and tensed as though he were about to leap across the coffee table, but she put a restraining hand on his knee. ''No, Travis, don't.''

''I had a long talk with Evan before I came here,'' her father went on, ignoring her stricken expression. ''Despite all you've done, he has generously offered to take you back. I want you to go pack your things, Rebecca. You're returning with me tonight. I've already booked us seats on the evening flight.''

She struggled to hold them back, but tears filled her eyes anyway. ''Father,'' she began in a shaky voice. ''Right after you left on your world trip, I learned I was pregnant.''

Travis jerked as though she'd slapped him, and his head snapped around in her direction. She could feel his gaze boring into the side of her face, but she kept her eyes focused on her father. For an instant joy lit his face, but the look faded when his gaze dropped to her flat abdomen.

''You can't imagine how thrilled I was,'' she went on doggedly, heedless of the tears that streamed down her face. ''I was finally going to have someone to love, someone who would love me back unconditionally. I wanted that baby so much.'' Her chin wobbled, and she put her hand over her mouth to control it. ''So much,'' she mumbled against her palm.

She looked at her father's wavering image through the wall of tears banked against her lower eyelids. ''I was in my fourth month when Evan threw me down a flight of stairs,'' she said in a stark monotone. ''When I woke up in the hospital they told me I'd lost the baby. I knew then that I had to leave.''

Her father waved his hand in a dismissive gesture. ''That was an irrational decision, made when you weren't thinking clearly. For Pete's sake, girl. You can have another baby, but husbands like Evan Hall don't grow on trees. Now, go pack your bags."

The trembling started deep inside. At its core was a hurt so deep Rebecca thought it would surely kill her. Whatever hope she still had that her father loved her withered and died on the spot, and she knew it would never be resurrected.

The awful shaking increased, and she folded her arms tightly across her midriff. Swallowing the knot in her throat, she raised her chin and in a quavering voice said, "No, Father. I won't go."

Richard shot to his feet. He looked ready to explode. "I'm warning you, girl. Either you get on that plane with me tonight or I wash my hands of you. Is that clear?"

"Why you sorry—"

"No, Travis." She laid her hand on his arm and shook her head. "Let me handle this."

Rebecca stood up on wobbly legs, still hugging herself tightly. She looked directly into Richard Quinn's furious eyes and drew a deep breath. "Goodbye, Father."

Chapter Twelve

Richard Quinn looked ready to explode. His jaw bulged, and his fierce stare stabbed into Rebecca. "You'll regret this," he snapped, and pivoted on his heel.

"Say, Quinn," Travis called after him. "Take a message to Evan for me, willya?"

Pausing with his hand on the doorknob, Richard glowered back over his shoulder. "What message?"

"Tell him that if he ever again gets within so much as a mile of Rebecca I'll break every bone in his body."

Rebecca's jaw dropped. She looked at Travis with a mixture of gratitude and fear. He had made the statement matter-of-factly, his voice mild, almost pleasant, yet the very calmness of his tone added a chilling menace.

"You wouldn't dare! Evan is a very important man—"

"Not only would I dare, I'd enjoy the hell out of it."

Richard clenched his jaw. He sliced a look of pure hatred between Travis and Rebecca, then turned to leave.

"Oh, one more thing," Travis called, stopping him again. "If I were you, I'd advise him against running for public office." Travis smiled coldly. "You see, I'm with the FBI. I promise you, if Evan Hall even tries to get elected dog-catcher I'll dig up every bit of dirt there is on him and feed it to the press, including his propensity for wife-beating. Somehow, I don't think the voting public would like that."

"How dare you. If you think your threats—"

"Oh, they're not threats. I mean every word."

Richard slammed the French door behind him with a force that rattled the glass panes. The finality of the sound struck Rebecca like a blow to the heart.

Woodenly, she walked to the doors and watched her father stomp down the steps and storm away out onto the pier.

It was over. Really over.

All of her life she had lived with the secret fear that her father would withdraw from her completely, that she would lose what little regard he felt for her. Now she had.

She had no illusions that he was bluffing, or that once he had cooled down he would retract his words; Richard didn't make idle threats. He would cut her out of his life with the same ruthless determination he employed to rid himself of an unprofitable investment.

"Why didn't you tell me about the baby?"

So lost was Rebecca in her painful thoughts, it took several seconds for Travis's question to penetrate. In truth, she had almost forgotten that he was there. Slowly, she turned halfway and looked at him over her shoulder.

"Why? Because losing my baby was too painful to talk about. It's still too painful." Her gaze returned to the pier in time to see her father climb aboard the *Juanita*. He said something to Raphael and slashed his hand through the air for emphasis. At once, the fisherman scurried down the gangplank and cast off the mooring lines. "Anyway, what would have been the point?"

"What would have been the point?" Travis repeated, incredulous. "The *point* is, I could have consoled you, or at least tried. Dammit, Rebecca, I thought we were getting close. That we'd come to mean something to each other. Now I find you've been keeping this secret."

Rebecca glanced back at him and felt a flicker of surprise when she saw his expression. For the first time she realized that she had hurt him. On some remote level she wanted to go to him and reassure him, erase that anguished look from his eyes, but her own pain was simply too overwhelming.

"It wasn't a secret. Not really. Oh, Travis don't you understand..." Out of the corner of her eye, Rebecca saw the boat pull away from the dock and head out to sea. She pressed her lips together and closed her eyes. "Please, Travis, I don't...I don't want to talk about this right now. I...I can't."

Travis's expression turned contrite. "Ah, sweetheart, I'm sorry. I shouldn't have—"

"No, don't!" she said quickly, and held up her hands when he took a step toward her. "I don't...that is...if you don't mind, I'd like to be alone for a while. I...I think I'll go to my room."

She felt fragile. And empty. Inside all that was left was one big ache. All she wanted was to find a dark place where she could curl up in a ball and shut out the world.

Travis frowned. "Rebecca...sweetheart, do you think that's wise? I know it hurts, but you need to let it all out—"

"No, really, I'm fine," she insisted shakily. "I just need a little time to myself to put everything into perspective. That's all." A wan smile of apology fluttered about her mouth for an instant before she turned to leave.

Travis watched her go, his concern growing when he saw the direction she was taking. Since becoming lovers, they had occupied his bedroom, but she was headed for her old room in the right wing.

She held her shoulders back and her head high, but she walked with stiff, precisely measured steps and a determined dignity that tore at his heart.

"Damn!" Travis swung away from the empty doorway, his hands balled into tight fists. He'd handled that all wrong. Jeez, McCall, you are a jerk. She'd just had her guts ripped out by her old man, for Pete's sake. So what do you do? Instead of comforting her right away like you should have, you light into her for not telling you about the baby. Great going, you jerk. Real sensitive.

All right, so it hurt that she hadn't confided in you. No matter how you feel or how much you want her to trust you, she has to deal with the past the best way she can. Hell, if you hadn't been so wrapped up in your own hurt feelings you would've noticed that it was agony for her to talk about losing her baby. She'd barely been able to get the words out to tell her father, and she'd only done that as a last ditch act of desperation.

Grimacing, Travis raked his hand through his hair, bringing it down the back of his head to massage the knotted muscles in his neck. It had cost her plenty, and for what? That bastard had brushed aside her suffering and loss as though she were a child whining over something as piddling as a skinned knee.

Travis thought about his own family. All of their lives he and the twins, Reilly and Ryan, and their younger sister, Meghan, had known the unconditional, unending love of both their parents. It had wrapped around them like a protective blanket, cushioning life's blows, giving them a sense of security and a comfortable confidence in themselves. That love had been so much a part of their lives, they had simply taken it for granted.

Travis frowned. He couldn't imagine what it would be like to have a father like Richard Quinn.

How the hell could a man treat his own child that way? How could he just put her out of his life?

Travis glanced at the entrance to the right wing. He didn't know what to do. It didn't set right with him for her to be suffering alone, yet what could he do, short of kicking the door down and forcing his company on her?

For the rest of the day, Travis prowled the living room, watching the right hallway entrance and straining to catch the slightest sound. Several times, he crept down the hall and stood outside her door. Had he heard weeping or any sign of anguish, he would have stormed inside and taken her in his arms, no matter what her objections, but from the other side of the door came only a tomblike silence.

He thought she would surely emerge after an hour or two, but darkness came with no sign of Rebecca. For dinner Travis opened a can of soup and made sandwiches, but when he tapped on her door and invited her to join him, he received a polite, "No thank you. I'm not hungry."

"At least you know she's still alive," he grumbled.

He ate alone sitting at the bar. After the dishes were done, he tried to read, but he couldn't concentrate, so he prowled some more. He wondered what Rebecca was doing in there. What she was feeling. What she was thinking. Dammit! Why wouldn't she talk to him? It wasn't healthy for her to withdraw into herself this way!

Nine o'clock came. Then ten. By eleven, Travis decided she wasn't coming out that night. He tiptoed down the hallway one last time and found there was no light coming from under her door. She probably fell asleep from emotional exhaustion, he told himself.

Travis showered and turned in himself, but an hour later he was still awake. He flounced and flopped and punched his pillow time and again, but it was no use. In the past ten days he'd grown used to having Rebecca beside him, and he couldn't sleep without her. Especially not when he knew she was just a few doors away, steeped in misery.

Finally Travis made a frustrated sound and left the bed. On bare feet, he crossed the hall into Erin and Max's room and stepped out through the French doors onto the deck. Braced stiff-arm against the railing, he sighed and gazed at the water.

Moonlight picked out the white foam of the breakers rolling in to shore. Its reflection and that of the stars spilled across the shining surface of the water like liquid gold and illuminated the sand an eerie iridescent blue. Lace-edge waves tumbled onto the shore with a whispery splash. Silhouetted against the lighter sky, the palm trees swayed in a gentle breeze like languid dancers, their tattered leaves rustling.

Absently, Travis studied the night sky for the Big Dipper, then let his gaze wander down the shoreline. He stiffened suddenly and stared, every muscle in his body springing to alertness. A hundred yards or so down the beach a lone figure stood at water's edge, her dark hair and long white robe billowing out behind her.

Rebecca.

The foamy edge of a wave tickled her toes before retreating. The next big one would probably cover her feet. Remotely, Rebecca knew she should probably step back a few paces, but she did not move. With her arms crossed over her midriff, she stared at the water, absently rubbing her elbows with her fingertips.

Her chest felt as though it were being squeezed in a vise. It doesn't matter. None of it matters! she told herself vehemently for perhaps the thousandth time. For heaven's sake, she had known for years that she meant less than nothing to her father. She had accepted that.

Rebecca closed her eyes and swallowed hard. So why couldn't she make this awful ache go away?

It would help, she knew, if only she could cry. But somehow she could not. She was too numb. The pain was too deep.

A prickly sensation ran up the back of her neck and over her scalp. She tensed, suddenly aware of him behind her.

''Rebecca.''

Travis whispered her name like a plea, his voice husky and beseeching, riddled with uncertainty and longing that tugged at her.

She turned slowly and looked across the few feet of sand that separated them, into pale eyes that glittered with loving concern. He had come to her as he slept—naked—and he looked impossibly beautiful standing there in the moonlight, like a magnificent Viking warrior, stunningly unselfconscious, his long blond hair lifting in the breeze, the dangling saber swaying from his left earlobe, his fit body gilded by the lunar glow.

"Rebecca," he repeated in an aching voice. "Sweetheart, for God's sake, let me hold you."

The concern and pleading in his eyes, the anguish in his voice reached out to her. Something shifted and gave way inside Rebecca, releasing a hot floodtide of emotion. It gushed up into her chest and clogged her throat. Her chin wobbled and tears filled her eyes. Trembling with desolation and wrenching pain, her gaze clung to him across the distance.

Finally her face crumpled. "Oh, Travis," she quavered piteously, and when he held his arms out to her, she took a stumbling step toward him.

Before she could take a second, he had covered the distance and snatched her into his arms.

"Oh, sweetheart! Dear God, I'm so sorry," he muttered fiercely. He clamped her to him with all his might, one arm wrapped around her waist, his other hand cupping the back of her head, pressing her face against his chest.

"Oh, Tra-Tra-Travis it hur-hurts so much," she gulped between sobs.

"I know, love. I know."

Great, wrenching cries rose up and tore from her. The sounds were raw and painful to hear, and the force of them shook her whole body.

The tears she had held in check for hours, years, came pouring out in a torrent. They saturated the mat of soft hair and trickled down his chest to the point where their bodies pressed together, soaking into the front of her terry cloth robe.

Rebecca clutched him as though she would climb right into his body, her fingers digging into his back. She burrowed against his chest, seeking the strength he gave so willingly. At that moment he was the bedrock of her life, her only source of comfort, and she clung to him with the strength of desperation.

Her sobs rent the peaceful night, harsh, heart-rending wails torn from the core of her being. They hurt her throat and interfered with her breathing, but she couldn't stop. Behind the tears was a lifetime of stored-up pain and disappointment and yearning.

Jaw clenched, Travis rubbed his cheek against her crown and waited for the storm to pass. "You just go ahead and cry, love," he crooned. "Let it all out. You'll feel better."

After a while, though, when her cries took on a hysterical edge and showed no sign of abating, he began to get worried. He rubbed her back and grimaced, wondering what he should do.

The problem resolved itself an instant later when a wave broke unexpectedly against the backs of her legs and washed around their feet.

Rebecca gasped and lifted her head from his chest. Bewildered, she looked around, her cries choking off to sharp hiccuping snuffles that caused her chest to jerk. "Wha—"

"Don't worry about it, love. C'mon. I'll take you home." Sweeping her up in his arms, Travis strode for the house.

Rebecca lay docile against his chest, too spent to move. By the time they reached the deck, her cries had diminished to sniffles and an occasional shuddering inhalation. He stood her on her feet only long enough to hose off their sandy legs. Then he scooped her up again and carried her inside.

Without the least hesitation or fumbling, he strode through the dark house to the bedroom they had shared for the past ten nights. Laying her down on the bed, he stretched out beside her and pulled her to him, tucking her firmly against his side and cradling her head on his shoulder. When they were settled he held her close and ran his hand up and down her arm and rubbed his jaw against the top of her head.

Rebecca accepted it all with a listless, almost zombielike calm. She lay limp against him, staring through the darkness, utterly exhausted. Her eyes felt gritty and swollen, and her nose burned, but the terrible ache in her chest had eased to a bearable level. She had needed the release of tears and the comforting support that only Travis could give her. Absently, she toyed with the hair on his chest and wondered why she had held herself apart from him for so long.

"You okay now?" His soft voice stroked over her like a caress and made her feel cherished and protected. His warm, moist breath filtered through her hair and feathered over her scalp. Rebecca shivered.

"Yes. I . . . I'm sorry I went to pieces like that."

"Hey. Don't worry about it. You were entitled."

"Maybe. But it's not as though I had no idea that I mattered so little to him. I realized that years ago." She gave a weak chuckle. "How could I not?"

"I still can't believe that he wanted you to go back to Evan, even after you told him how the bastard had mistreated you. Why, for Pete's sake? Does he like him that much?"

"Oh, yes. Evan is Father's idea of the perfect son—rich, successful, sophisticated, powerful. He has a lot of influence with some very important people. My father has benefited from Evan's connections more than once."

"Money and social position? For that he's willing to sacrifice his own daughter? That's sick. Did he honestly believe that he could just snap out an order and you'd go meekly back to that monster and let him knock you around some more?"

"Probably. I've never crossed him before." Several seconds ticked by in silence. When she spoke again, her voice had the soft, faraway quality of one adrift in painful memories. "But then I lost the baby, and everything changed. I changed." Her fingers curled into the hair on his chest and her voice dropped to a low pitch that vibrated with passion. "Nothing could make me go back," Rebecca vowed, and a shudder rippled through her. "Nothing. I'd rather die first."

Travis continued to rub her arm from wrist to elbow with slow, hypnotic strokes. "Don't worry, sweetheart. You'll never have to go through anything like that again. I promise."

A weak smile tugged at her mouth. It was sweet of him to want to protect her, but did he really believe that his threat would keep Evan away? "Thank you, Travis. I hope you're right. I just wish I could be as confident. Unfortunately, Evan doesn't easily give up what he considers to be his. I'm sure I'll be hearing from him again soon," she said with weary acceptance.

Travis reached out and snapped on the bedside light, then rolled her onto her back and propped up on his elbow beside her. Tenderly, he touched her cheek with his fingertips. Rebecca looked up at him, and her heart skipped a beat. His habitual, lazily amused expression had given way to taut eagerness, and his silvery eyes glittered down at her with an intensity she had never seen before. "He would have to accept that he's lost you if you were married to another man."

"Ma— Travis! What in the world are you talking about? I'm—" Rebecca caught her breath at the look in his eyes.

"Marry me, Rebecca."

She stared at him in utter disbelief, a panicky feeling rising inside, suffocating her. "Travis, you . . . you can't be serious. You don't marry someone just so you can protect her." She gave a nervous little laugh and tried to scoot away from him, but he would not let her brush the matter aside that easily.

He shifted his hand from her face to her shoulder and held her in place, his gaze boring into her. "That's not why I want to marry you. At least, not the main reason." His eyes delved into hers, and Rebecca felt her heart squeeze. "I love you," he said with a soft sincerity that stole her breath. "I think I always have. I've just been running scared all these years."

"Oh, Travis."

"And I think you love me, too. Don't you, Rebecca?"

She gave him a desperate look, silently pleading with him to stop. "Travis, please . . ."

"Don't you?"

"All right, yes. Of course I do, but—"

"Then marry me."

Rebecca bit her lower lip and gazed at him in anguish. Dear, Lord. For years she had dreamed of him saying those words to her. What cruel irony it was to hear them now, when it was too late. "I...I can't," she whispered. Her throat worked, and fresh tears filled her eyes. "I just...can't."

"Why not? If we love each other—"

"Love isn't enough, Travis. We're too different. We want different things from life. Marriage between us would never work."

He started to argue, but she placed four fingers over his mouth and looked at him with infinite sadness. "Oh, my darling, don't you see? You thrive on excitement and danger. And variety—in your work and..." Her lips twisted in a wry grimace. "...let's face it, in women. You enjoy the challenge of each new assignment, of moving from place to place, and of charming the next woman you meet."

"That's not true." At Rebecca's skeptical look his mouth twisted. "All right. So maybe it was at one time, but not anymore. I like women, yes. I admit that. But I've never been in love before, nor have I ever said those words to another woman. I already told you that I haven't been happy with my life lately, and that I was thinking of making a change."

"Yes, and to what? Another job that will keep you bouncing around the globe, as rootless as ever. The only difference is you won't be in danger all the time."

"Dammit, Rebecca—"

"Please understand, Travis, I'm not blaming you." She took his face between her palms and looked deep into his eyes. "You're drawn to excitement and adventure. It's your nature. And I would never try to change you. But if I ever marry again, I want a full-time husband. One who'll be there for me through good times and bad. Someone who will be around for Little League games and dance recitals, and be home for dinner every evening. Someone who'll still love me, and only me, when I'm ninety. Travis, I want—no, I *need*—a quiet, peaceful life. I need the stability and security of an ordinary existence.''

"Don't you think I want those things too? Hell, I realized months ago that I'd reached a crossroad in my life. It's time for me to take a different direction. I just didn't realize until now what I wanted it to be. I'm ready to settle down, Rebecca. I swear it. Believe me, I've had enough excitement to last a lifetime." He looked at her tenderly, his handsome face full of emotion. "I love you, sweetheart," he whispered. "And I will when I draw my last breath. Whatever kind of life you choose is fine with me, just as long as you let me share it."

Smiling sadly, she smoothed her thumb over one of his silky eyebrows. "Oh, my love. You say that now, but you would hate it. Within six months you'd be miserable."

The eager hopefulness faded from his expression, along with every trace of tenderness. Muscle by muscle, his face tightened and his eyes turned hard. Watching him, Rebecca felt a knot forming in the pit of her stomach.

Travis sat up and swung his legs over the side of the bed. The stiffness of his back and the rigid set of his shoulders loudly proclaimed his anger. He sat with his hands braced on his thighs, staring straight ahead. Lying motionless, apprehension growing by the second, Rebecca watched the taut muscles in his jaw work. The awful silence seemed to stretch out endlessly.

"You know what I think?" he said in a tight voice, startling Rebecca. He turned his head and looked at her over his shoulder. "I think that's all a bunch of bunk. You're not worried about my job or the differences between us, or us not being able to make a marriage work. Or even that I might stray. You're afraid of being loved."

"That's not true!"

"I think it is. You claim to want love, but when I offer you mine you shy away from it. You don't want to make the commitment because you're afraid I'll turn out to be like Evan. Isn't that right?"

"No. Travis, no. I . . . I know you're not like him. You're nothing like him," Rebecca insisted, but even to her own ears her protests sounded unconvincing.

Sadly, they both knew there was a grain of truth in his accusation. She *was* afraid of binding herself to another man, of giving a man, *any* man, any kind of power over her life. It gave her cold chills to think about it.

She loved Travis with all her heart and soul. He was a good man. He would never hurt her physically. She knew that . . . but still . . .

"Do you really?" he asked skeptically. "Then prove it. Marry me, Rebecca. Let me love you the way you deserve to be loved."

Rebecca swallowed hard. Unable to hold his steady gaze, she looked down at her hands, twisting a corner of the sheet. A shiver she was powerless to prevent rippled through her, and Travis's mouth thinned. "I . . . I . . ."

"That's what I thought," he snapped, and the bitterness in his voice wrung her heart. He stood up abruptly and stomped to the dresser. After pulling on a pair of briefs he went to the closet, put on jeans and a shirt, which he didn't bother to tuck in or button, and stuffed his feet into his holey sneakers.

Sitting up in the bed, Rebecca tucked the sheet up under her arms and watched him, her uneasiness growing. Without even looking in her direction, he headed for the door.

"Travis, where are you going?" she called after him.

"Out."

He didn't slow down or even look back. He simply walked out, leaving Rebecca sitting in the middle of the bed staring at the empty doorway, hurting for him, hurting for herself. Her heart felt like a lead weight in her chest, and her eyes slowly filled with tears.

She heard the French door in the living room slam. A short while later the speedboat motor roared to life. Within moments the powerful rumbling receded into the distance.

By dawn Travis had not returned. Rebecca told herself it was just as well. At least they would be spared the awkwardness and pain of saying goodbye. But in unguarded moments she wondered where he'd spent the night . . . and with whom, and the heavy ache in her heart would increase tenfold.

During the long hours of waiting for Travis to return, Rebecca had reached a painful decision; the time had come for her to leave. Their idyll was over. They were at an impasse. There was no going back to the way things had been, and, no matter how much she might yearn to, she couldn't do what Travis wanted. Rather, what he thought he wanted.

So she had spent the night packing and hauling her cases out to the end of the pier. Just before dawn, when she knew the fishermen would be preparing to go out for the day, she had telephoned Señor Delgado, the proprietor of the one and only tiny grocery-cum-cantina in the village, which also happened to boast the only telephone.

After receiving assurance from Señor Delgado that he would make arrangements for one of the boats to take her to Alhaja Verde, Rebecca placed another call, this one to Erin and Elise. Then she locked the house, went out on the pier and sat down on one of her suitcases to watch the sunrise and wait for her ride.

On the dock in San Cristobal, she hired a taxi to take her to the airport, but on the way she made one stop. She could not leave without saying goodbye to Constanza and Pepe.

It was still early, and only Constanza and three of her daughters were in the cantina, setting up tables and sweeping up, getting ready for the day. The Mexican woman did not seem at all surprised to see her. The minute Rebecca stepped inside she came bustling over, wiping her hands on her apron.

"Ah, Señora, you are here. *Muy bueno.* You are looking for Señor Travis, no?"

"Travis is here?" Rebecca glanced around at the empty tavern, her heart beginning to pound.

"Ah, *sí.* We were closing for the night when the *señor,* he arrived. He was *un hombre desdichado, señora*—a very unhappy man. All night the *señor* and Pepe, they drink te-

quila and talk of love and women. Ai yi yi!'' Constanza
rolled her eyes and threw up her hands. "They both get *muy
borracho* ... how you say ... drunk-as-skunks."

"Oh, dear. Where are they now?"

Constanza tipped her head toward the family living
quarters behind the cantina. "In the back, sleeping it off."
She patted Rebecca's arm. "You wait here, *señora*. I will go
wake the *señor* for you?"

"No! Please, don't do that!"

Constanza's eyebrows shot upward. "You do not wish to
take the *señor* home?"

"No. That is ... I didn't come for that. I, uh ... I just
stopped in to say goodbye."

Constanza's expressive face registered shock. "Ah, no,
señora, you must not go! This quarrel, you and Señor
Travis, you will make it up. It is nothing. *Nada.*"

"There's more to it than just a quarrel, Constanza."
Swallowing hard, Rebecca shook her head. "This ... this is
the only way. I have to leave."

"But, the *señor,* he loves you."

"And I love him. But it just won't work." A tear slipped
over onto her cheek. She dashed it away and surged forward to give Constanza a hug. "Tell Pepe goodbye for me,"
she said tearfully. "And all the others."

"Si, si. Adios, señora. Vaya con diõs," the motherly
woman murmured sadly, patting Rebecca's shoulder.

Almost blinded by tears, Rebecca whirled and hurried
from the cantina. Behind her, Constanza sighed heavily and
mumbled a string of mournful Spanish.

"She claims she loves me, dammit. So tell me how she
could think I would ever hurt her?" Slumped on his spine
in an overstuffed chair, Travis glared at his cousins.

He saw the worried glance that passed between Erin and
Elise. They'd been exchanging the same kind of looks ever
since he showed up, unannounced, on the doorstep of Elise
and Sam's sprawling ranch house, two hours before.

Travis's mouth turned down at the corners. He knew he looked a little rough around the edges. Hell, after the thirty-six hours he'd just had, who wouldn't? He was disheveled from traveling all night, unshaven, and in one rip-roaring bitch of a mood, but the way they were acting you'd think he was ready for a straitjacket.

"Travis, I've never seen you like this before," Elise said, her soft voice riddled with concern.

"Yeah," her twin piped in. "You're so . . . so *angry*. This isn't like you, Travis."

"Dammit! I've got a right to be angry!" he roared, thumping the arm of the overstuffed chair with his fist.

"Okay. Okay. Take it easy. Sam won't like it if you demolish his favorite chair. Trust me, you don't want to rile my brother-in-law."

"Erin, don't tease," Elise scolded, but her expression remained troubled.

Travis scowled at both of them, but deep down, he understood their confusion. He'd never experienced emotions this strong before. Love, rage and frustration roiled through him, creating a painful pressure in his chest. He damn well felt ready to explode.

In the past he had pretty much taken life and its ups and downs in stride. Occasionally he had experienced mild anger or disgust, a touch of sadness, an occasional twinge of excitement or fear. He loved his family and he had usually felt a warm affection for the women he dated. He had enjoyed life with all its pitfalls and absurdities and generally he'd been a happy man. When they'd experienced extremes of emotions he had commiserated with friends and family but he'd never truly understood what all the fuss was about. Until now.

Before accepting his feelings for Rebecca, he'd never felt such piercing joy . . . or such black despair.

Travis dragged both palms down over his face and sighed. Hell, now he knew what people meant when they talked about being heartbroken. His felt as though someone had cleaved it in two with an ax.

The twins were eyeing him warily and waiting for him to speak. He shot them a disgruntled look. "She left me a note. Did I tell you that?"

"Only six times."

"A damned note," he muttered, ignoring Erin's sarcasm. "I poured out my heart to her and asked her to marry me, and she takes off without a word the minute my back is turned."

"Well after all, Travis, you did stomp off in a huff first."

"Erin." This time Elise's voice held a warning. She aimed a quelling look at her sister, but her expression softened when she turned to him.

"Travis, I'm sure in her heart Rebecca knows that you would never hurt her, but her fear has little to do with rational thought or even emotion. It's the result of six horrible years of enduring pain and degradation that most of us probably can't even imagine. Don't you see, it's ingrained and instinctive. You shouldn't take it personally."

"That's right," Erin chimed in. "You're just going to have to give Rebecca time."

"Time! Time for what? If she doesn't trust me by now, she never will."

"You have to give her time to heal," Elise said gently. "Time to recover—from that hideous six years and from the loss of her baby. Time to build her self-confidence, her self-esteem." Elise went to Travis and knelt beside his chair. Taking his fist in her hands, she gazed at him, her brown eyes full of sympathy and entreaty. "Rebecca needs a chance to stand on her own two feet, to prove to herself that she can make it on her own. Once she has, the fear will fade and she'll be able to trust again."

"Elise is right."

Travis swept them both with a sour look. "Oh, great. You two practically railroaded David into marriage, but you advise me to wait. Thanks a lot."

"That was different," Erin sniffed. "Abigail and David were ready for marriage. David just needed a little push, is all. Rebecca, on the other hand, is afraid of making another mistake, which even you have to admit is understandable.''

''I suppose,'' Travis conceded grudgingly.

''And I wouldn't be so quick to dismiss her other concerns either, if I were you. Face it, Cuz. We love you dearly, and God knows, you do set feminine hearts aflutter, but you're hardly the type to inspire much hope in a woman who dreams of picket fences and station wagons and a passel of kids. Frankly,'' Erin stated with her usual irrepressible bluntness, ''if I were in her shoes, I wouldn't consider you likely husband material either.''

''Hey! Bachelorhood is not an unalterable condition, you know. You make it sound like some kind of incurable disease. For your information, the single life was beginning to pale for me even before Rebecca and I fell in love. That was one of the reasons I took the summer off—to reevaluate my life.''

''And what did you decide?''

Her gaze swinging from Erin to Travis, Elise sat back on her heels and waited to hear how he would answer her twin's question.

Travis did not hesitate. ''That a house in Crockett with a picket fence around it and Rebecca inside sounds like heaven.''

''Then, Cuz, if I were you, I'd make sure that Rebecca knew how I felt.''

''And just how do you suggest I do that? I've already told her that I love her and that I wanted to settle down with her and raise a family and she didn't believe me.''

Erin smiled smugly. ''Don't tell her, you jerk. Show her.''

Chapter Thirteen

"Rebecca!" Joe Blaine hollered up the stairs. "Shake a leg, girl, or we'll be late for church!"

Rebecca jumped at the bellowed command and picked up her already frantic pace. With a moan, she rushed to the four-poster bed, dumped the contents of one purse onto the candlewick bedspread, snatched up what she needed from the pile and began stuffing it into another purse.

"Rebecca!"

"I'm coming! I'm coming!" She grabbed up the gray suede clutch bag, a lipstick, tissue, wallet and keys and dashed out the door. Hurrying, she crammed the last items into the purse as she clattered down the stairs.

"There you are. It's about time," Joe grumbled.

Arriving breathless at the bottom of the stairs, Rebecca found David and Abigail, Elise and Sam already in the foyer.

"Here, put this on," Joe said. "Time's awasting."

Obediently slipping her arms into the coat he held for her, Rebecca glanced at the grandfather clock. "Goodness, Joe, service doesn't even start for another forty-five minutes."

David grinned and winked. "It's the same every Sunday. Dad thinks 'Thou salt not be late for church' should be the eleventh commandment. He's always in a dither about it, especially when it comes to holiday services, but I can't remember a time when we were ever late."

"That's right," Joe snapped. "And this family has me to thank for it."

He looked around and gave an aggravated snort. "Now, where the devil did those two women go? They were here just a minute ago. Dorothy! Erin!" he yelled. "It's time to leave!"

The kitchen door swung open and Dorothy came bustling out, followed by Erin, who made a face at her father. "There's no need to shout, darling," Dorothy said calmly. "We're right here. I was just basting the turkey one last time."

"Good heaven's, woman. You've been working in the kitchen since before dawn. Aren't you done yet?"

Unperturbed by her husband's mouthing, Dorothy slipped her arms into the coat he held for her and calmly pulled on her gloves. "Meals do not cook themselves, Joseph. It's Christmas, after all. Maggie and Colin and their family will be over right after church. I want everything to be ready for our Christmas dinner when they arrive."

"Humph. You've been cooking for the past week. There's already enough food in that kitchen to feed an army."

Joe was right. The smells of roasting turkey and dressing, candied sweet potatoes, wassail, mince, pecan and pumpkin pies permeated the big old Victorian house. Mingled with the cooking smells were the sweet aroma of bayberry candles and the pungent scents of the pine Christmas tree in the parlor and the evergreen boughs draped over the mantle and the banisters.

Rebecca inhaled deeply of the heavenly smells. Christmas in the Blaine home was the fulfillment of every fantasy she'd ever had of what holidays should be. The past weeks had been hectic and wonderful, and she had loved every minute of them—the shopping, wrapping gifts, tromping through the woods and cutting down the tree, putting up the decorations, helping Dorothy with the cooking, getting the rooms ready for the Blaine offspring and their spouses. It was the most wonderful Christmas Rebecca had ever had.

If it were not for the persistent ache in her heart for Travis, the holiday season would have been perfect.

In unguarded moments Rebecca found herself daydreaming of how it would be to share this time with Travis, of the two of them together as a couple, living the same sort of simple, day-to-day life that had brought his parents and Joe and Dorothy so much joy and contentment. Always, though, the instant Rebecca realized the drift her thoughts had taken she impatiently dismissed the foolish dreams. Travis simply was not the domestic type, and no amount of wishful thinking would make it otherwise. Nor, despite her heart's yearning, was she ready to chance marriage again.

"Well, come on. Everybody get a move on."

Elise and Erin rolled their eyes, and Sam tolerated his father-in-law's prodding with a sardonic half smile, but they all headed for the door.

"Where's Max?" Dorothy asked, looking around for Erin's husband.

"He's out warming up the van. He's the only one in this family besides me who knows what punctual means."

"Punctual, my patootie," Erin snorted. "He's just trying to get on your good side."

"Whatever. At least he's ready on time. Now, out. Out, all of you." Joe shooed them all out to the van, including Rebecca in his parental haranguing as though she, too, were one of his and Dorothy's brood.

All the way to church, Erin and the others razzed Joe, and he bantered back good-naturedly. Settled in the back of the van, Rebecca listened to it all with a smile on her face, and thought, not for the first time, how lucky she was to be included in this warm family.

Returning to her father's house had been out of the question after their argument on Rincon. In his typical ruthless fashion, he had wasted no time in cutting ties with her. Rebecca returned to Crockett to find the big house with a "For Sale" sign on the front lawn.

At first, when Erin and Elise had suggested that Rebecca move in with their parents, she had been reluctant, but they had brushed aside all her reservations.

"Don't be silly. Mom and Dad would love to have you," Erin had declared breezily. "Since David and Elise and I left home, they've just been rattling around in that big old house."

"That's right," Elise had concurred. "There's nothing Mom and Dad love more than having someone to see after. I'm sure they'll welcome you with open arms."

Reluctantly, Rebecca had agreed to let them broach the subject to their parents. She hadn't much choice, since she hadn't known how she was going to manage otherwise. She could not afford a place of her own on a part-time teacher's pay.

Erin and Elise's predictions had been right on target. The minute Dorothy and Joe learned of her predicament they had insisted that Rebecca stay with them.

It was, Rebecca reflected, the best move she had ever made. The twins' parents treated her as though she were a third daughter, showering her with love and attention, encouraging her, worrying over her, scolding her when they thought she needed it.

Smiling to herself, Rebecca recalled the gruff lecture Joe had given her when he'd discovered that the spare tire on the old secondhand clunker she'd bought was not only flat, but bald as a cue ball. He had driven her straight to the auto supply store and purchased a new one for her.

Rebecca sighed. The only disadvantage to living with the couple was that it made her dread the thought of moving out into a place of her own next fall, if she should manage to secure a fulltime teaching position.

They arrived at church with plenty of time to spare, and Joe ushered his family into one of the two empty pews near the front, which, for almost forty years, had been unofficially reserved for the Blaines and McCalls. In the shuffle for position, Rebecca somehow ended up on the end next to Abigail, with the aisle seat on her right, which Joe usually occupied, vacant. They had barely taken their seats, when the McCall family arrived and began filing into the pew behind them.

The peace of the sanctuary settled over Rebecca. Her senses absorbed the soft organ music, the winter sunshine seeping through the stained glass windows, the smell of flowers and candles and evergreen boughs. Her gaze was drawn to the bright spots of color provided by the poinsettias scattered all around, to the manger scene set up on one side of the altar, and she smiled.

The parishioners filing in murmured hushed greetings and brought with them the scents of perfume and winter woolens and the cold freshness of outdoors. Gertrude Paterson stumped down the aisle, trailing the combined scents of mothballs and lavender, her ancient pillbox hat perched atop white corkscrew curls, its stiff veil hooked under the end of her nose.

Talking quietly to Abigail, Rebecca was only vaguely aware of a man slipping into the seat beside her as the organist played the flourish that signaled the start of service and the first hymn. The choir and the congregation rose as one, but when Rebecca reached for a hymnal, a dark-suited arm extended in front of her, an open songbook clasped in the masculine hand extending from the snowy white cuff.

"Here, sweetheart, we'll share."

Rebecca gasped and jumped, shock jolting through her like a zap from a lightning bolt at the sound of that familiar deep voice in her ear. Her head whipped around, and her eyes grew huge.

"Travis! Wha—?"

All around them voices raised in song, drowning out her words. Travis, his gray eyes twinkling, gave her a devilish smile before turning his attention to the altar and adding his rich baritone to the throng of voices.

Rebecca's heart boomed and her head whirled. Mouth open, she stared up at his profile for a full half minute before gaining the presence of mind to fix her gaze on the hymnal.

The notes and words ran together in a blur before her eyes. Her lips moved in sync with the other singers, forming the lyrics automatically, but her voice emerged in a quavering whisper.

She stared blindly at the open songbook, trembling inside. Travis. Here. Why hadn't anyone mentioned he was coming home for Christmas?

Somehow she got through the song. Moving like an automaton, she took her seat along with the rest of the congregation. She sat ramrod straight on the padded bench seat and stared straight ahead, her hands folded atop her purse in her lap, her chest so tight she could barely breathe.

Of course, she had known that she was bound to see him again someday, especially living as she was with his aunt and uncle. Crockett was Travis's hometown as well as hers. Most of his family lived there, and many of his old friends.

She had expected to see him at Thanksgiving, had braced for it, but when she had cautiously inquired of his mother when he would be arriving, Maggie had told her that he was on an important assignment and would not be home for the holiday. When no mention had been made of him coming home for Christmas, she had assumed that he was still unable to get away.

Rebecca peeked at Travis out of the corner of her eye. Shock gave way to amazement as, one by one, the changes in his appearance began to register. He wore a beautifully tailored dark gray suit, teamed with a crisp white shirt and a paisley print silk tie in maroon, silver and gray. He was clean shaven, and the dagger earring was gone. Most amazing of all, he'd cut his long lion's mane of silvery blond hair to a stylishly short length that fell just shy of being conservative.

She swallowed hard. He looked breathtakingly hand-some...and so very dear she ached to throw her arms around him and never let go.

Travis turned his head and caught her staring at him. The corners of his mouth turned upward, and he lowered one eyelid in an outrageous wink. Rebecca jerked her gaze away from those twinkling eyes and stared straight ahead.

Not one word of Reverend Dixon's Christmas sermon registered on her, not did any of the hymns or carols sung by the choir, nor was she more than distantly aware of the children's Christmas pageant that followed the service. She was only conscious of Travis sitting straight and tall beside her, looking so stunningly handsome, of his thigh pressing against hers, the faint citrusy smell of his after-shave and that unique male scent that was all his own that drifted to her on the overheated air.

After the service there was no chance for them to speak. Travis was quickly surrounded by family and old friends and greeted with thumps on the back and exuberant hugs, and she lost sight of him as they made their way outside through the throng.

In a panicked daze, Rebecca rode home in the van, barely conscious of the talk around her or the sly looks she received from Erin and Elise or the ones the sisters exchanged.

She was given no chance to recover her equilibrium. They had barely walked into the house when the McCall clan arrived.

As had the Blaine offspring, all the McCalls had made it home for Christmas. The noise level was horrendous and for several minutes pandemonium reigned while boisterous greetings and hugs and kisses were exchanged. Not wanting to draw attention to herself, Rebecca stood to one side and watched it all, her eyes eating Travis, her stomach churning with excitement and dread.

"Hey! Look who else is here. Och! Come here, Rebecca, you gorgeous creature, and give us a hug." Before she could evade him, Reilly McCall had clamped his hands around her waist, lifted her up above his head and swung her around in a circle. A startled cry that was half laughter and half fright escaped her, and she clutched his brawny shoulders.

"Reilly, you idiot, put her down before you make her dizzy," Meghan, the youngest sibling, ordered.

He obeyed, but not before he placed a smacking kiss on Rebecca's lips.

"Here now, none of that." Standing on tiptoe, Meghan cuffed him upside the head. Releasing his captive, Reilly laughingly dodged another blow and backed away, and his sister rolled her eyes. "Trust Casanova to zero in on the only female in the room who's not a relative."

She flashed Rebecca her contagious grin. It lit up her whole face, showing her crooked teeth and tilting up the corners of her blue eyes. For that brief instant she looked exactly like the rambunctious tomboy she had been as a child, instead of the hard-driving young career woman Rebecca knew her to be.

"Hi, Rebecca. It's great to see you." With a toss of her bright red hair she lunged forward and caught Rebecca in a hug.

When they drew apart, Meghan turned and gave her brother Ryan a pointed look. "Well? Are you going to say hello to Rebecca, or are you just going to stand there looking fierce?"

Undaunted by his baby sister's acerbic tongue, Ryan turned his remote gaze on Rebecca and nodded. "Hello, Rebecca." The corners of his mouth tilted up in the faintest of smiles that did not reach his eyes.

She returned the greeting just as sparely. He made no attempt to touch her, nor did she expect him to. Though Ryan and Reilly were identical twins, they were as different in their own way as Erin and Elise were.

Devilish, good-natured Reilly was an extrovert who could charm his way out of almost any situation. Which was fortunate since he had a talent for attracting trouble . . . and women . . . usually at the same time.

Ryan had always been the reserved one, the serious one, but since his wife had walked out on him and their then eight-year-old son Mike, five years ago, he had become an embittered man with little use for women, outside of those within his family.

Oddly, although Ryan had always attracted his share of women, now his cold disdain and brooding intensity seemed to draw them like flies to honey. Rebecca supposed it was the irresistible lure of the unattainable.

She had only seen Mike once before, and he'd been a baby at the time. When they were introduced the gangly boy gravely shook her hand and uttered a polite response in his cracked voice.

At thirteen, Mike was the image of his father and uncle, who—unlike Travis, who favored Colin—had inherited their grandfather Monahan's black hair and blue eyes. It was obvious, even now, that the boy was destined to be a heartbreaker someday.

Finally, when she had greeted everyone else, Travis sauntered forward. Rebecca's heart banged against her ribs like a sledgehammer. It skipped a beat, then took off at a gallop when she met his sexy gaze.

"Hello, sweetheart," he said in a husky voice that dripped intimacy. He glanced at the gold locket she wore around her neck and smiled. "I'm glad you're wearing my gift."

Rebecca's eyes widened, and her hand lifted automatically and closed around the lovely heart-shaped locket. Of all the Christmas gifts she'd received, it had been her favorite. "This is from you?"

When they had opened the presents under the tree early that morning, her name had been on the tag attached to the tiny box containing the necklace, but the name of the giver had been left blank. She had assumed it was an extra gift from Dorothy and Joe, but in the hubbub and the rush to get ready for church, she hadn't had a chance to ask.

"Uh-huh. Erin sneaked it under the tree for me. I'm surprised you didn't know who sent it when you looked inside."

"I...I didn't realize it opened. Travis you really shouldn' have—"

He took the locket from her hand and pressed the center of the heart between his thumb and forefinger, and Rebecca caught her breath when it snapped open. On one side there was a picture of her and Travis that Pepe had taken last summer. He had captured them embracing on the beach at sunset, the look of love on their faces as they gazed into each other's eyes so vivid it leaped out at you. Engraved on the opposite half of the heart were the words, *Some things are meant to be.*

Tears filled Rebecca eyes. She looked up at Travis's blurry image, so choked with emotion she could barely speak "Oh, Travis."

"Do you like it?"

"Of course I like it. I love it, but—"

"Shh. No buts." Without the least hesitation or reserve, he slipped his arms around her and pulled her to him.

Rebecca sucked in her breath at the feel of his body against hers and unconsciously braced her forearms against his chest, her splayed fingers flexing against the wool fabric of his suit coat. Too stunned to protest, she stared up at him.

A cocky, purely masculine smile spread over Travis's face. "Merry Christmas, sweetheart," he murmured, and lowered his mouth to hers.

Everything inside Rebecca seemed to turn to hot liquid. Her knees wobbled and her stomach went woozy. She sagged against him, her whole body afire with pleasure and burning for more.

Taking his time about it, Travis kissed her long and thoroughly, savoring every touch, every taste, every texture, making up for the long, lost months they'd been apart. His tongue tested the curving roof of her mouth, the slightly serrated edges of her teeth, the silken membrane in her cheek. His lips rubbed and rocked, his teeth nipped.

Mindlessly, Rebecca returned each stroke, each caress. After five endless, empty months without him, she was starved for the feel of him, the taste of him, the smell of him. She couldn't seem to get enough. Her hands crept up over his shoulders and around his neck, her fingers sifting through the thick, newly clipped hair at his nape. Her body pressed against his, wanting, needing, to get closer.

Neither was aware of the stunned silence around them, or of the discreet coughs and "ah-hems" that followed it. Not until the kiss ended and they were bombarded with hoots and hollers did they even remember their audience. Unperturbed, Travis simply looked around at his relatives and grinned.

David was the first to comment. He stared, flabbergasted, at his cousin. "Good Lord, Travis. Don't tell me, after all those years of detesting her, that you've got the hots for Rebecca?"

Erin snorted and rolled her eyes. "Oh, brother! Some super FBI man you must have been. For pity's sake, David. Of course he's got the hots for her, as you so elegantly put it. He's been nuts about her for years, ever since we were in Junior High. Any fool could see that."

All the males exchanged baffled looks, and Erin sighed. "Well, Elise and I have known it for ages, and I suspect that Mother and Aunt Maggie and Meghan have, too."

"Well I'll be damned," David muttered.

Reilly gaped, for once at a loss for words.

"Don't fight it men," Joe advised sagely. "It's the female mind at work. I learned years ago to just accept it."

Ryan scowled and fixed his younger brother with a hard look. "Are you sure you know what you're doing?"

"Positive."

"Travis, let me go." Mortified by her wanton behavior, Rebecca tried to free herself from Travis's embrace, but he hooked an arm around her waist and clamped her tight against his side. Grinning, he looked around at his family. "I can see you're all curious so, here's the story. Rebecca and I spent most of last summer together at Elise and Erin's summer place on Rincon Island."

"Travis!" Rebecca gasped, but the shocked protest had no effect on him.

"I love her, and she loves me."

The announcement caused raised eyebrows among the men and brought ooohs and ahhhs from the women, especially Maggie McCall. She had long since given up hoping that Ryan would remarry, and in recent years she had begun to despair of any of the others ever settling down and providing her with more grandchildren.

"Travis! Will you stop!" Rebecca pleaded. "You can't do this!"

She might as well have saved her breath.

"I've asked Rebecca to marry me," Travis continued, and Rebecca groaned as a rapturous look lit up his mother's face.

"Oh, Travis, that's wonderful! Rebecca, you naughty thing, why didn't you tell us?" Maggie turned a beaming look on her youngest son. "She never said a word."

"That's because she turned me down."

"What!"

"But you just said—"

The happy exclamations quickly turned into a chorus of disappointed grumbles, and Travis raised his hand for silence.

"Hey, it's okay. I realize now that I shouldn't have rushed her. Rebecca had been divorced for only a few months at the time. The marriage was a bad experience, one she's afraid of repeating. Plus, for some reason, she's convinced herself that I'm not husband material."

"Now I wonder where she got that idea?" David drawled.

Meghan winked at Rebecca. "I always knew you were a bright woman."

Travis grinned, unfazed by the comments or the other hoots of agreement from his kin. Her face burning, Rebecca squirmed, at a loss to know what to say.

"I've stayed away these past five months to give her time to get over the past, but now I've come home, and I intend to prove to her that I'm serious about wanting to settle down.''

"This ought to be interesting," Meghan quipped. "Just how do you plan to accomplish that in a two-day visit?"

"Ah, but you see, this isn't a visit." Travis looked at his father and uncle and received a subtle nod from both. Grinning, he swept his gaze over the others. "You are looking at the new partner in the law firm of McCall and Blaine. As of January first, it will be official."

"You're going into partnership with Dad and Uncle Joe!" Meghan's face lit up in a dazzling smile. All around, an excited babble erupted from the others.

"Hey, that's great!"

"Congratulations!" Speaking at once, his brothers slapped him on the back.

"Yeah, that's terrific news, Cuz," David said. "They've been wanting one of us to go in with them for years now. I have to admit, though, I sure never expected it would be you." He grabbed Travis's hand and pumped it, then muttered an "Aw, what the hell" and caught his cousin in a bear hug.

Rebecca stared at him, her heart doing a crazy dance in her chest. "You...you mean you're going to work here? In Crockett? You're going to live here?"

Smiling tenderly, Travis placed one finger beneath her chin and lifted her sagging jaw. His eyes twinkled with amusement and love. "That's right. It seemed like the wisest thing to do. It'd be kind of a tough commute from D.C. every day," he teased. "Besides, I've already given up my apartment there."

"I can't believe this. I just can't believe it," she babbled.

"Why not? I have a law degree. All I have to do is pass the Texas Bar and I'm set. Anyway, I don't know why you're so surprised. I told you that I was thinking of making a change."

"Yes, but for another exciting job. Then, when you went back to the Bureau, I figured you'd changed your mind. I never expected you to move back to Crockett."

"I gave my notice as soon as I went back, but I got involved in a touchy assignment and couldn't shake loose as quickly as I'd planned."

Rebecca shook her head as though to clear it. "You love the excitement and challenge of being an agent. Why would you give that up to practice law here?"

Travis sighed. "We've been through all this before." Cupping her face in his hand, he looked into her eyes. "Now listen up, love of my life, because I'm only going to say this one more time. First of all, I was getting tired of risking life and limb on undercover assignments and of moving around all the time. I guess I'm getting too old for that kind of stuff. Or maybe I've just grown up. I want what Dad and Uncle Joe have—a stable life, a home and family, old friends and neighbors around." He paused, and his voice lowered to a husky caress. "Most of all . . . I want you."

"Me?" Rebecca's heart pounded painfully.

"Yes, you. I'm glad you came back to Crockett, because I like the idea of working with my dad and uncle and being close to my family. Plus, I like this town. But if you had moved to Santa Fe, or New York City, or even Nome, Alaska, then I would have gone there," he said with a quiet conviction that left no room for doubt. Heat and longing and an aching tenderness simmered in his gray eyes. He touched the gold locket that lay against her chest. "As this says, some things are meant to be."

"Oh, Travis," she whispered. "We went through all this that last day on Rincon. I told you—"

"I know what you told me, but I'm not giving up on us, Rebecca. Look, I understand that you're scared to commit yourself again. I understand that you don't trust your own judgment where men are concerned. I even understand your reservations about me. But none of that matters.

"Sooner or later, sweetheart, you're going to realize that I'm serious about wanting to settle down. I think you already know that I'd never lift a hand to hurt you." Releasing her waist, he framed her face with both his palms. His voice dropped another notch. "You can fight it all you want, sweetheart, but sooner or later I'll wear you down."

"Travis—"

"You love me, dammit! And I love you. And I'm going to marry you."

Before she could utter a response, he tilted her head up and his mouth swooped down on hers. The kiss was heated and thorough and utterly possessive. When he finally raised his head they were bombarded with teasing comments from his family, and Rebecca blushed scarlet. "Travis!" she whispered urgently. "Will you behave! You're embarrassing me."

Ignoring the others, Travis grinned and gave her cheek a pat. "Not a chance. Get used to it, honey, because starting as of now, I'm coming courting."

Chapter Fourteen

Court her, he did. In the weeks that followed, Travis spent more time at his aunt and uncle's house than he had as a child. It seemed to Rebecca that he was always there. No matter whether she was grading papers or helping Dorothy in the kitchen or just watching television, he lounged nearby and watched her with a smoldering look.

How he managed it was a mystery, but on the days when she taught school there was always a fresh red rose on her desk. He called her the minute she got home from work and again every night before she went to bed, even though he spent part of every evening with her.

Wherever Rebecca went, Travis turned up: at the grocery store, the computer shop, the library, the service station. She suspected that Joe and Maggie were supplying him with information about her. The suspicion was confirmed when her car wouldn't start one morning and she bummed a ride to school with Joe. That afternoon when school let out, she found Travis in the hallway outside her classroom, leaning against the wall, waiting to drive her home.

His determined pursuit rattled Rebecca. She never knew where he would pop up next, or what he would take it into his head to do. He sent her candy and flowers for no reason, he sat beside her in church every Sunday, he called her darling and sweetheart in public and kissed her as though it were the most natural thing in the world and his right. He came to school and ate lunch with her in the cafeteria, which drew giggles from the children and speculative looks from the other teachers.

Over and over, Rebecca told him to cease and desist, but she might as well have been talking to the wind for all the good it did. Resisting his charm took every ounce of fortitude she possessed, and daily the task grew harder. The problem was, she was fighting not only Travis, but herself. She loved him desperately, yet the mere thought of marrying again sent cold chills through her.

Gossip about them was flying fast and thick around town, and Rebecca had no idea what to do about it, or how to make Travis stop his determined courtship. Worse, though she told herself it was the wisest course, she really didn't want him to stop.

The admission merely served to make her more miserable and string her nerves out even more. Which, she supposed, was why it seemed like the final straw when Travis showed up at the beauty parlor.

Lerleen Perkin's shop was not one of those unisex establishments, so prevalent in the big city, where men and women sat elbow to elbow to get their hair styled. Oh no. The Beauty Boutique was an old-fashioned, three-station, gossip pit of a salon that reeked of permanent wave solution, peroxide and nail polish, one of the last exclusively female strongholds where women in ill-fitting, passion-pink smocks that gaped open and showed their underwear, sat around with their hair in various stages—from dripping wet to plastered with gunk to twisted in rollers or rods, all of which looked ghastly—dishing the dirt.

Most men of Rebecca's acquaintance would have quailed at entering such a bastion of female mystique. Not Travis.

Without the least trace of discomfort, he lounged against the wall beside the shampoo bowl and flirted with Vera Mae while she washed Rebecca's hair.

He had attended high school with Lerleen and Edith Ann Polson, one of the other beauticians, and with several of the customers, as well. He laughed and chatted with them all, flashing that eye-crinkling smile and ignoring Rebecca's dark looks while he supervised the hair trim Lerleen was giving her.

His presence put the women, beauticians and customers alike, in a tizzy. They fluttered and carried on coyly about him seeing them with their hair wet or in curlers, but they lapped up his every word and vied shamelessly for his attention.

Wynona Watley, a thirtyish blonde whose husband was the pharmacist and owner of a local drugstore, flirted with Travis so brazenly Rebecca was sure they had once been lovers. From the woman's body language and provocative innuendos, it was obvious she would not object to renewing the relationship.

As always, Rebecca's heart pulled her one way and her head another. On the one hand, she wanted to slap the woman, and threaten to put a bug in her husband's ear if she didn't quit making cow eyes at Travis. On the other hand, she knew that she had no right to be upset, given the stance she'd taken. By the time Rebecca left the shop she was so agitated and confused, her nerves were twanging like a struck gong.

Travis sauntered after her when she stormed out the door, his long stride eating up the distance between them with ease. He strolled along the sidewalk beside her, his hands in his trouser pockets, oblivious to her ruffled feathers.

"Go away, Travis," she snapped. She was fighting a ridiculous urge to cry, and whipping up her anger helped. Staring straight ahead, she marched for her car, parked around the corner of the square, the stacked heels on her boots hammering the pavement.

As usual, he paid no attention to the command. "It's almost noon. Whaddaya say we stop at the café for lunch?"

Rebecca stopped dead in her tracks and swung on him, oblivious to the people walking by. "Travis, you have to stop this!"

"Stop what?" he asked innocently, his eyes dancing.

"Stop following me around. Stop sending me flowers. Stop acting as though we are a couple. Stop...stop..." She waved her hands in frustration. "Stop..."

"Courting you?" he supplied helpfully.

"Yes!"

He grinned and rocked back on his heels. Eyeing her lazily, he shook his head. "Uh-uh. Not a chance."

"Travis—"

"Save your breath, sweetheart. I know that you love me. And I love you. And I'm going to marry you." He looked around at the passing shoppers, then threw his head back and shouted at the top of his lungs, "You hear that, people? Travis McCall loves Rebecca Quinn and wants to marry her!"

Rebecca gasped, but before she could utter a word, he grasped her shoulders, hauled her up against him and covered her mouth with his. He kissed her long and thoroughly, right there on the sidewalk in the center of town, with people streaming around them like water seeking its course.

They drew a loud "Humph!" from a passing farmer in overalls, but applause from several of the women and a couple of whistles and encouraging cheers from two young men cutting across the courthouse lawn.

"Travis!" Rebecca gasped when he let her up for air. Casting a quick look around, she saw several familiar faces and blushed scarlet. "Have you lost your mind? What do you think you're doing?"

He flashed an unrepentant grin. "I'm letting the whole town know how I feel and what my intentions are."

Rebecca's frayed nerves snapped. Tears welled in her eyes and spilled over. She looked at him pleadingly, her chin wobbling. "Please, Travis. Don't do this to me. I . . . I can't take anymore."

"Hey, take it easy, love." His cocky grin vanished, his handsome face darkening with concern at the sight of her tears. "Ah, sweetheart, don't. Don't cry." He wiped away a crystal drop with his thumb, but more streamed down her cheeks.

"I can't...I can't marry you, Travis. I love you, but I just can't. Why won't you accept that?"

"Okay. Okay, you win." He stepped back and held his hands up. "I'll leave you alone if that's what you really want."

Pain and weary acceptance etched his features, and the sight wrung Rebecca's heart. She laid her hand on his arm. "Travis...it doesn't have to be the end. Couldn't...couldn't we just go back to the way things were on Rincon?"

"You mean just be lovers? No. No, I don't think so." He shook his head sadly and gave a mirthless chuckle. "This must be what's called poetic justice. I've had affairs, Rebecca. Lots of them. Until now I've never wanted anything more from a woman. But for the first time in my life I'm in love, and as tempting as your offer is, it's just not enough. I want you to be my wife, the mother of my children. I want us to grow old together. I want marriage and all that goes with it."

The words sent a quiver of longing through Rebecca, and she pressed her lips together to keep from crying. She wanted that, too, wanted it so much her heart felt as though it were breaking in two.

But her fear was stronger. "I . . . I can't."

He removed her hand from his arm and held it in a gentle grip. For a moment he just stood there, staring at her hand, brushing his thumb back and forth over the delicate skin on the back. He looked up, and his eyes held a world of sadness and hurt. "Well, I guess that's that. If you change your mind, you know where to reach me," he said softly.

Reaching out, he lifted a tear from her cheek, touched the corner of her mouth with his thumb, then turned and walked away.

She told herself over and over she'd done the right thing, that in time she would get over Travis, but as weeks passed and winter faded into spring, the terrible pain did not lessen. She realized that, deep down, she had not really believed Travis would stay away. She had been wrong.

He no longer came to his aunt's house. No more red roses appeared on her desk. There were no more impromptu lunches at school or "accidental" meetings around town.

Every time the telephone rang, Rebecca's heart leaped, but it was rarely for her, and even when it was, the caller was never Travis. In church on Sundays he sat with his family, and somehow he always managed to avoid her afterward.

Crockett was not a big town, and occasionally she saw him, usually at a distance. On those few occasions when they did bump into one another, he was so excruciatingly polite she wanted to cry. After what they had been to each other, it distressed Rebecca to her very soul to realize that they had become just distant acquaintances living in the same town. His open animosity of the past had hurt less.

She had her freedom, her independence; she should have been happy...but she wasn't. She missed Travis dreadfully, and the love she felt for him stubbornly refused to fade.

It was, of course, inevitable that Travis's family would learn of the rift between them. When the call came from Santa Fe, Rebecca was not surprised, since Erin and Elise had never been shy about giving her advice, but she was braced for their arguments and deflected them with little trouble.

Not quite so easy to take was Maggie McCall's coolness. Even Dorothy seemed to have withdrawn from her. Rebecca had the panicky feeling that she was losing everyone she loved.

"Do you want me to move out?" she blurted one evening while she and Dorothy were cooking dinner.

"Of course not." Dorothy turned from stirring a pot on the stove, a look of genuine shock on her face. "Why on earth would I want that?"

"Well...I know that you and Mrs. McCall are angry with me because of Travis."

"I see." Dorothy sighed. "We're not angry with you, child. Just disappointed. To be frank, I think your behavior is cowardly, and I had thought better of you than that."

"Dorothy!" The disdainful words hit Rebecca like a slap in the face. Hurt to the quick, she stared, white-faced, at the woman she had come to regard almost as a mother. "How can you say that? Don't you understand how horrible my marriage was? How terrified—"

"Horse feathers! That's an excuse. A crutch you use to avoid facing the truth."

"What!" Shocked to the core, Rebecca stared at the older woman with her mouth agape.

"Come now, child. Can you look me in the eye and honestly say that you're afraid of Travis?"

Confusion and panic swirled through Rebecca. "I...I..." Her mouth worked, but the words would not come out.

"I thought not." Dorothy nodded with grim satisfaction. "It's not Travis you're afraid of at all. You're afraid of being happy."

"That's not true!"

"Isn't it? All your life you've been like that little match girl out in the cold, always on the outside looking in, weaving dreams about what it would be like to love and be loved. Now you've got a chance to find out, and you haven't the courage to take it. What are you afraid of, Rebecca? That reality won't live up to your dreams? That Travis will disappoint you?" Dorothy's eyes narrowed shrewdly. "Or that you'll disappoint him?"

"I..." Rebecca swallowed hard and blinked back tears. "I don't know."

"If you marry Travis things won't always be wonderful, Rebecca. Life isn't like that. You'll get angry and you'll fight. You might have to face hard times, or grief and sorrow, but you'll do it together. Marriage is never easy or idyllic, but it's comforting and warm to know that, no matter what, there is someone who loves you." She took Rebecca's hand and patted it. "Travis does love you, Rebecca, and he'll make you happy if you let him. Don't you think it's time to come in from the cold, child?" she asked gently.

Dazed and speechless, Rebecca sagged against the counter. Could it be true? Had she been using the past to cover up her real fear? Certainly, now that Dorothy had forced her to take a good hard look at them, her arguments against marrying Travis no longer seemed valid.

She supposed that all along, in her heart of hearts, she had known that she did not really fear Travis. She had tried to tell herself that he was not serious about settling down in Crockett, that he would tire of the quiet life, of the town, of working in the law firm...of her. But he was still there, and though she had refused him, he showed no sign of leaving.

Since divorcing Evan, she had prided herself on her courage, but now she wondered. Was she so timid and lacking in backbone that she was afraid to reach out for a little happiness? If so, she didn't deserve it.

The thought was so unpalatable she straightened away from the counter with her jaw set and headed for the door.

"Where are you going?" Dorothy called after her.

"To the McCall's. I have to talk to Travis."

"He's not there."

Rebecca halted and spun around. "What do you mean, he's not there?" Her heart began to pound. Oh, Lord, had he gotten tired of waiting for her to come to her senses and given up?

"He bought the old Martin place, down the road from his folks' house. He moved into it two months ago. I would've thought you'd heard by now."

Rebecca nearly sagged with relief. "No. No, I hadn't."

"I guess everyone's avoided talking about Travis around you lately. The old place has been vacant for years and needs a lot of work. Travis spends his evenings and weekends renovating it." Dorothy paused to let that soak in, then added pointedly, "Doesn't sound much like a man who plans to move on, does it?"

A beaming smile lit up Rebecca's face. "No. It certainly doesn't."

The McCall house was only ten minutes away if you used the shortcut through the woods, and the old Martin place was only another five minutes farther, but Rebecca was in too much of a hurry to walk.

Twilight was settling in when she brought her car to a halt in the drive. Like Dorothy and Joe's home, the Martin place was a rambling old Victorian, set far back from the country lane among a veritable forest of trees and overgrown shrubs.

Whatever work Travis had done, Rebecca realized, must have been on the inside. The wraparound porch sagged, and the place obviously hadn't seen a coat of paint in years. The siding and gingerbread were a uniform weathered gray. Except for the light spilling from the uncurtained windows of the parlor, the place looked forlorn and deserted.

Rebecca climbed the steps and crossed the sagging porch, her heart pounding like a wild thing in her chest. The doors and windows were open to the cool April night, and when she peeked through the screen door, she saw Travis in the parlor bent over a pair of sawhorses, marking a board. She drew a deep breath and tapped on the door frame. "Hello."

Travis straightened and looked around, and his eyes widened. "Rebecca." He tossed down the pencil and straight edge and walked into the foyer. "This is a surprise."

His voice carried not the slightest inflection. Halting on the other side of the door, he studied her through the screen, his expression carefully neutral. Rebecca hadn't a clue as to how he felt about her being there, and panic began creeping in. Oh, Lord. What if he didn't want her there? What if he didn't love her anymore?

She cleared her throat and pasted a smile on her face. "May I come in?"

He shrugged and stepped aside, pushing the screen door open with one hand. "Sure. C'mon in."

As she stepped past him, her senses were assaulted by his familiar scent, and she felt her insides tremble. He was dressed in tattered jeans and a paint-splattered shirt that was unbuttoned to the waist. Sawdust covered his forearms below the rolled-up sleeves. More clung to the faded chambray shirt and to the hair on his chest. Rebecca had to fight to keep her gaze away from that enticing strip of bare flesh. She wanted nothing so much as to throw herself into his arms.

She forced herself to turn away and look around. Except for the power saw, the sawhorses and a pile of lumber in the corner, the room was empty. "I heard you had bought this place and were fixing it up. Are you doing all the work by yourself?"

"I had it rewired and the plumbing replaced before I moved in. The rest I'm doing." He stood with his feet braced wide, his arms crossed over his chest, watching her. In his demeanor there was no trace of the easygoing devil she had grown to know.

Rubbing her sweaty palms on the seat of her jeans, Rebecca stepped to the archway that led to the foyer and pretended an interest in the fretwork that ran along the top. "They don't build places like this anymore. I'm sure it will be beautiful when you've finished."

"Why are you here, Rebecca? I know you didn't drop by to talk about remodeling."

She turned to face him. His set expression was not encouraging, and his intimidating stance had not eased one iota. She had hoped that he would bring up the matter of their relationship, or at least give her an opening, but his silent stare put the onus squarely on her.

"I, uh . . . I came to ask you something."

"What?"

"Do you..." She stopped to clear her throat. "Do you still want to marry me?"

He looked at her steadily. "Why do you want to know?"

"Because, if you... Travis, I love you so much."

"I know," he said in that flat, emotionless voice, but his expression did not alter one whit. "But that doesn't answer my question. Why are you here, Rebecca?"

"Oh, Travis, why are you doing this? You know why," she cried.

He didn't give an inch. His unyielding stare demanded that she say the words, and in her heart she knew he deserved to hear them.

She was trembling so, she could barely stand. Her heart clubbed her ribcage. She drew a shaky breath, swallowed hard and looked him in the eye. "I... I came to ask you to marry me."

Something flickered in his eyes, but still he didn't move. "You're not afraid I'll mistreat you?"

"No."

"Or that I'll get bored?"

"No."

"Or run out on you?"

She pressed her lips together and shook her head.

For an agonizing length of time he simply stared at her. Rebecca felt sick. Then, slowly, his mouth curved up in that sexy smile that crinkled the corners of his eyes, and he held out his arms. "Then what're you doing way over there? Come here, woman."

Before he finished speaking, Rebecca closed the distance between them and flung herself against his chest. "Oh, Travis, I love you so. And I've missed you so much, my darling," she cried. "I've been miserable without you."

"I know, sweetheart. So have I. So have I," he groaned against her neck.

He held her so tight she could barely breathe, but Rebecca didn't care. She burrowed against his chest, greedily drawing in his wonderful smell, along with the sharp scent of sawdust. She clung to him fiercely, her restless, caressing hands running over him, slipping beneath the open shirt, learning anew the texture of his skin, the firmness of his hard flesh, the silky smoothness of his hair. She had not expected to be in his arms ever again. It was heaven.

"Oh, Travis, I'm sorry. So sorry," Rebecca murmured. "I've been such a fool."

"Shh. It's okay. You had things you had to work through on your own." Travis lifted his head, and their eyes met in a look that spoke of past regret and pain. "But all that's over now."

The look of love on his face as he gazed down at her pierced Rebecca's heart with a sweet, sweet pain. A smile of wonder curved her mouth, and she reached up and touched his face with her fingertips. "I do love you, Travis. So much. I always have." Their eyes delved, blue into gray, soft with emotion, seeking solace for the long months apart, promising love beyond forever, saying without words all that was in their hearts.

Then, subtly, the look changed. The air around them seemed to crackle. Fire leaped in Travis's eyes, and Rebecca sucked in her breath as her body went weak and warm.

Travis's gaze dropped to her mouth. Rebecca's lips parted. Her eyes drifted shut.

She moaned at the first touch of his lips against hers and looped her arms around his shoulders. The kiss began tenderly, but quickly became hot and hungry, open and wet, as each sought to make up for the lonely weeks apart.

Tongues dueled in a rough caress, twisting and twining, speaking of need that had grown to near desperation since last they loved. Their lips rocked together in greedy passion, their hearts thudded and their blood rushed hotly through their veins as the kiss went on and on.

Travis nipped at Rebecca's lower lip, then drew it into his mouth and sucked gently. She made a low, throaty sound in the back of her throat and burrowed her fingers through the hair at his nape, telling him without words of the depth of her feelings.

To her shock, Travis suddenly broke off the embrace. "C'mon," he growled, and before she could react, he grabbed her hand and headed for the door, towing her along with him.

"Travis! What are you doing?"

"I want to show you what I've done to the house."

"Now?"

"Uh-huh. I'm doing one room at a time, according to priority." At the bottom of the stairs he swooped her up in his arms. Pausing with one foot on the bottom step, he flashed her a wicked grin. "I started with the master bedroom."

Rebecca laughed, her heart swelling with happiness. His face was alive with devilish amusement and passion. With a sigh, she looped her arms around his neck and laid her head on his shoulder. Her old carefree, charming, outrageously roguish Travis was back.

He gave her little chance to admire the work he'd done in the bedroom. He carried her straight to the bed, and as they tumbled onto the mattress, their lips meshed in a long, sizzling kiss.

"Oh, Travis. Travis," Rebecca gasped, almost sobbing with frustration.

"I know, sweetheart. I know." He trailed his open mouth down her neck, and she felt the nip of his teeth on her skin.

Desperation and a wild hunger drove them. With shaking hands, buttons, hooks and zippers were swiftly dealt with. They rolled together across the king-size bed in a frenzy of passion, discarding clothes helter-skelter. When at last there were no more barriers between them, they came together at once in a blaze of desire and love so intense Rebecca thought its heat would surely consume them both.

The inferno burned brightly, quickly. Together, they caught fire, and when the shattering explosion of joy came, rocking them to the depths of their souls, each called out the other's name.

A long while later, when thundering hearts had calmed and breathing had returned to normal, Travis raised up on his forearms and they smiled at each other with lazy contentment. He touched the sides of her neck and ran his fingers over the velvety rims of her ears, all the while looking deep into her eyes.

"When will you marry me?"

"Any time you say." The sense of freedom the words brought amazed Rebecca. She felt as though an icy shackle had been removed from her heart.

"Tomorrow?" Travis asked hopefully.

"Yes. Yes!" She threw her arms around his neck and hugged him tightly. Tears of joy filled her eyes as she basked in the warmth of his love. Heat cascaded through her body, filling every cell, every pore, and she shivered.

"Are you cold, sweetheart?"

Rebecca smiled over his shoulder, her gaze blurred with happy tears. "No, my love," she said in a voice that wobbled with emotion. "I don't think I'll ever be cold again."

* * * * *

Silhouette Special Edition

salutes

MOMENTS OF GLORY

from Lindsay McKenna

In a country torn with conflict, in a time of bitter passions, these brave men and women wage a war against all odds . . . and a timeless battle for honor, for fleeting moments of glory, for the promise of enduring love.

February: RIDE THE TIGER (#721) Survivor Dany Villard is wise to the love-'em-and-leave-'em ways of war, but wounded hero Gib Ramsey swears she's captured his heart . . . forever.

March: ONE MAN'S WAR (#727) The war raging inside brash and bold Captain Pete Mallory threatens to destroy him, until Tess Ramsey's tender love guides him toward peace.

April: OFF LIMITS (#733) Soft-spoken Marine Jim McKenzie saved Alexandra Vance's life in Vietnam; now he needs her love to save his honor. . . .

SEMG-1

NORA ROBERTS

Love has a language all its own, and for centuries, flowers have symbolized love's finest expression. Discover the language of flowers—and love—in this romantic collection of 48 favorite books by bestselling author Nora Roberts.

Starting in February 1992, two titles will be available each month at your favorite retail outlet.

In February, look for:

Irish Thoroughbred, Volume #1
The Law Is A Lady, Volume #2

Collect all 48 titles and become fluent in the Language of Love.

LOL192

THE LANGUAGE of LOVE